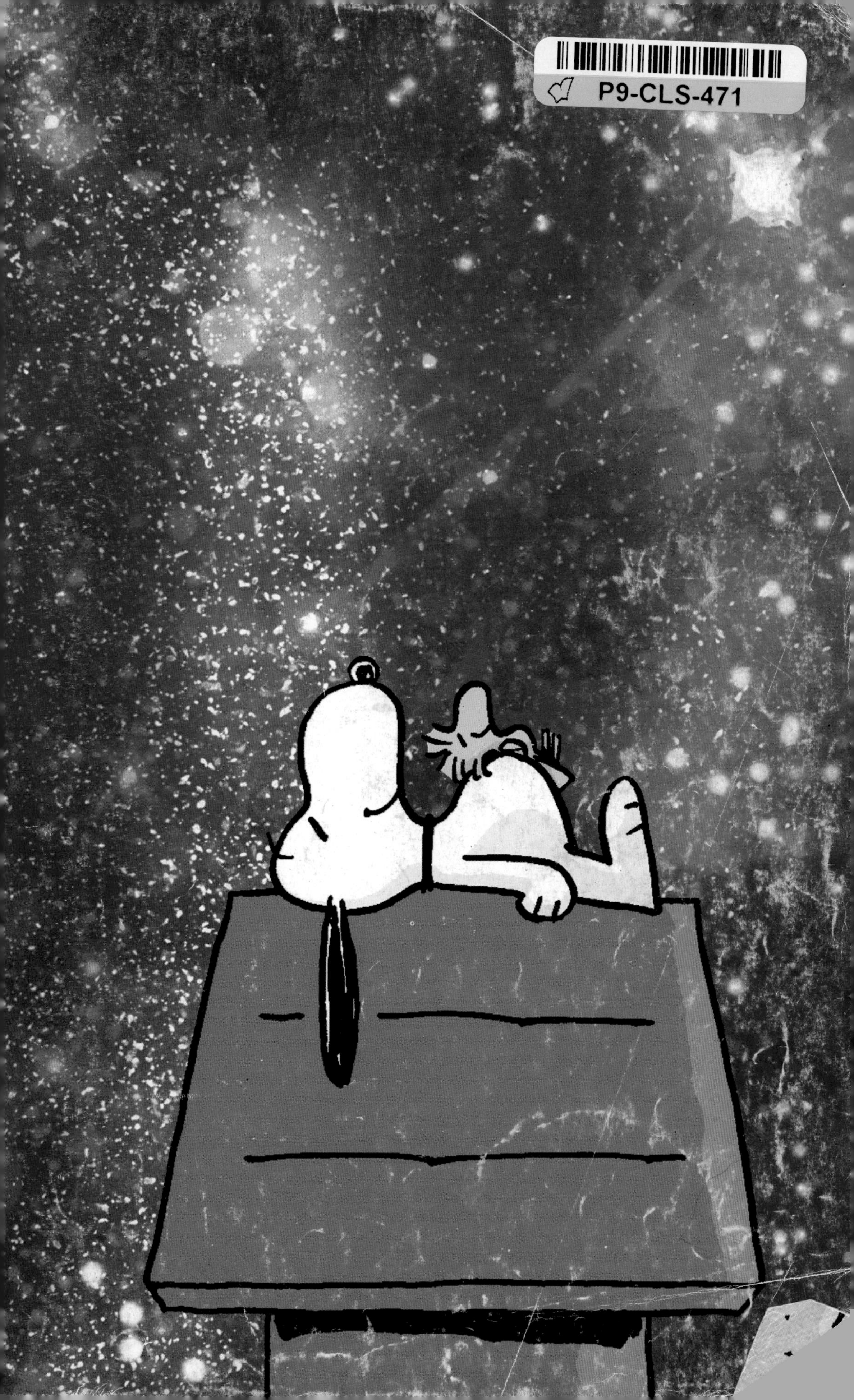

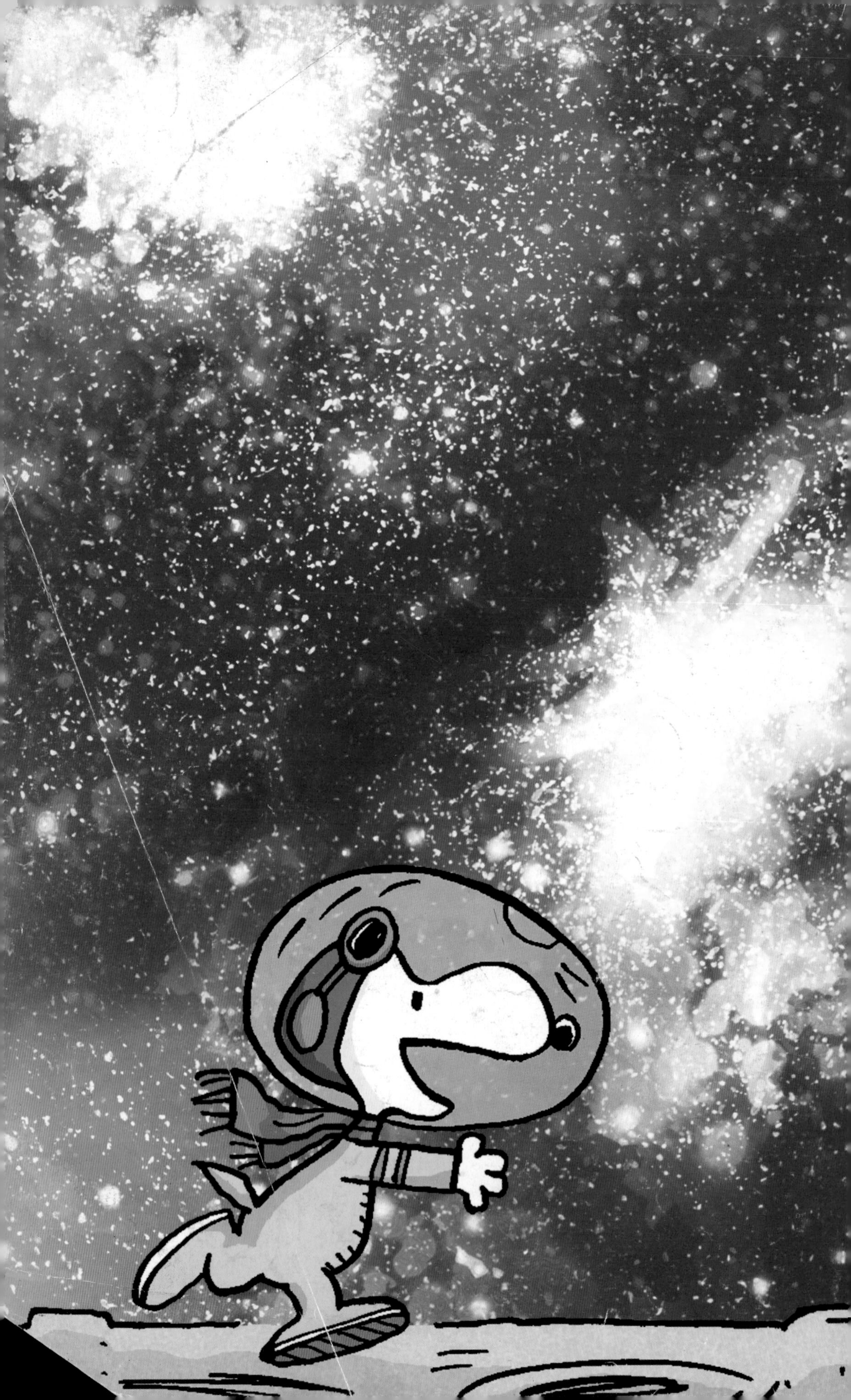

Charles M. Schulz

PEANUTS™

THE BEAGLE HAS LANDED, CHARLIE BROWN!

ROSS RICHIE CEO & Founder • JACK CUMMINS President • MARK SMYLIE Founder of Archaia • MATT GAGNON Editor-in-Chief • FILIP SABLIK VP of Publishing & Marketing • STEPHEN CHRISTY VP of Development
LANCE KREITER VP of Licensing & Merchandising • PHIL BARBARO VP of Finance • BRYCE CARLSON Managing Editor • MEL CAYLO Marketing Manager • SCOTT NEWMAN Production Design Manager • IRENE BRADISH Operations Manager
DAFNA PLEBAN Editor • SHANNON WATTERS Editor • ERIC HARBURN Editor • REBECCA TAYLOR Editor • IAN BRILL Editor • CHRIS ROSA Assistant Editor • ALEX GALER Assistant Editor • WHITNEY LEOPARD Assistant Editor
JASMINE AMIRI Assistant Editor • CAMERON CHITTOCK Assistant Editor • HANNAH NANCE PARTLOW Production Designer • KELSEY DIETERICH Production Designer • EMI YONEMURA BROWN Production Designer
DEVIN FUNCHES E-Commerce & Inventory Coordinator • ANDY LIEGL Event Coordinator • BRIANNA HART Executive Assistant • AARON FERRARA Operations Assistant • JOSÉ MEZA Sales Assistant • ELIZABETH LOUGHRIDGE Accounting Assistant

kaboom!™

A catalog record of this book is available from OCLC and from the KaBOOM! website, www.kaboom-studios.com, on the Librarians Page.

BOOM! Studios, 5670 Wilshire Boulevard, Suite 450, Los Angeles, CA 90036-5679. Printed in China. First Printing.

ISBN: 978-1-60886-334-1, eISBN: 978-1-61398-188-7

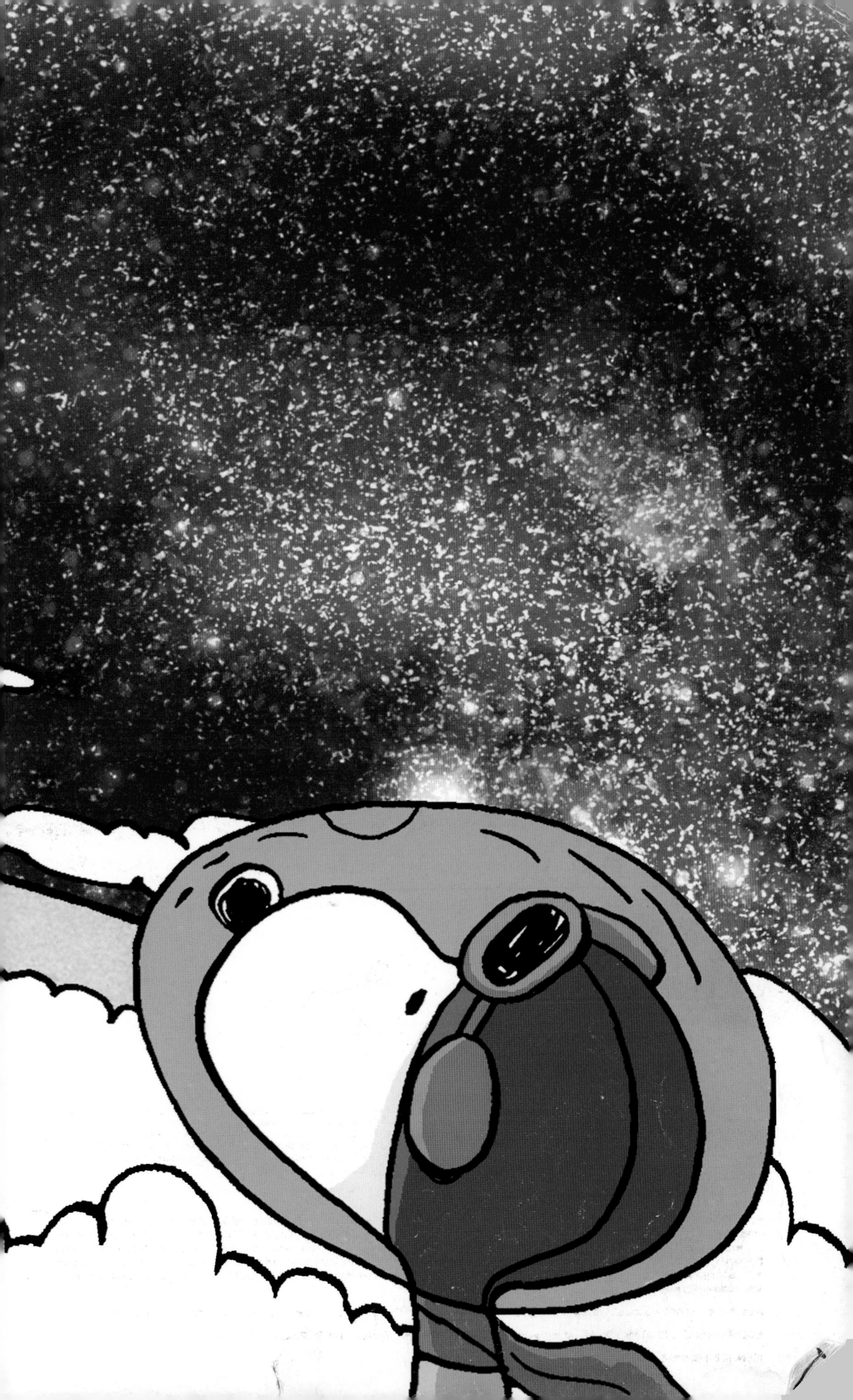

Based on the comic strip, Peanuts, by
Charles M. Schulz

Story by
Andy Beall, Bob Scott, and Vicki Scott

Pencils & Layouts by
Vicki Scott

Inks by
Paige Braddock

Colors by
Nina Kester and Donna Almendrala

Letters by
Donna Almendrala

Cover

Pencils by
Bob Scott

Inks By
Justin Thompson

Colors by
Nina Kester

Assistant Editor **Alex Galer**
Editors **Matt Gagnon & Shannon Watters**
Trade Design **Emi Yonemura Brown**

For Charles M. Schulz Creative Associates:
Creative Director **Paige Braddock**
Managing Editor **Alexis E. Fajardo**

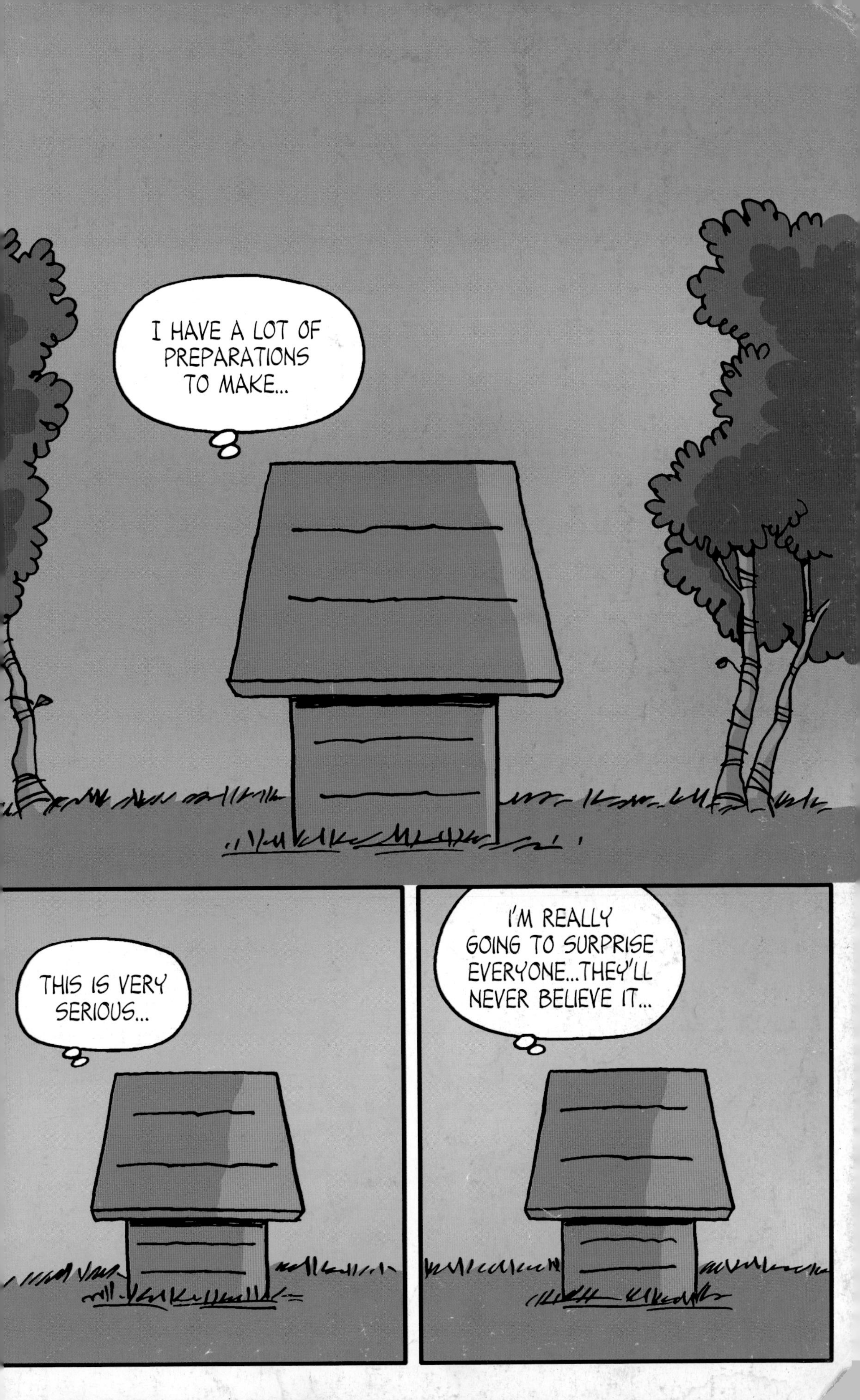
I HAVE A LOT OF PREPARATIONS TO MAKE...
THIS IS VERY SERIOUS...
I'M REALLY GOING TO SURPRISE EVERYONE...THEY'LL NEVER BELIEVE IT...

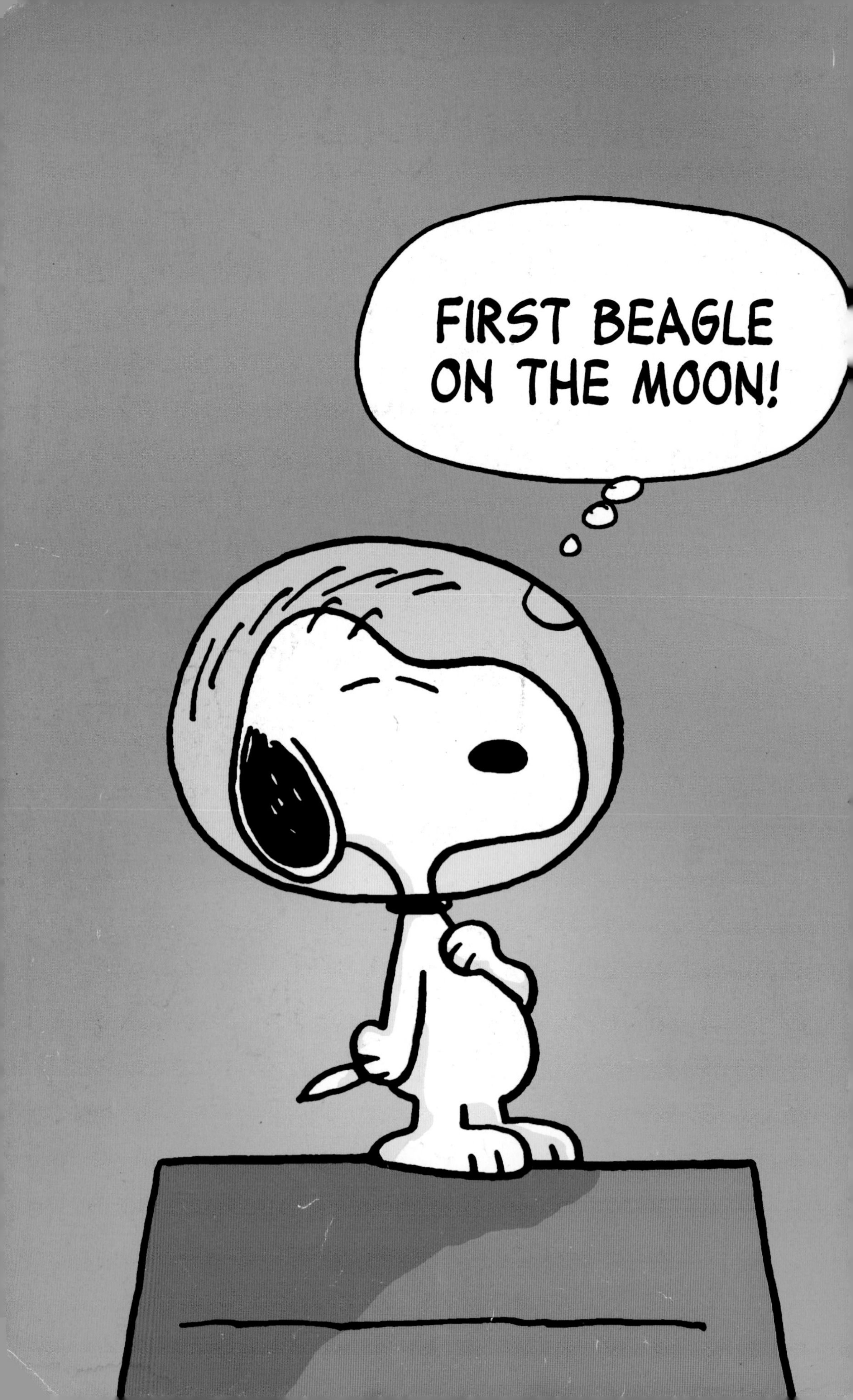
FIRST BEAGLE ON THE MOON!

Charles M. Schulz

PEANUTS™

THE BEAGLE HAS LANDED, CHARLIE BROWN!

I DID IT! I BEAT THE RUSSIAN WOLFHOUNDS! I BEAT THE COYOTES!
I BEAT EVERYONE!
I EVEN BEAT THE STUPID CAT NEXT DOOR!

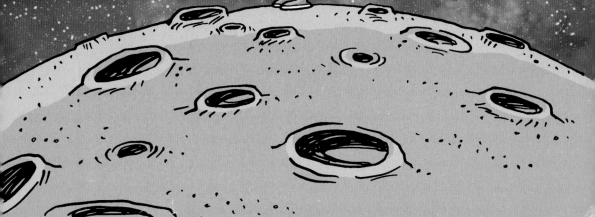

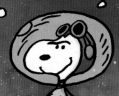

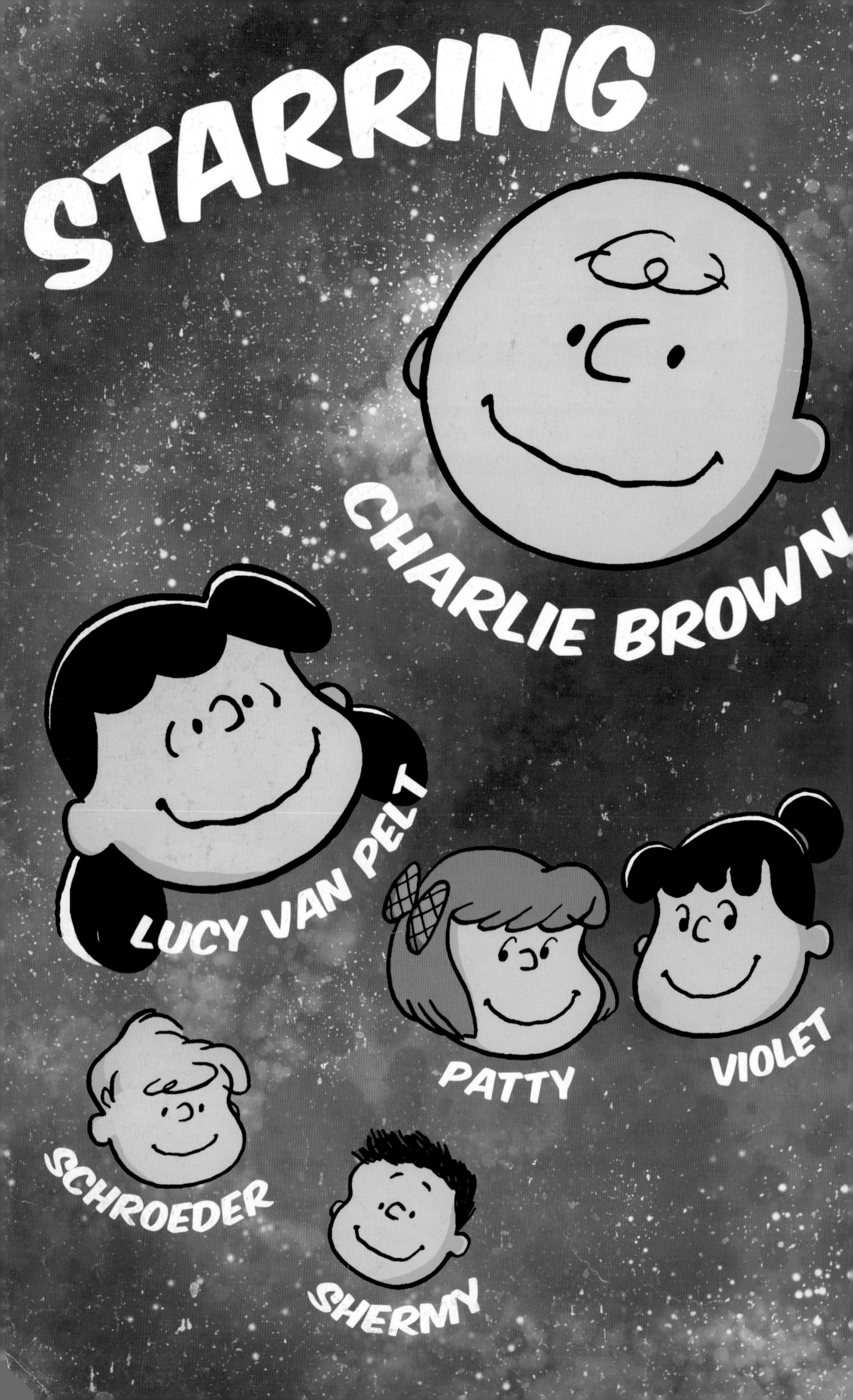
STARRING
CHARLIE BROWN
LUCY VAN PELT
PATTY
VIOLET
SCHROEDER
SHERMY

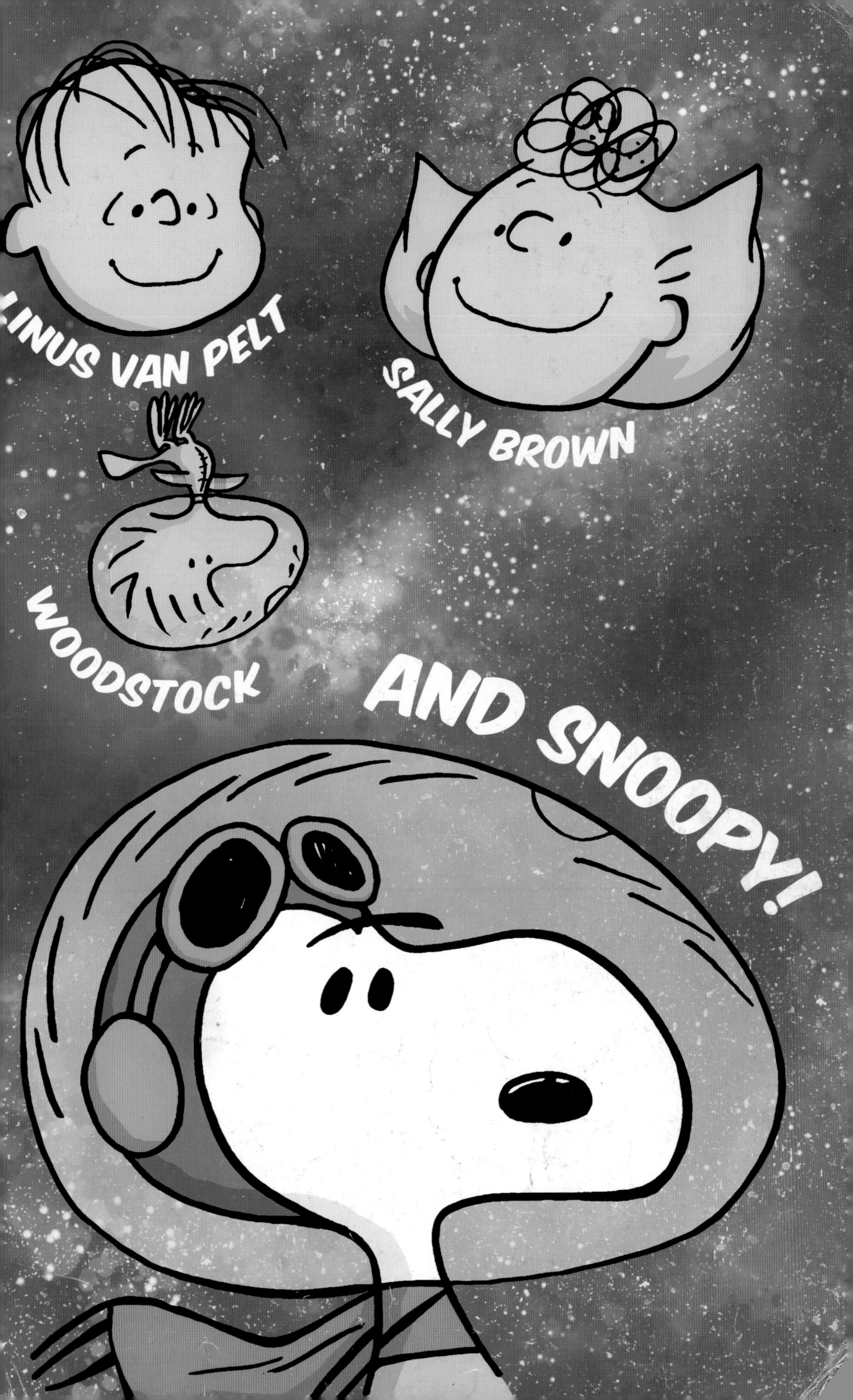
LINUS VAN PELT
SALLY BROWN
WOODSTOCK
AND SNOOPY!

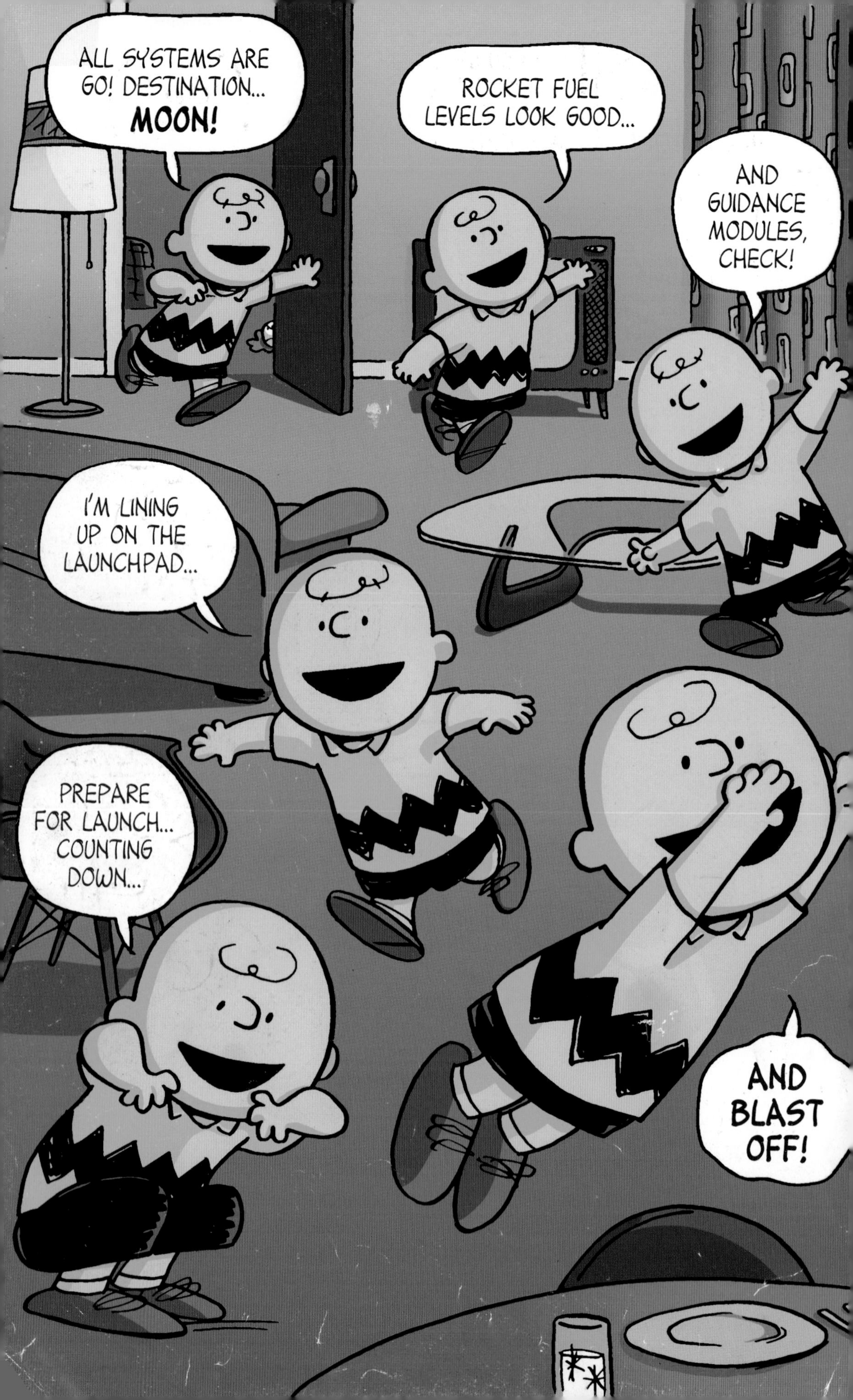
ALL SYSTEMS ARE GO! DESTINATION... MOON!
ROCKET FUEL LEVELS LOOK GOOD...
AND GUIDANCE MODULES, CHECK!
I'M LINING UP ON THE LAUNCHPAD...
PREPARE FOR LAUNCH... COUNTING DOWN...
AND BLAST OFF!

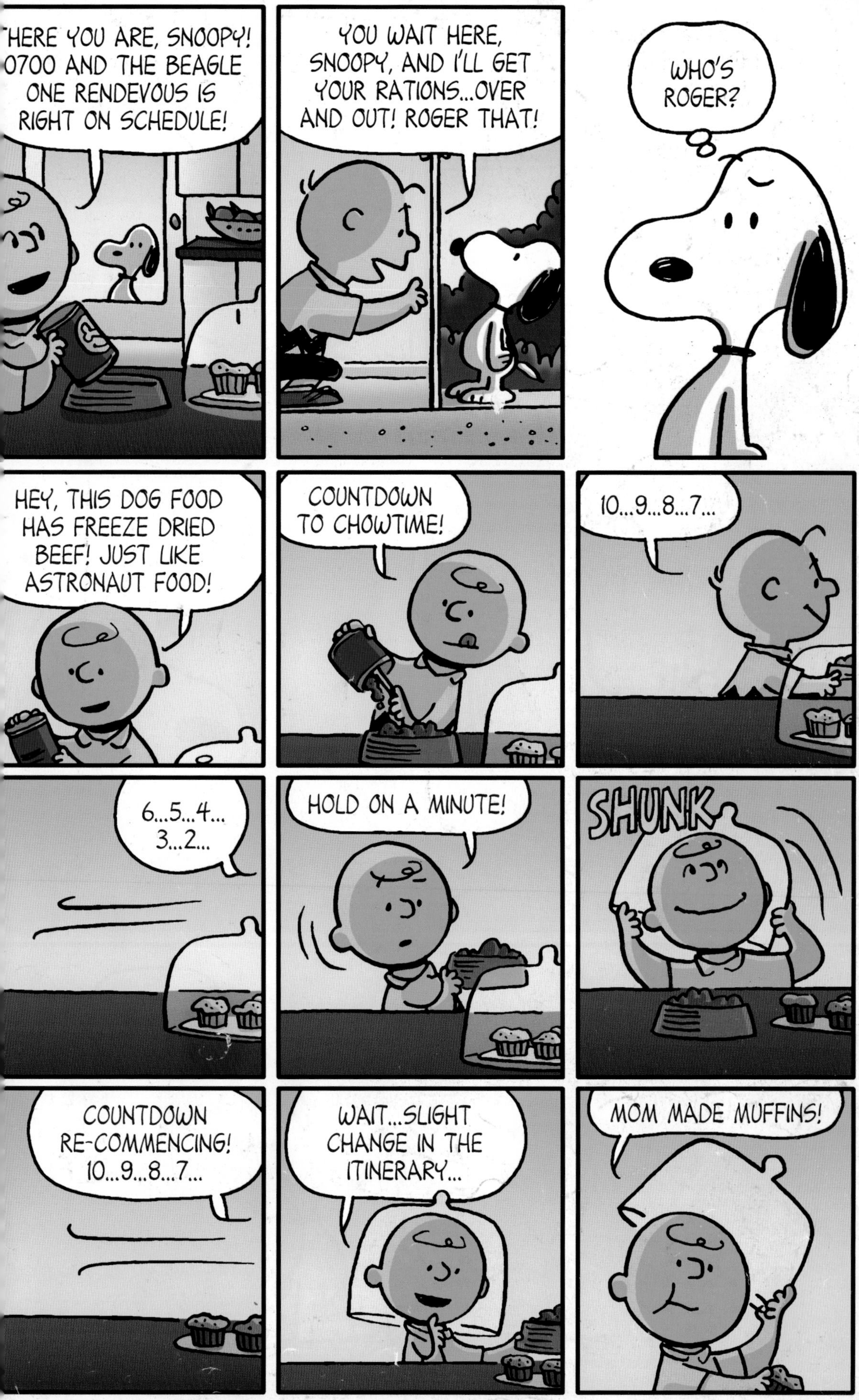
HERE YOU ARE, SNOOPY! 0700 AND THE BEAGLE ONE RENDEVOUS IS RIGHT ON SCHEDULE!
YOU WAIT HERE, SNOOPY, AND I'LL GET YOUR RATIONS...OVER AND OUT! ROGER THAT!
WHO'S ROGER?
HEY, THIS DOG FOOD HAS FREEZE DRIED BEEF! JUST LIKE ASTRONAUT FOOD!
COUNTDOWN TO CHOWTIME!
10...9...8...7...
6...5...4... 3...2...
HOLD ON A MINUTE!
SHUNK
COUNTDOWN RE-COMMENCING! 10...9...8...7...
WAIT...SLIGHT CHANGE IN THE ITINERARY...
MOM MADE MUFFINS!

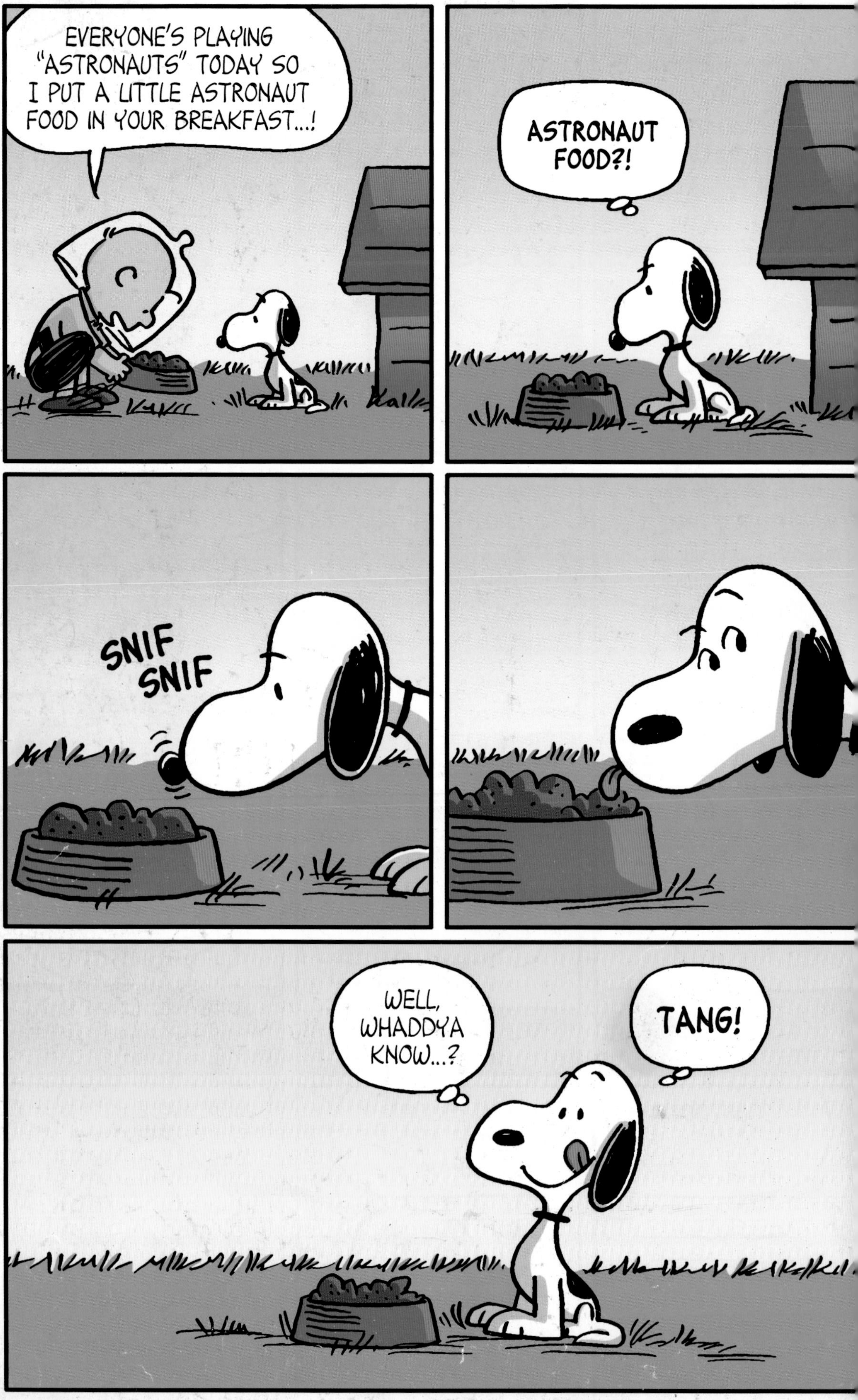
EVERYONE'S PLAYING "ASTRONAUTS" TODAY SO I PUT A LITTLE ASTRONAUT FOOD IN YOUR BREAKFAST...!
ASTRONAUT FOOD?!
SNIF SNIF
WELL, WHADDYA KNOW...?
TANG!

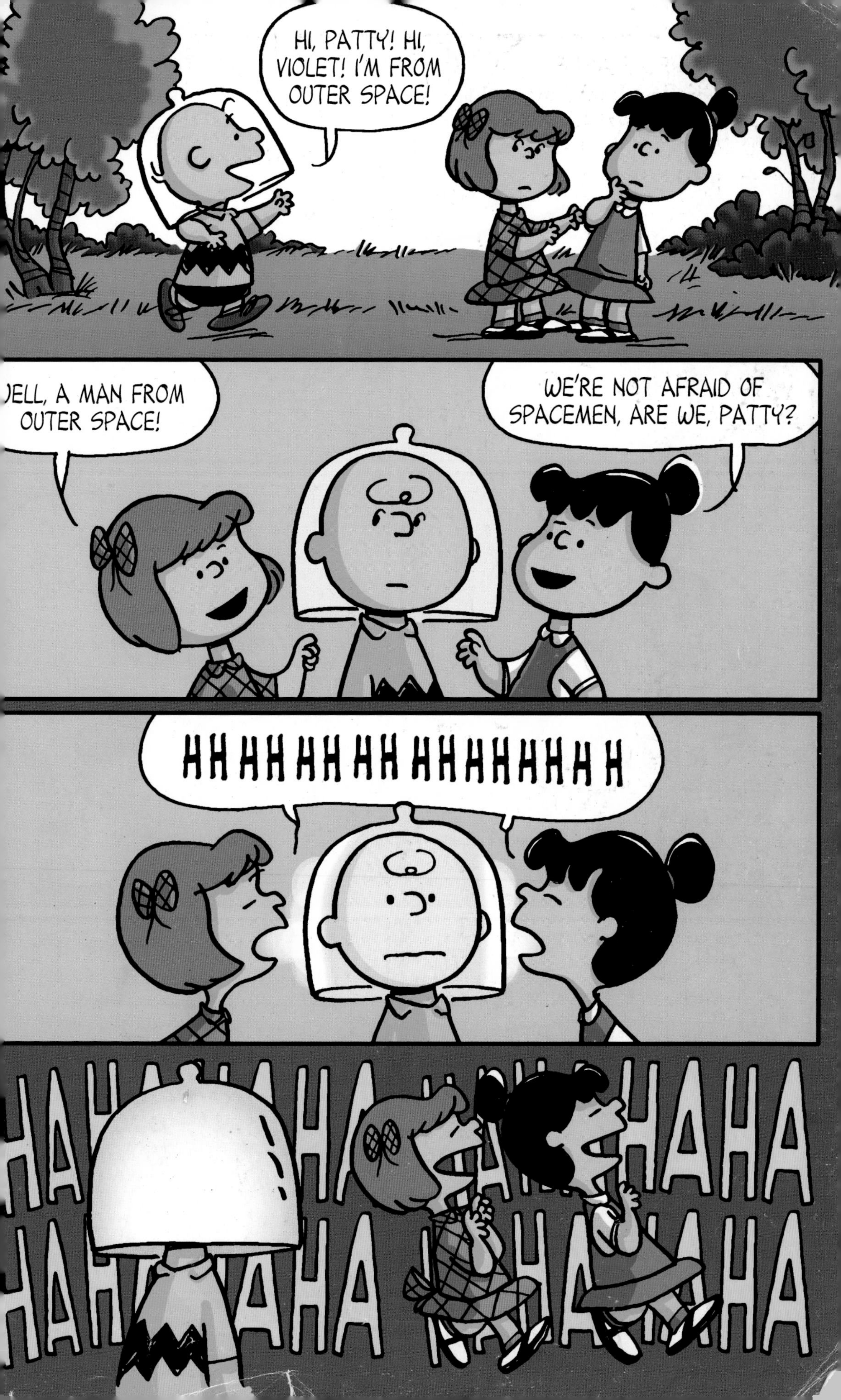

HI, PATTY! HI, VIOLET! I'M FROM OUTER SPACE!
)ELL, A MAN FROM OUTER SPACE!
WE'RE NOT AFRAID OF SPACEMEN, ARE WE, PATTY?
HHHHHHHHHHHHHHHH
HAHAHAHAHAHAHAHA
HAHAHAHAHAHAHAHA

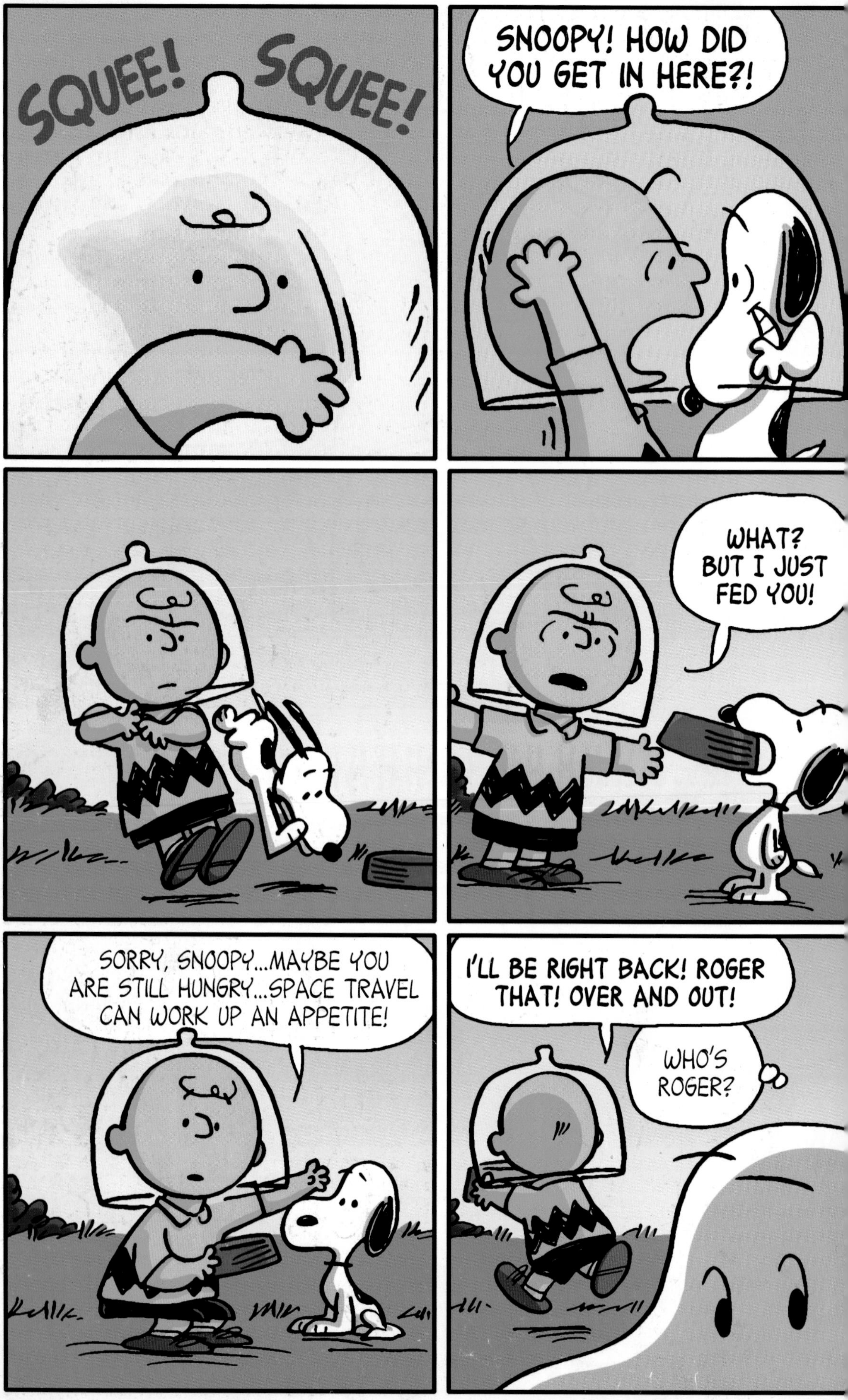
SQUEE! SQUEE!
SNOOPY! HOW DID YOU GET IN HERE?!
WHAT? BUT I JUST FED YOU!
SORRY, SNOOPY...MAYBE YOU ARE STILL HUNGRY...SPACE TRAVEL CAN WORK UP AN APPETITE!
I'LL BE RIGHT BACK! ROGER THAT! OVER AND OUT!
WHO'S ROGER?

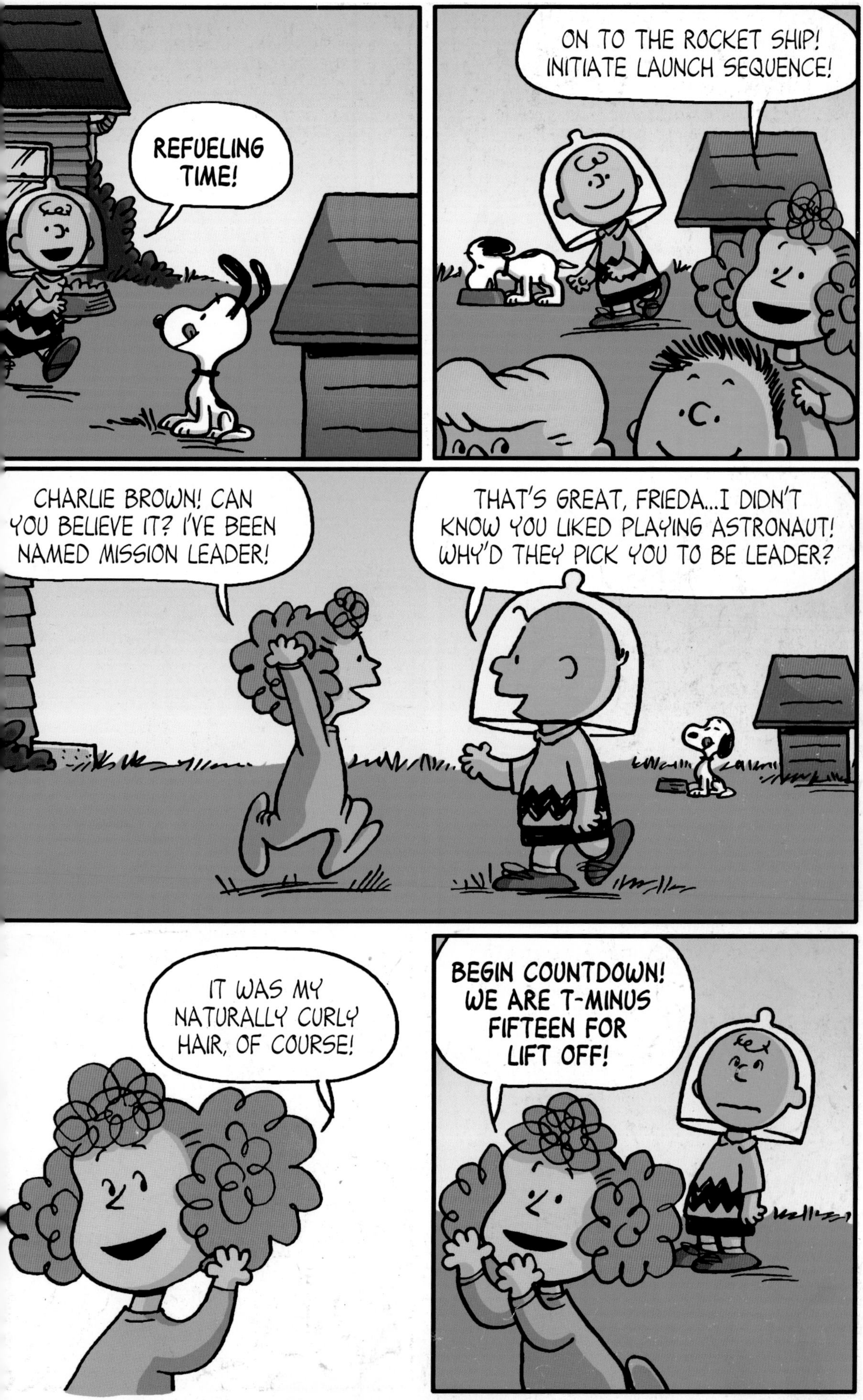

REFUELING TIME!
ON TO THE ROCKET SHIP! INITIATE LAUNCH SEQUENCE!
CHARLIE BROWN! CAN YOU BELIEVE IT? I'VE BEEN NAMED MISSION LEADER!
THAT'S GREAT, FRIEDA...I DIDN'T KNOW YOU LIKED PLAYING ASTRONAUT! WHY'D THEY PICK YOU TO BE LEADER?
IT WAS MY NATURALLY CURLY HAIR, OF COURSE!
BEGIN COUNTDOWN! WE ARE T-MINUS FIFTEEN FOR LIFT OFF!

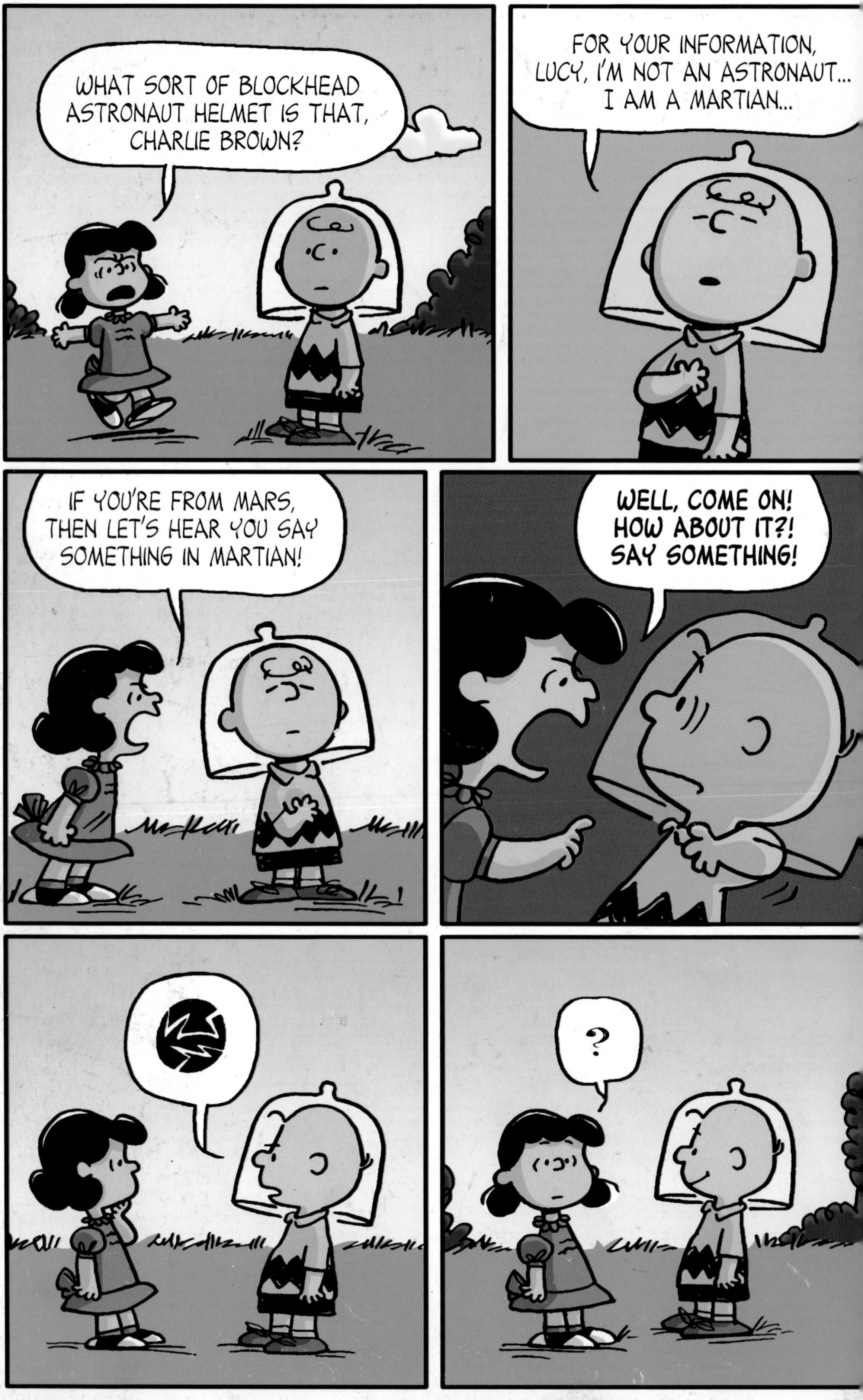
WHAT SORT OF BLOCKHEAD ASTRONAUT HELMET IS THAT, CHARLIE BROWN?
FOR YOUR INFORMATION, LUCY, I'M NOT AN ASTRONAUT... I AM A MARTIAN...
IF YOU'RE FROM MARS, THEN LET'S HEAR YOU SAY SOMETHING IN MARTIAN!
WELL, COME ON! HOW ABOUT IT?! SAY SOMETHING!
?

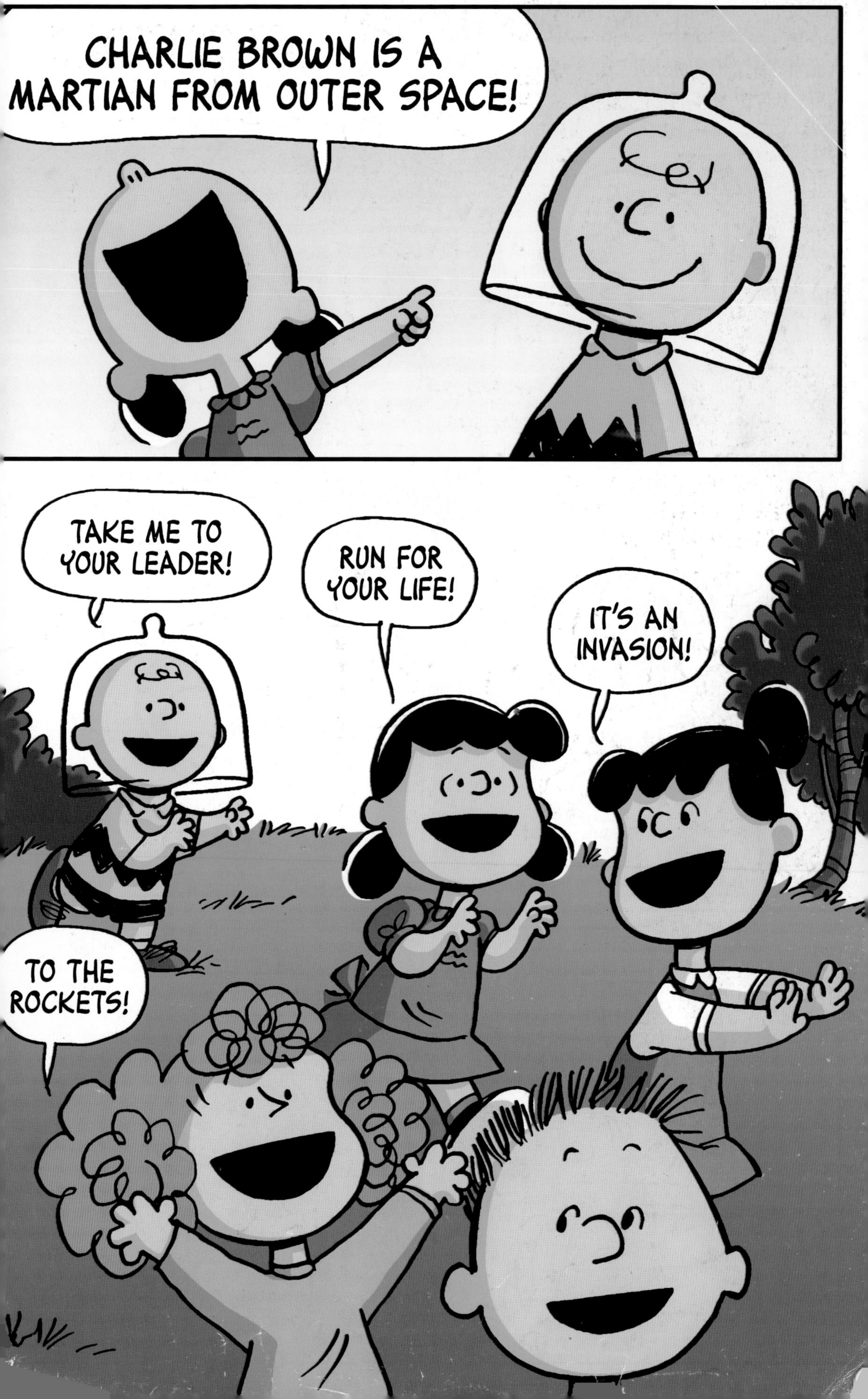
CHARLIE BROWN IS A MARTIAN FROM OUTER SPACE!
TAKE ME TO YOUR LEADER!
RUN FOR YOUR LIFE!
IT'S AN INVASION!
TO THE ROCKETS!

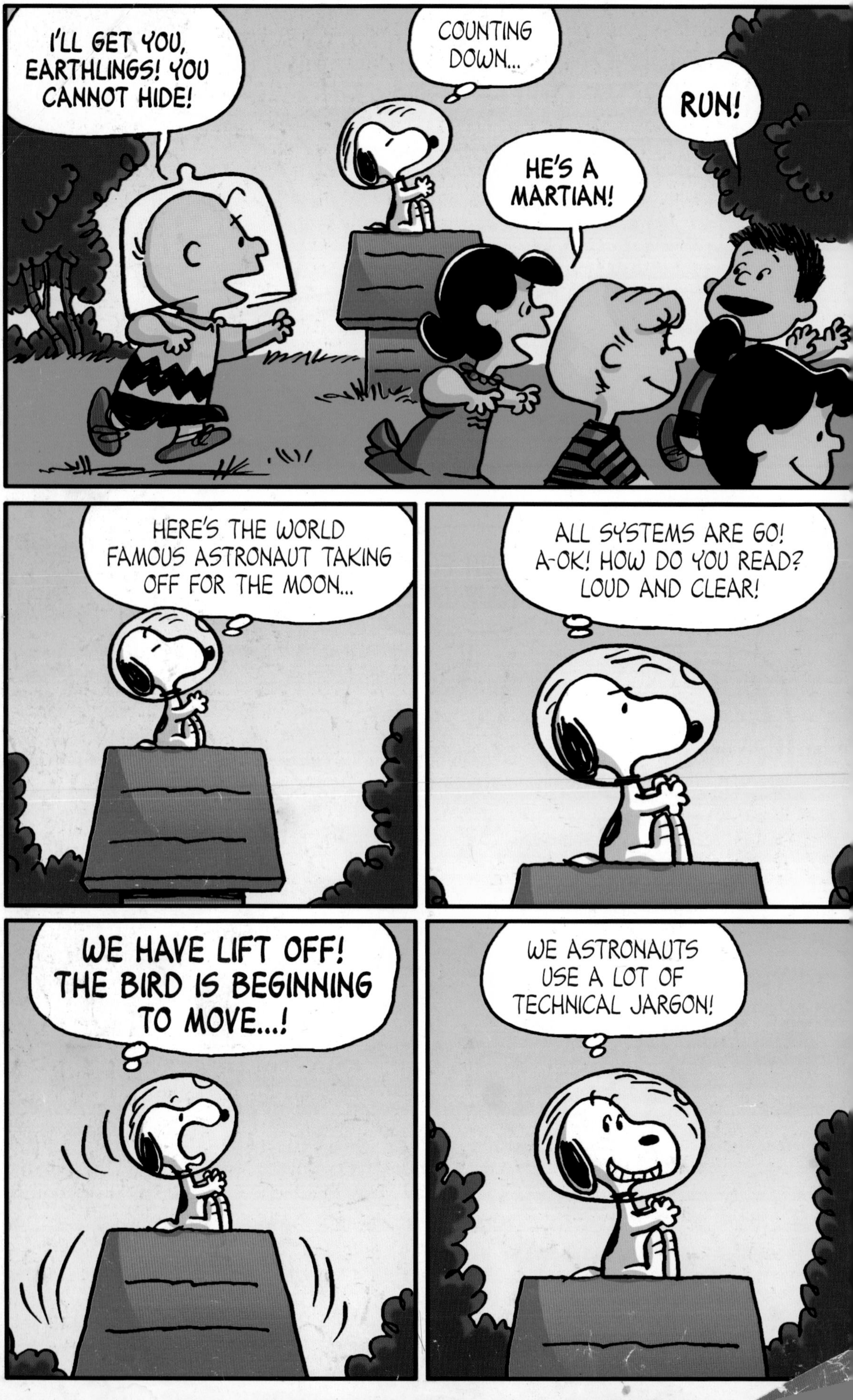
I'LL GET YOU, EARTHLINGS! YOU CANNOT HIDE!
COUNTING DOWN...
HE'S A MARTIAN!
RUN!
HERE'S THE WORLD FAMOUS ASTRONAUT TAKING OFF FOR THE MOON...
ALL SYSTEMS ARE GO! A-OK! HOW DO YOU READ? LOUD AND CLEAR!
WE HAVE LIFT OFF! THE BIRD IS BEGINNING TO MOVE...!
WE ASTRONAUTS USE A LOT OF TECHNICAL JARGON!

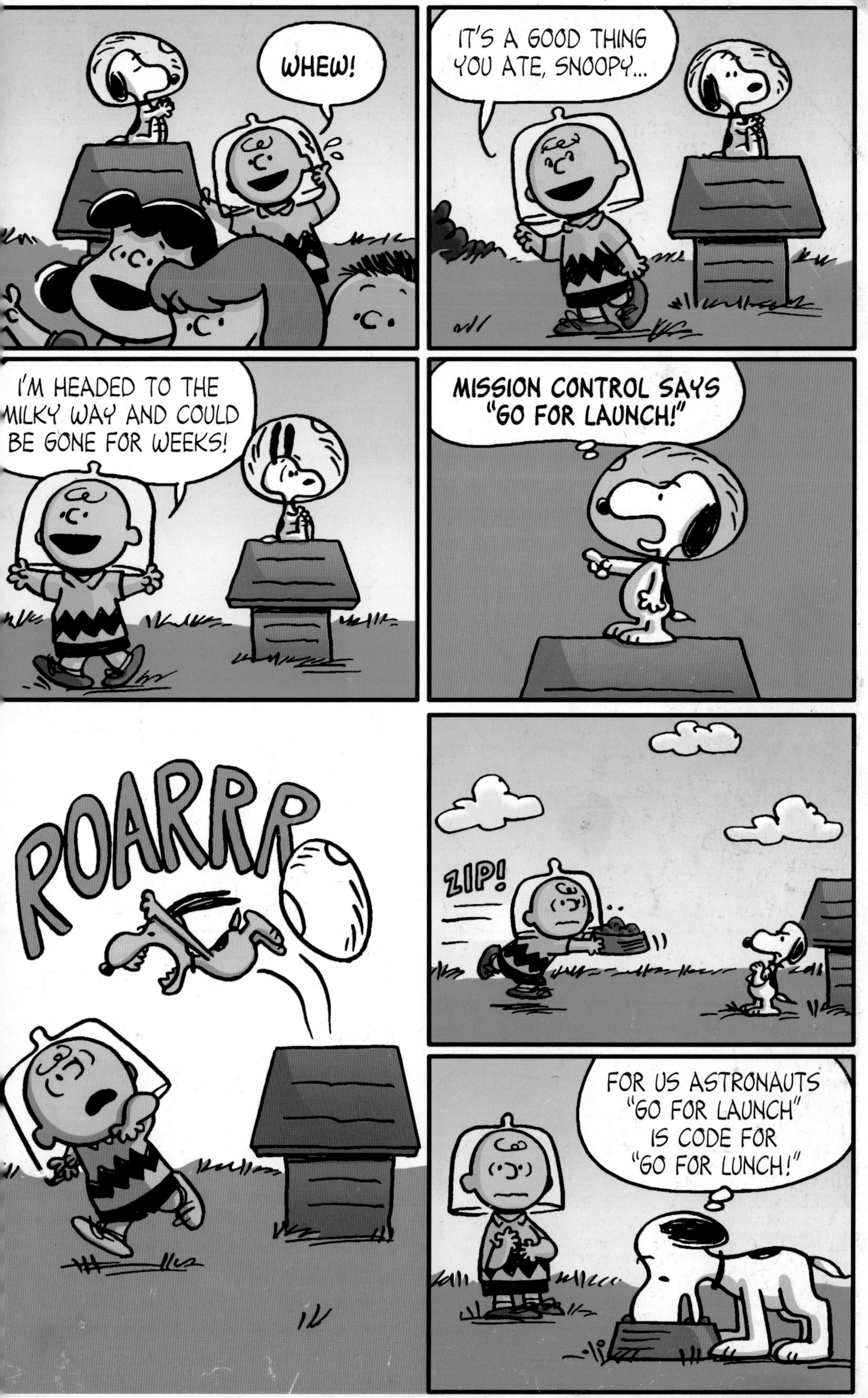
WHEW!
IT'S A GOOD THING YOU ATE, SNOOPY...
I'M HEADED TO THE MILKY WAY AND COULD BE GONE FOR WEEKS!
MISSION CONTROL SAYS "GO FOR LAUNCH!"
ROARRR
ZIP!
FOR US ASTRONAUTS "GO FOR LAUNCH" IS CODE FOR "GO FOR LUNCH!"

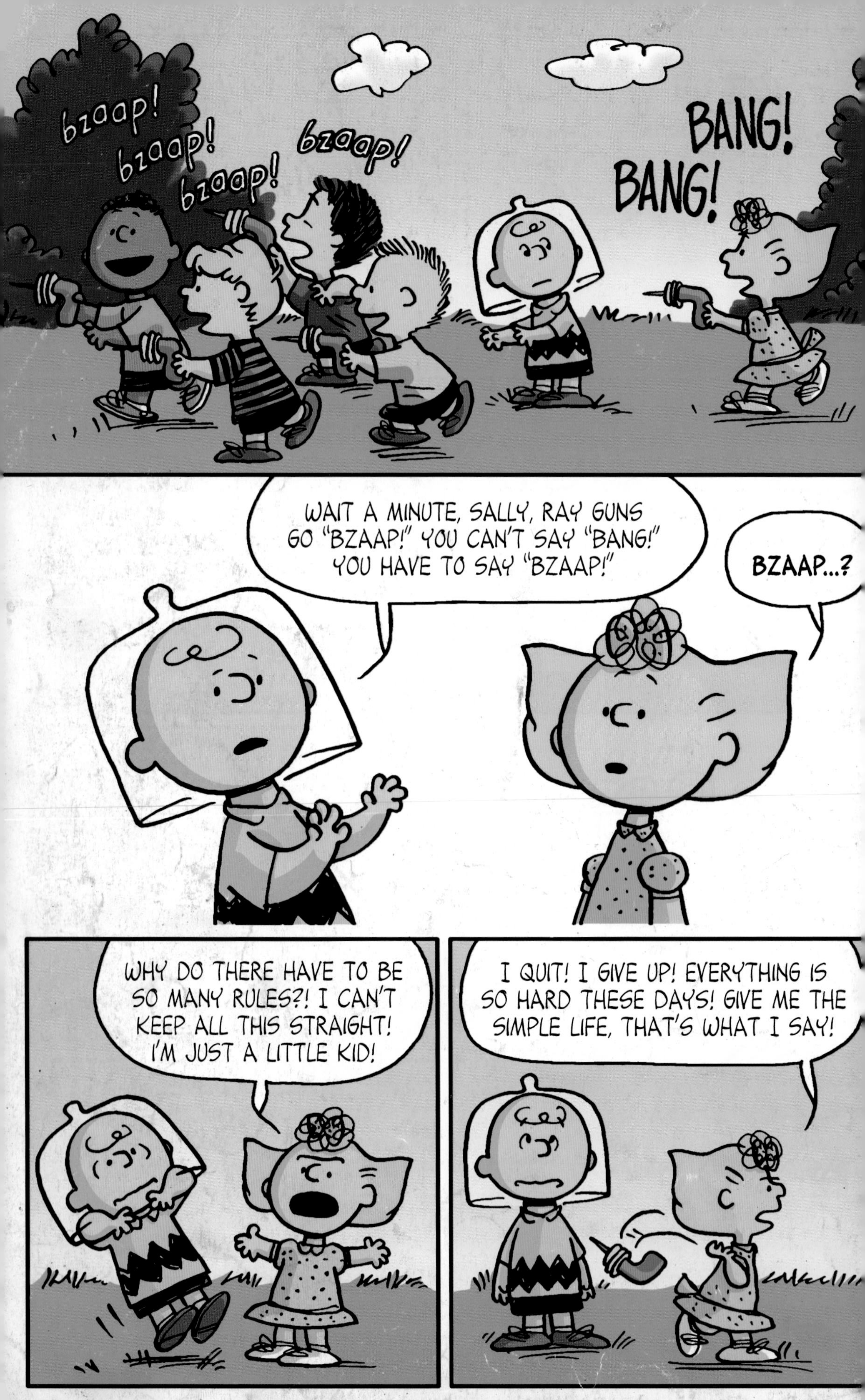
bzaap!
bzaap!
bzaap!
bzaap!
BANG!
BANG!
WAIT A MINUTE, SALLY, RAY GUNS GO "BZAAP!" YOU CAN'T SAY "BANG!" YOU HAVE TO SAY "BZAAP!"
BZAAP...?
WHY DO THERE HAVE TO BE SO MANY RULES?! I CAN'T KEEP ALL THIS STRAIGHT! I'M JUST A LITTLE KID!
I QUIT! I GIVE UP! EVERYTHING IS SO HARD THESE DAYS! GIVE ME THE SIMPLE LIFE, THAT'S WHAT I SAY!

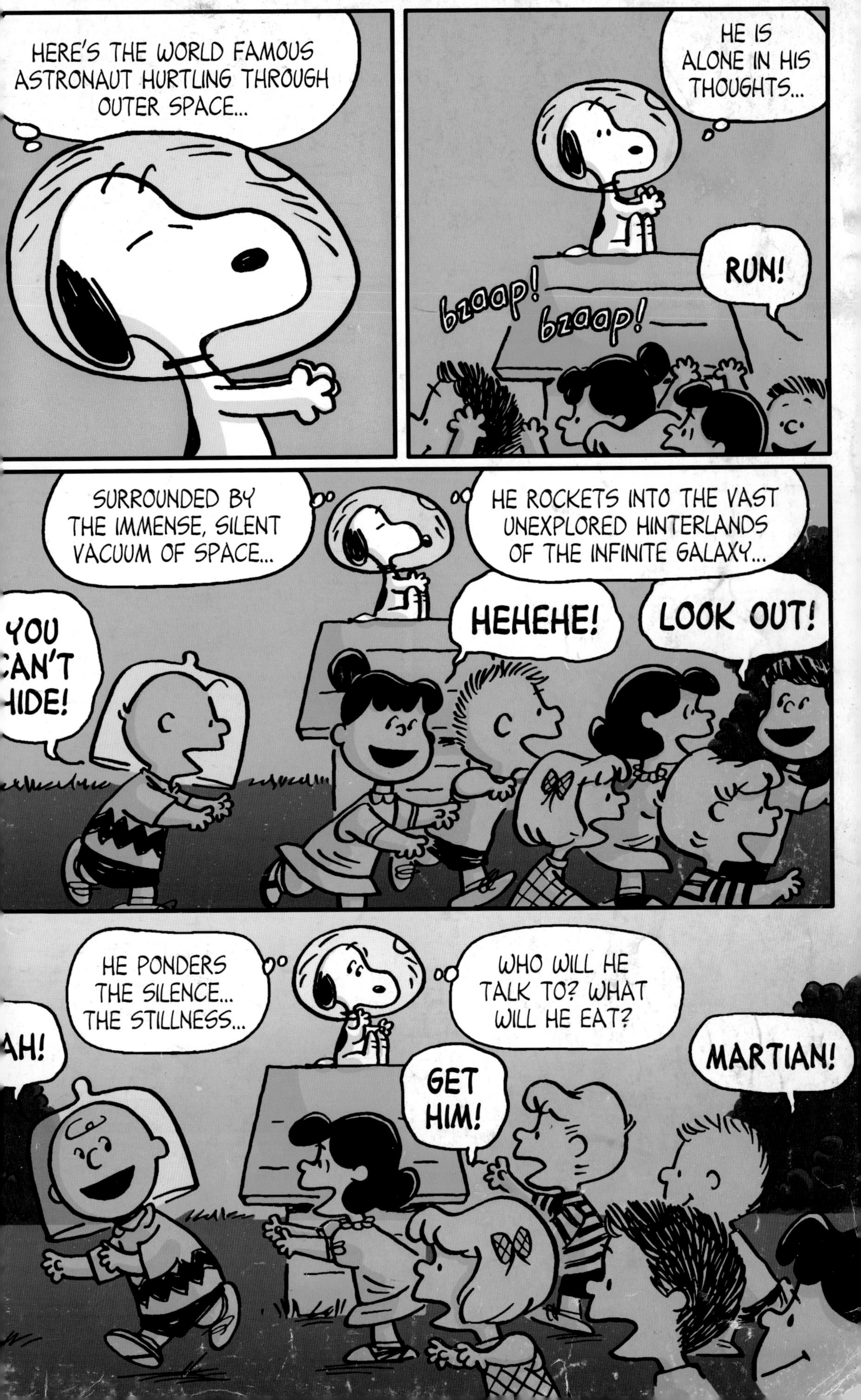
HERE'S THE WORLD FAMOUS ASTRONAUT HURTLING THROUGH OUTER SPACE...
HE IS ALONE IN HIS THOUGHTS...
bzaap!
bzaap!
RUN!
SURROUNDED BY THE IMMENSE, SILENT VACUUM OF SPACE...
HE ROCKETS INTO THE VAST UNEXPLORED HINTERLANDS OF THE INFINITE GALAXY...
YOU CAN'T HIDE!
HEHEHE!
LOOK OUT!
HE PONDERS THE SILENCE... THE STILLNESS...
WHO WILL HE TALK TO? WHAT WILL HE EAT?
AH!
GET HIM!
MARTIAN!

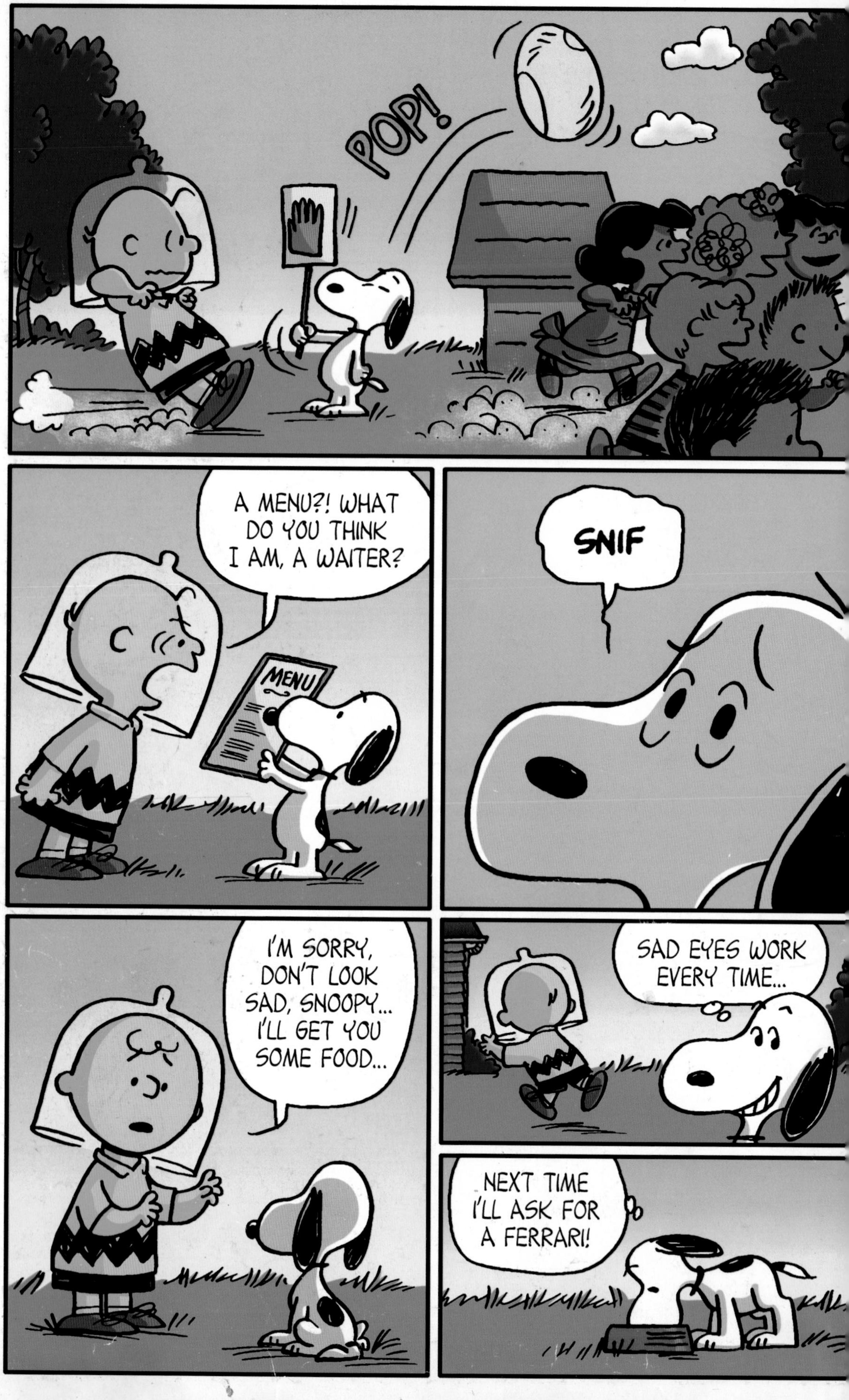
POP!
A MENU?! WHAT DO YOU THINK I AM, A WAITER?
MENU
SNIF
I'M SORRY, DON'T LOOK SAD, SNOOPY... I'LL GET YOU SOME FOOD...
SAD EYES WORK EVERY TIME...
NEXT TIME I'LL ASK FOR A FERRARI!

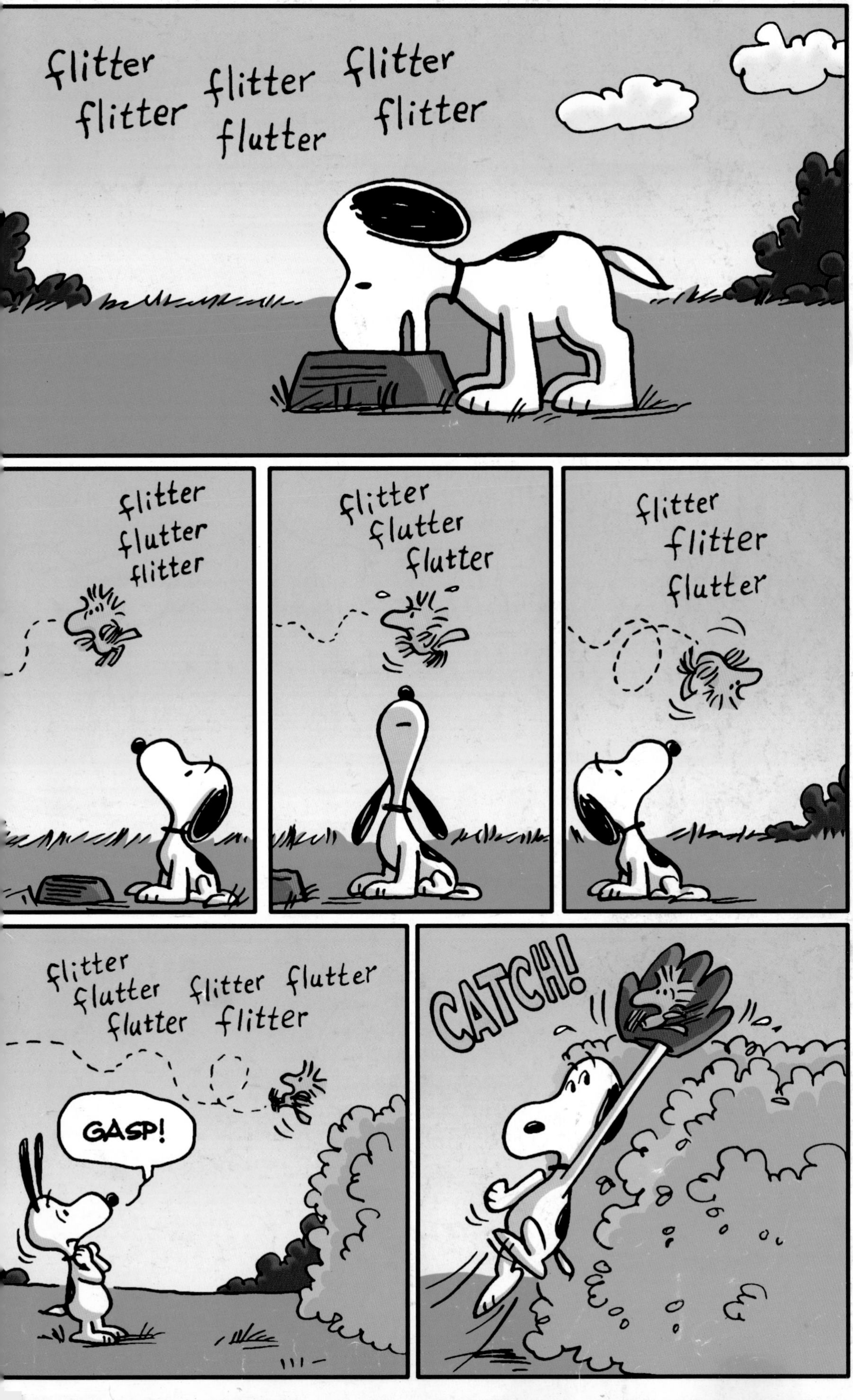
flitter flitter flitter flitter flutter flitter
flitter flutter flitter
flitter flutter flutter
flitter flitter flutter
flitter flutter flitter flutter flutter flitter
GASP!
CATCH!

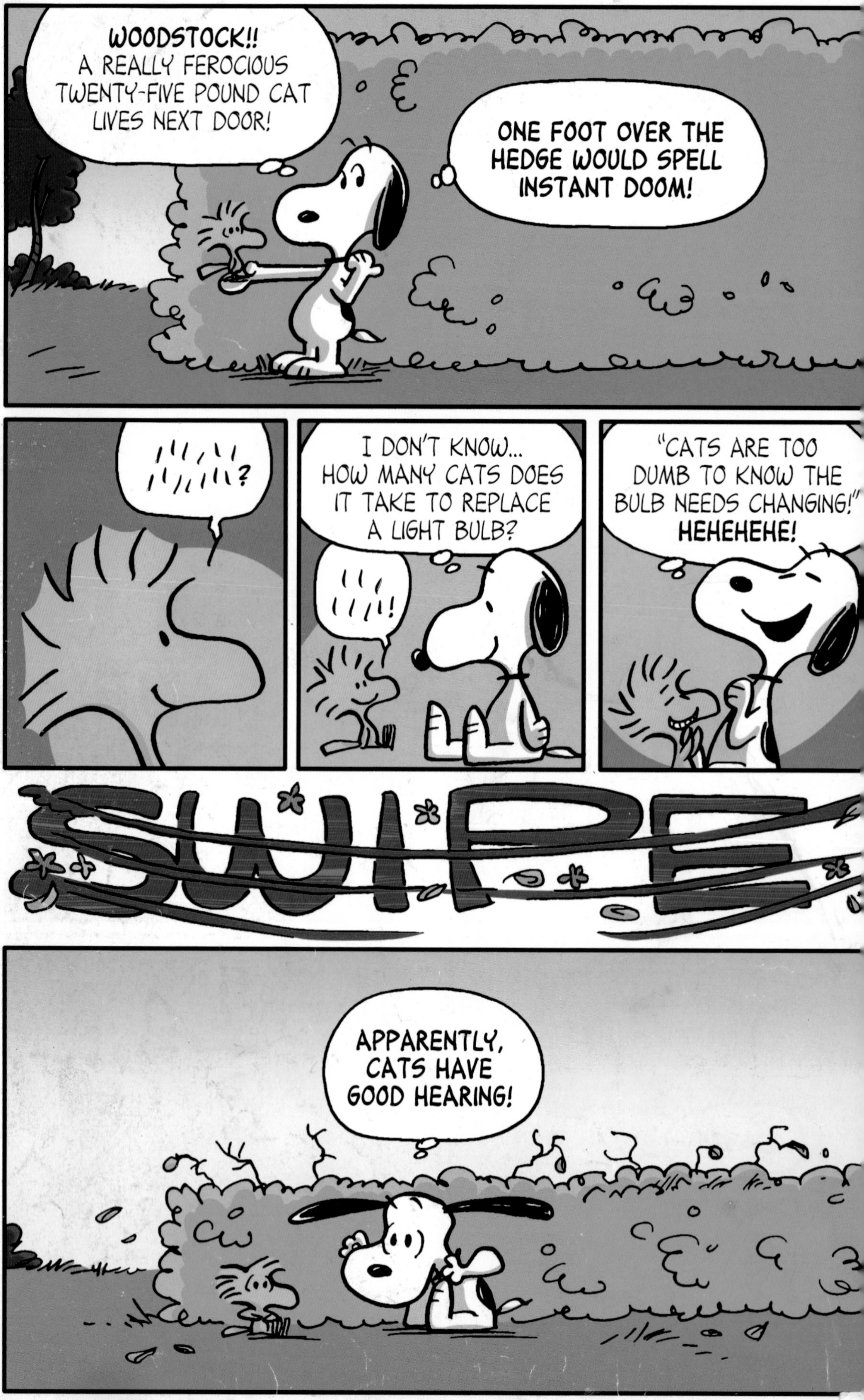
WOODSTOCK!! A REALLY FEROCIOUS TWENTY-FIVE POUND CAT LIVES NEXT DOOR!
ONE FOOT OVER THE HEDGE WOULD SPELL INSTANT DOOM!
?
I DON'T KNOW... HOW MANY CATS DOES IT TAKE TO REPLACE A LIGHT BULB?
!
"CATS ARE TOO DUMB TO KNOW THE BULB NEEDS CHANGING!" HEHEHEHE!
SWIPE
APPARENTLY, CATS HAVE GOOD HEARING!

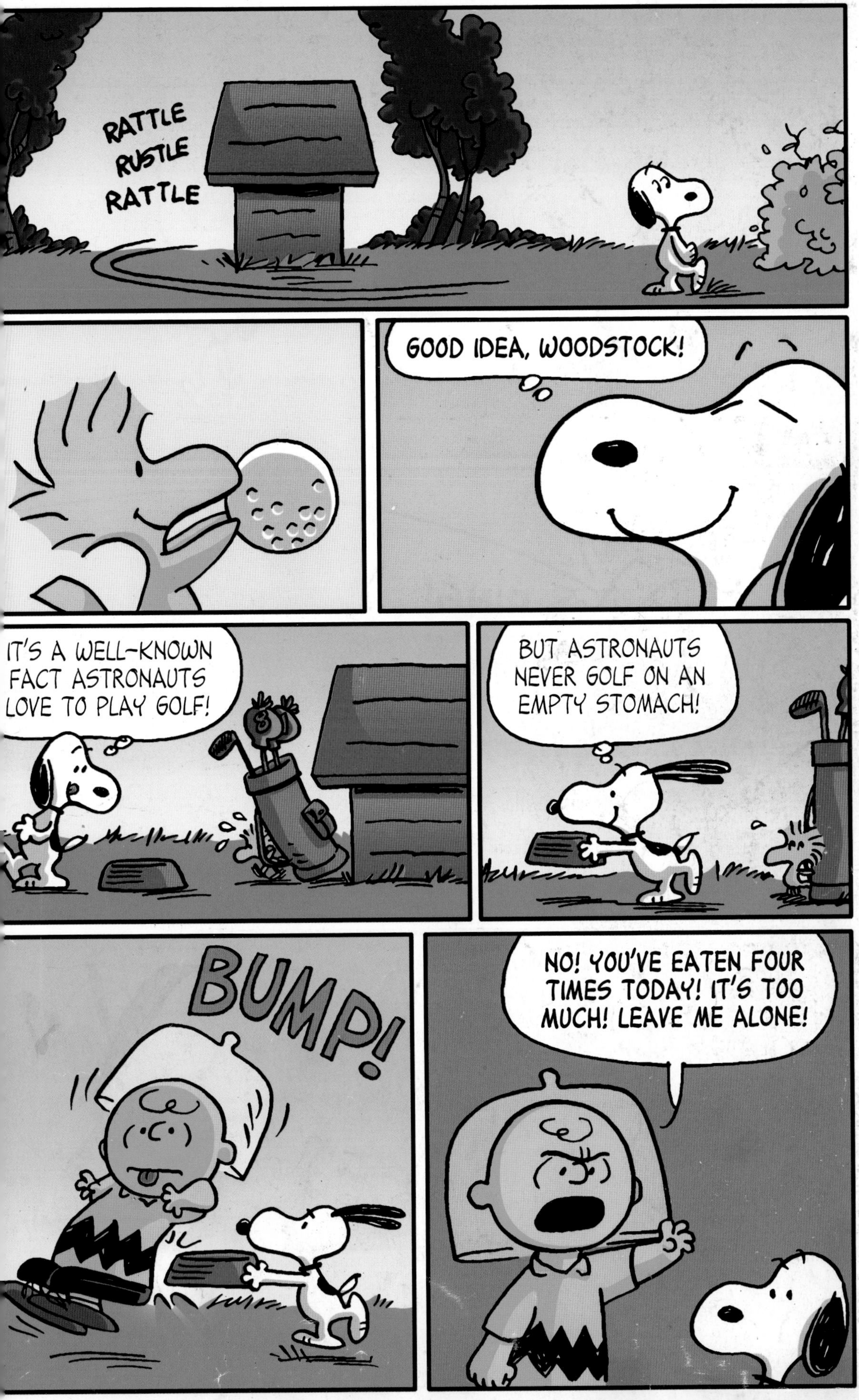
RATTLE
RUSTLE
RATTLE
GOOD IDEA, WOODSTOCK!
IT'S A WELL-KNOWN FACT ASTRONAUTS LOVE TO PLAY GOLF!
BUT ASTRONAUTS NEVER GOLF ON AN EMPTY STOMACH!
BUMP!
NO! YOU'VE EATEN FOUR TIMES TODAY! IT'S TOO MUCH! LEAVE ME ALONE!

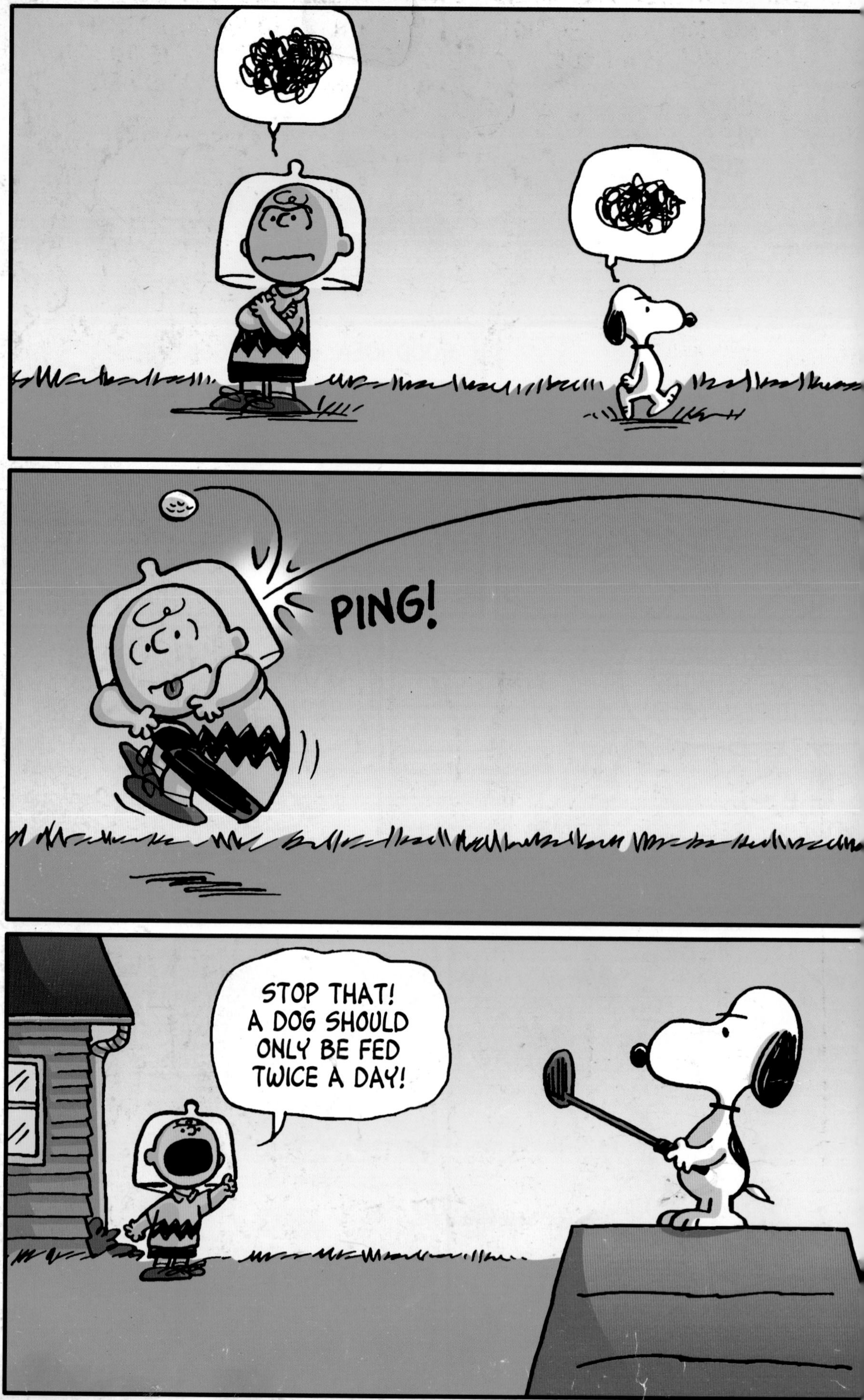
PING!
STOP THAT! A DOG SHOULD ONLY BE FED TWICE A DAY!

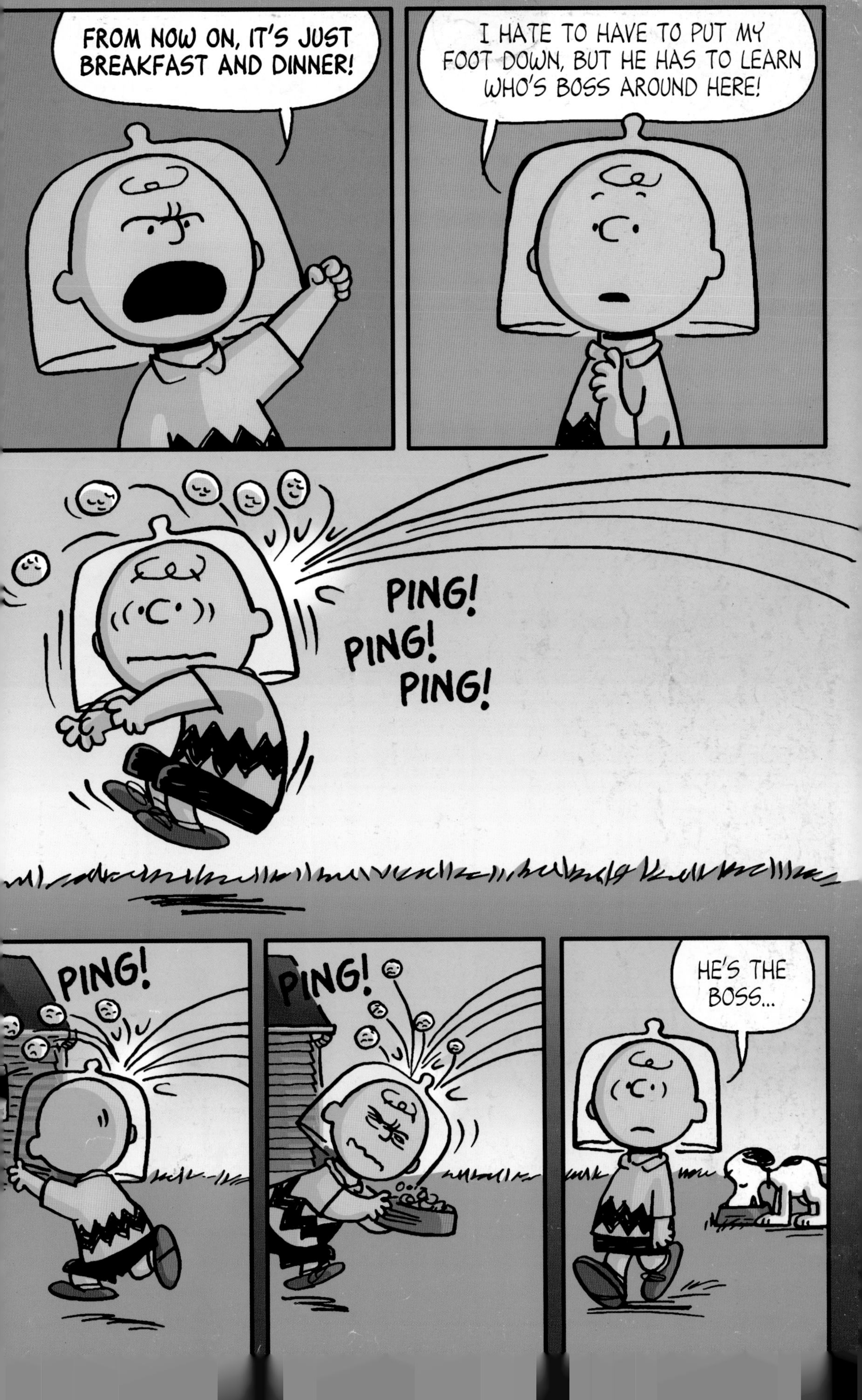
FROM NOW ON, IT'S JUST BREAKFAST AND DINNER!
I HATE TO HAVE TO PUT MY FOOT DOWN, BUT HE HAS TO LEARN WHO'S BOSS AROUND HERE!
PING!
PING!
PING!
PING!
PING!
HE'S THE BOSS...

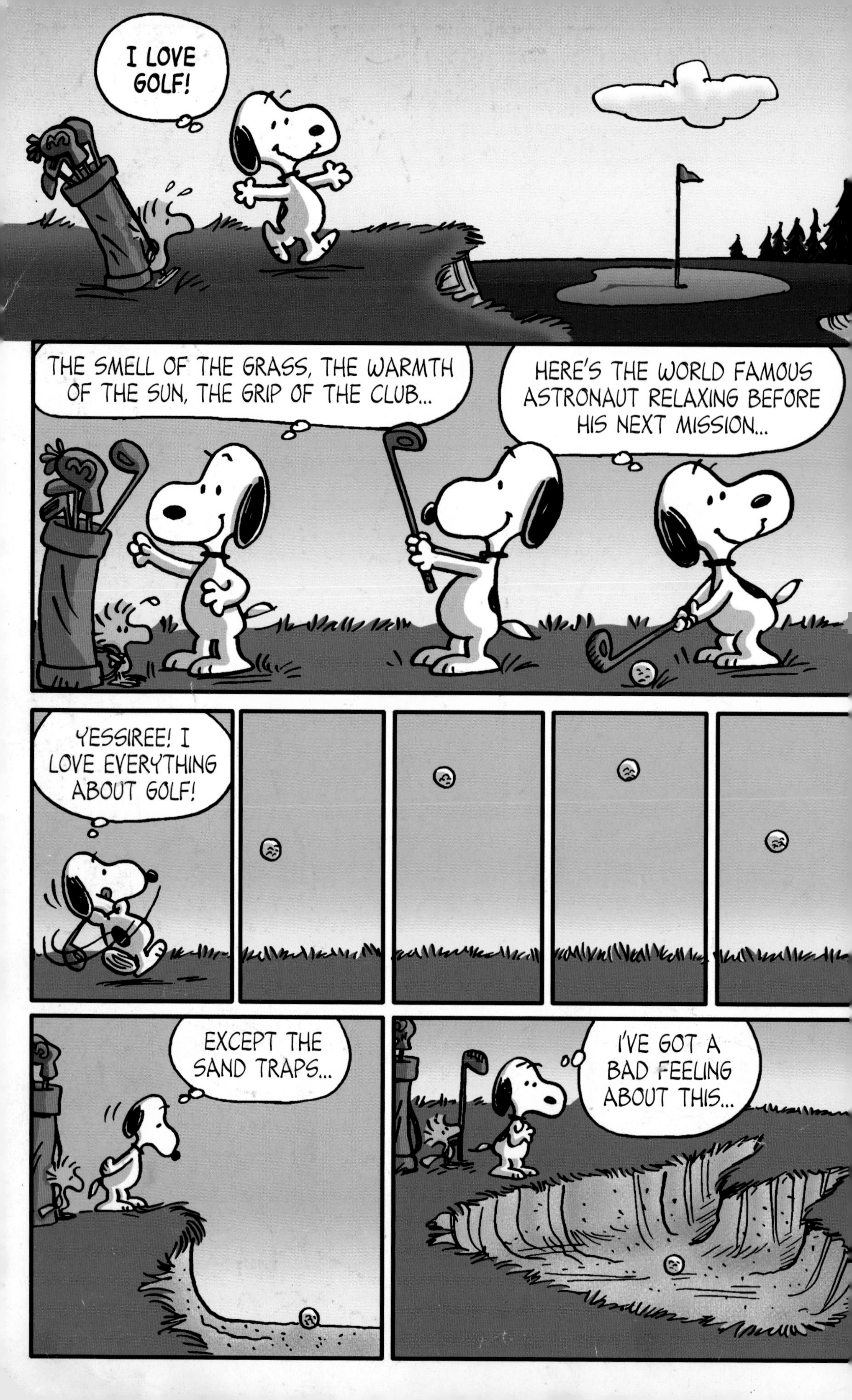
I LOVE GOLF!
THE SMELL OF THE GRASS, THE WARMTH OF THE SUN, THE GRIP OF THE CLUB...
HERE'S THE WORLD FAMOUS ASTRONAUT RELAXING BEFORE HIS NEXT MISSION...
YESSIREE! I LOVE EVERYTHING ABOUT GOLF!
EXCEPT THE SAND TRAPS...
I'VE GOT A BAD FEELING ABOUT THIS...

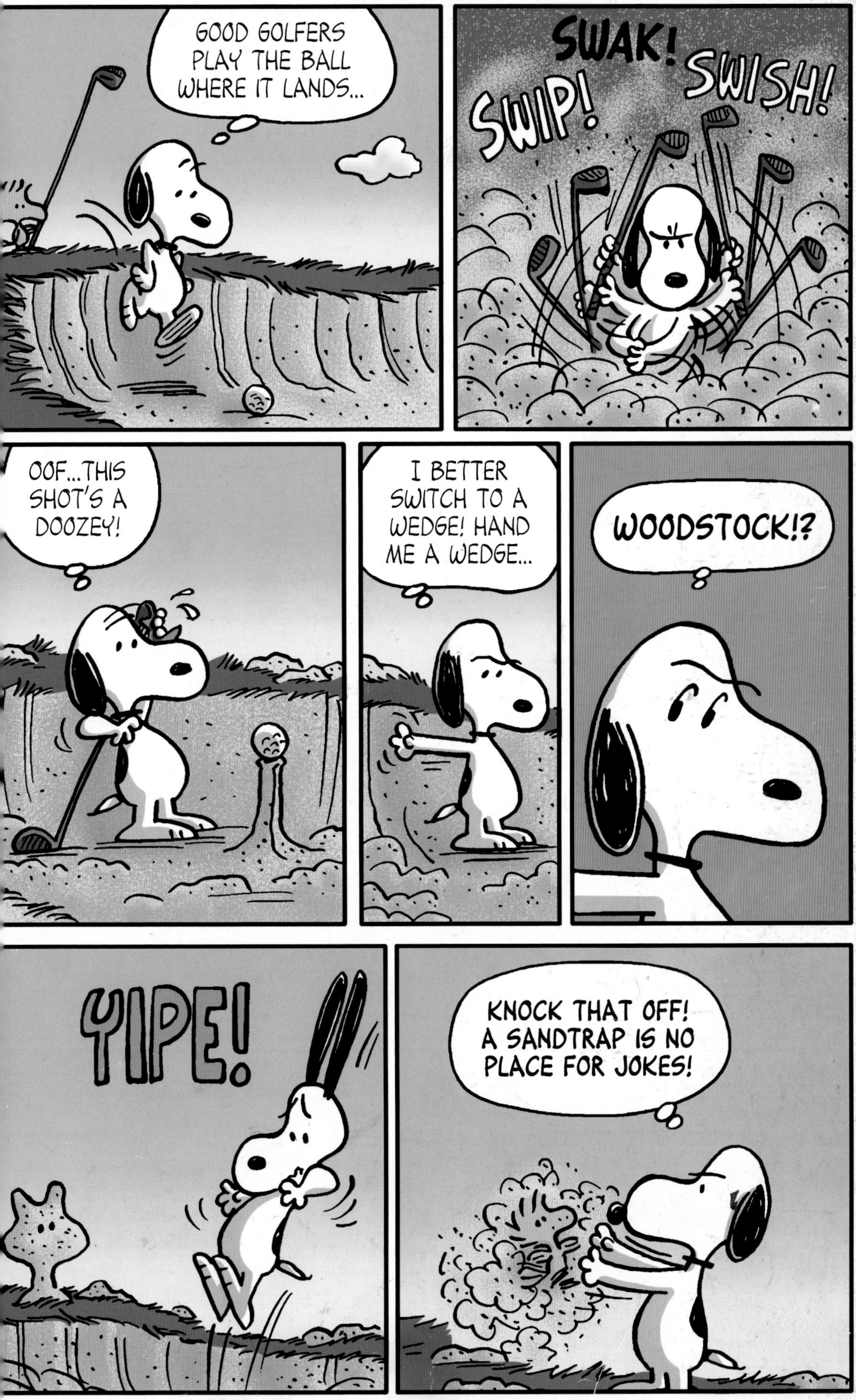
GOOD GOLFERS PLAY THE BALL WHERE IT LANDS...
SWAK!
SWIP!
SWISH!
OOF...THIS SHOT'S A DOOZEY!
I BETTER SWITCH TO A WEDGE! HAND ME A WEDGE...
WOODSTOCK!?
YIPE!
KNOCK THAT OFF! A SANDTRAP IS NO PLACE FOR JOKES!

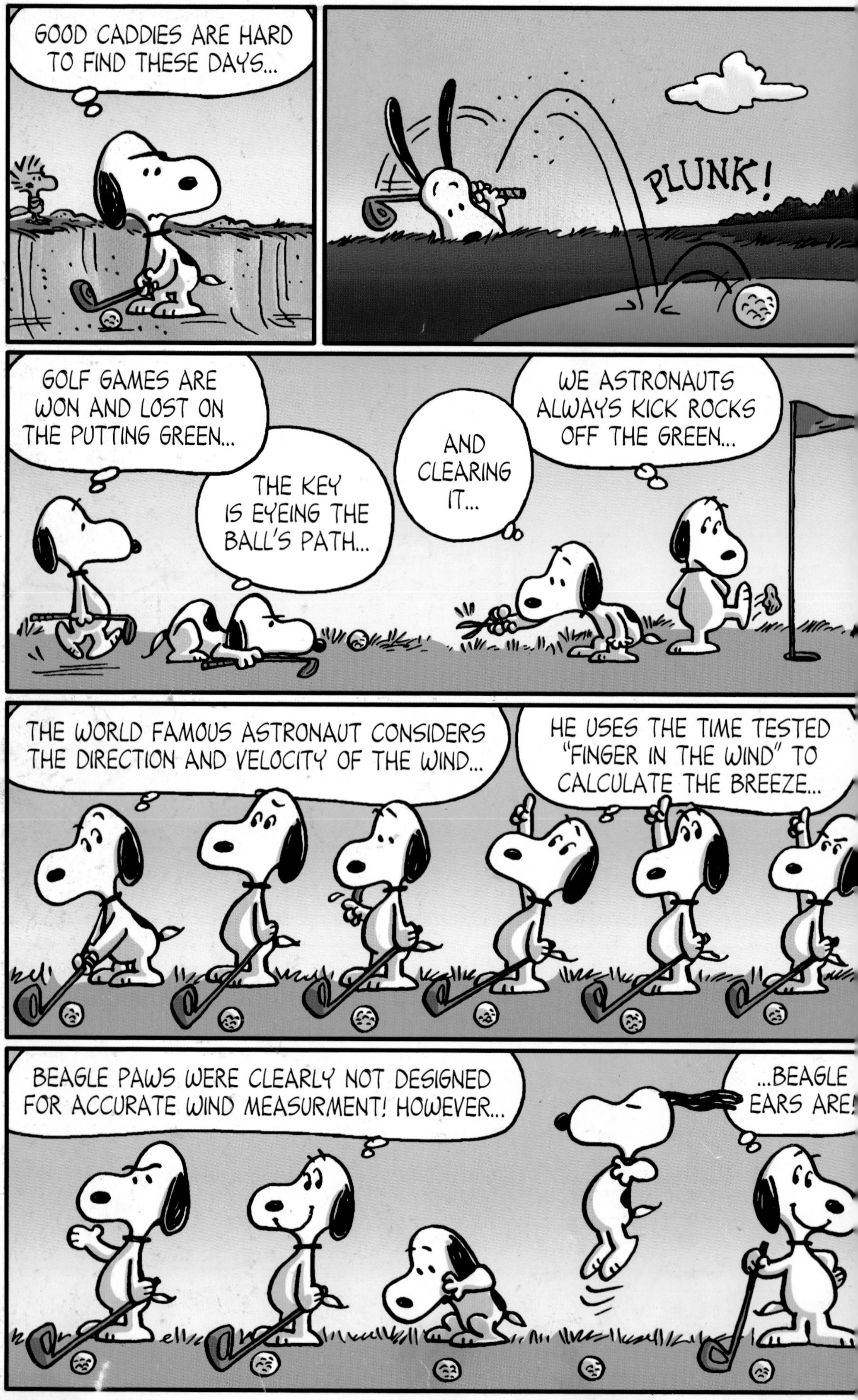
GOOD CADDIES ARE HARD TO FIND THESE DAYS...
PLUNK!
GOLF GAMES ARE WON AND LOST ON THE PUTTING GREEN...
THE KEY IS EYEING THE BALL'S PATH...
AND CLEARING IT...
WE ASTRONAUTS ALWAYS KICK ROCKS OFF THE GREEN...
THE WORLD FAMOUS ASTRONAUT CONSIDERS THE DIRECTION AND VELOCITY OF THE WIND...
HE USES THE TIME TESTED "FINGER IN THE WIND" TO CALCULATE THE BREEZE...
BEAGLE PAWS WERE CLEARLY NOT DESIGNED FOR ACCURATE WIND MEASURMENT! HOWEVER...
...BEAGLE EARS ARE!

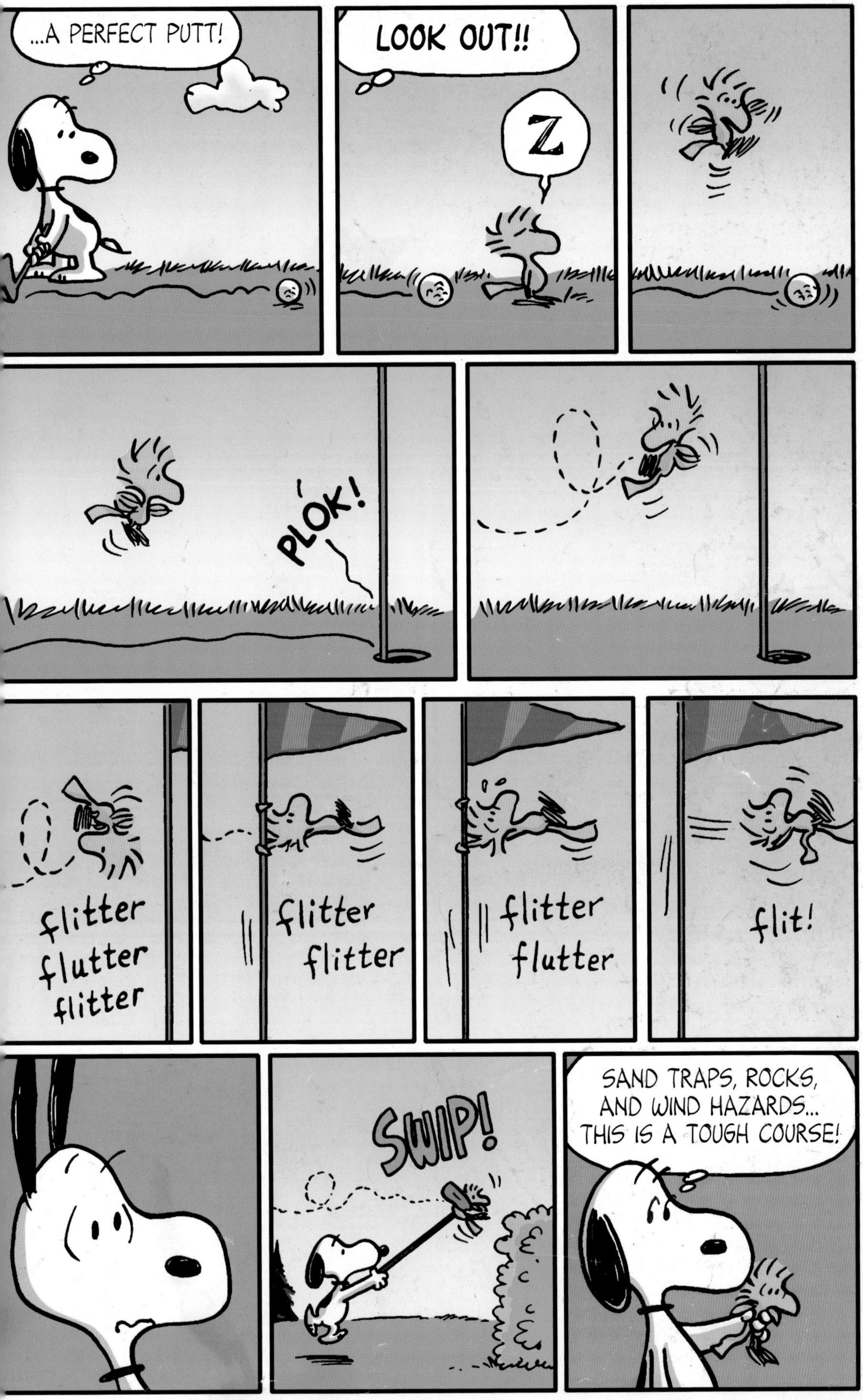
...A PERFECT PUTT!
LOOK OUT!!
Z
PLOK!
flitter flutter flitter
flitter flitter
flitter flutter
flit!
SWIP!
SAND TRAPS, ROCKS, AND WIND HAZARDS... THIS IS A TOUGH COURSE!

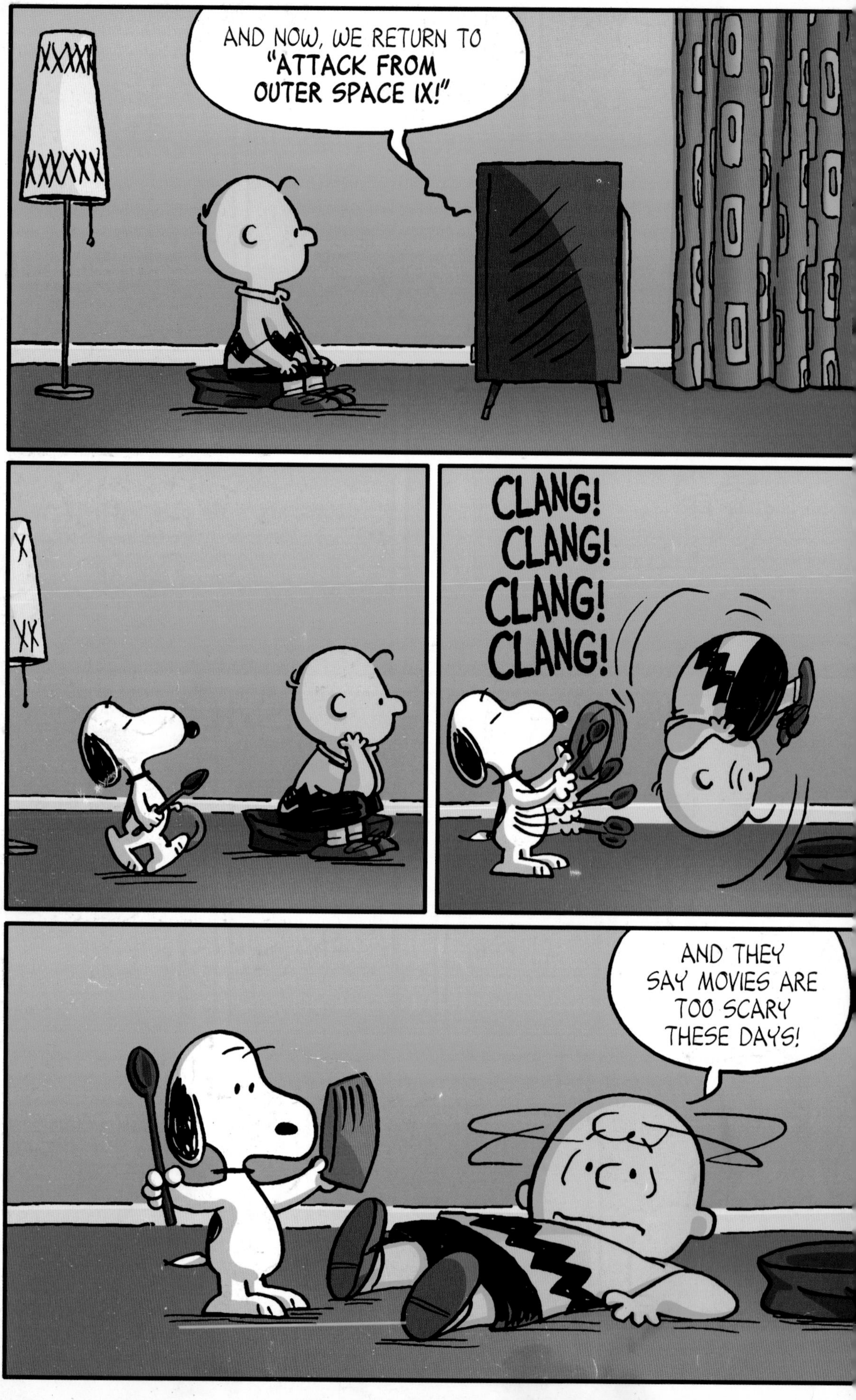
AND NOW, WE RETURN TO "ATTACK FROM OUTER SPACE IX!"
CLANG! CLANG! CLANG! CLANG!
AND THEY SAY MOVIES ARE TOO SCARY THESE DAYS!

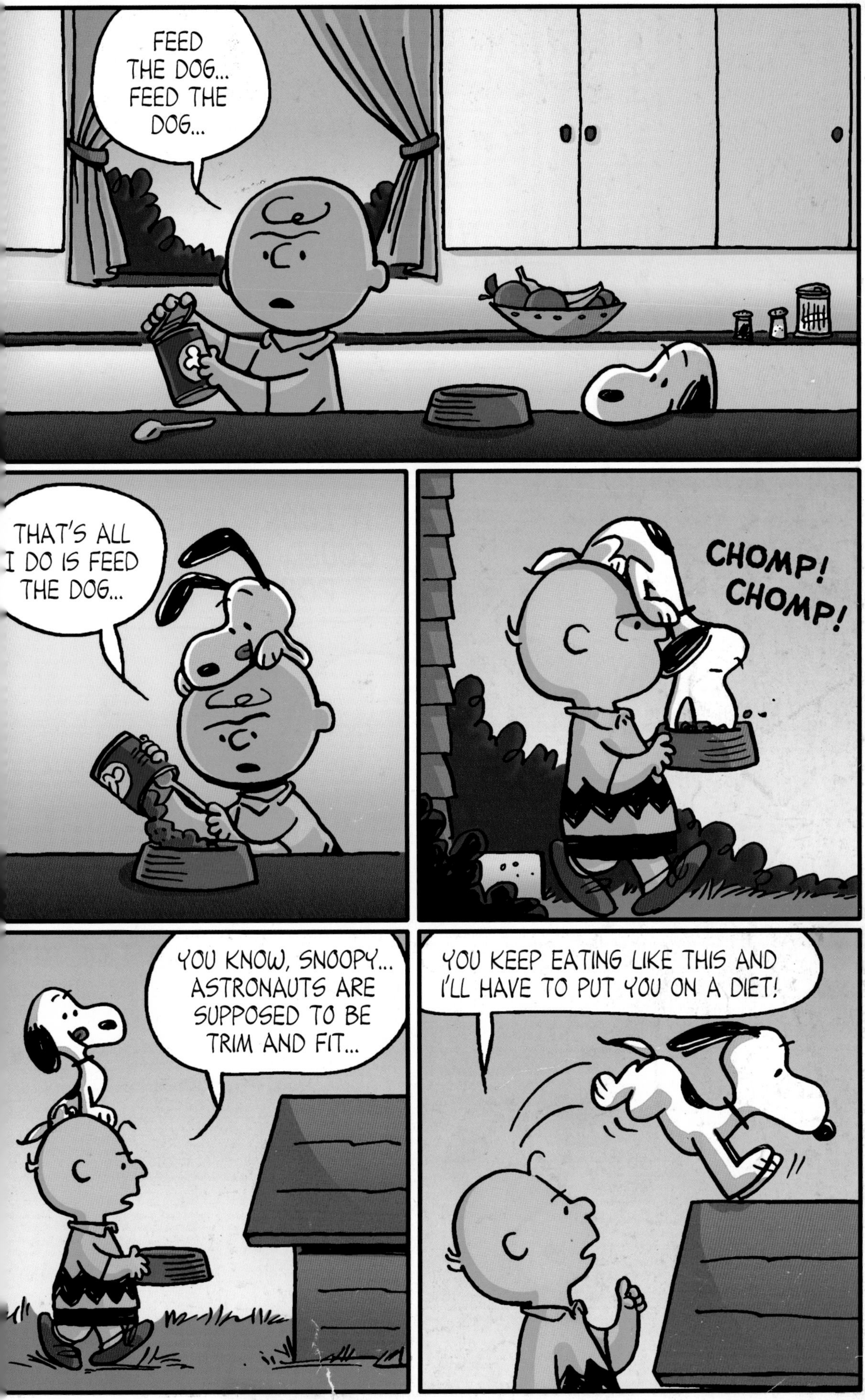
FEED THE DOG... FEED THE DOG...
THAT'S ALL I DO IS FEED THE DOG...
CHOMP! CHOMP!
YOU KNOW, SNOOPY... ASTRONAUTS ARE SUPPOSED TO BE TRIM AND FIT...
YOU KEEP EATING LIKE THIS AND I'LL HAVE TO PUT YOU ON A DIET!

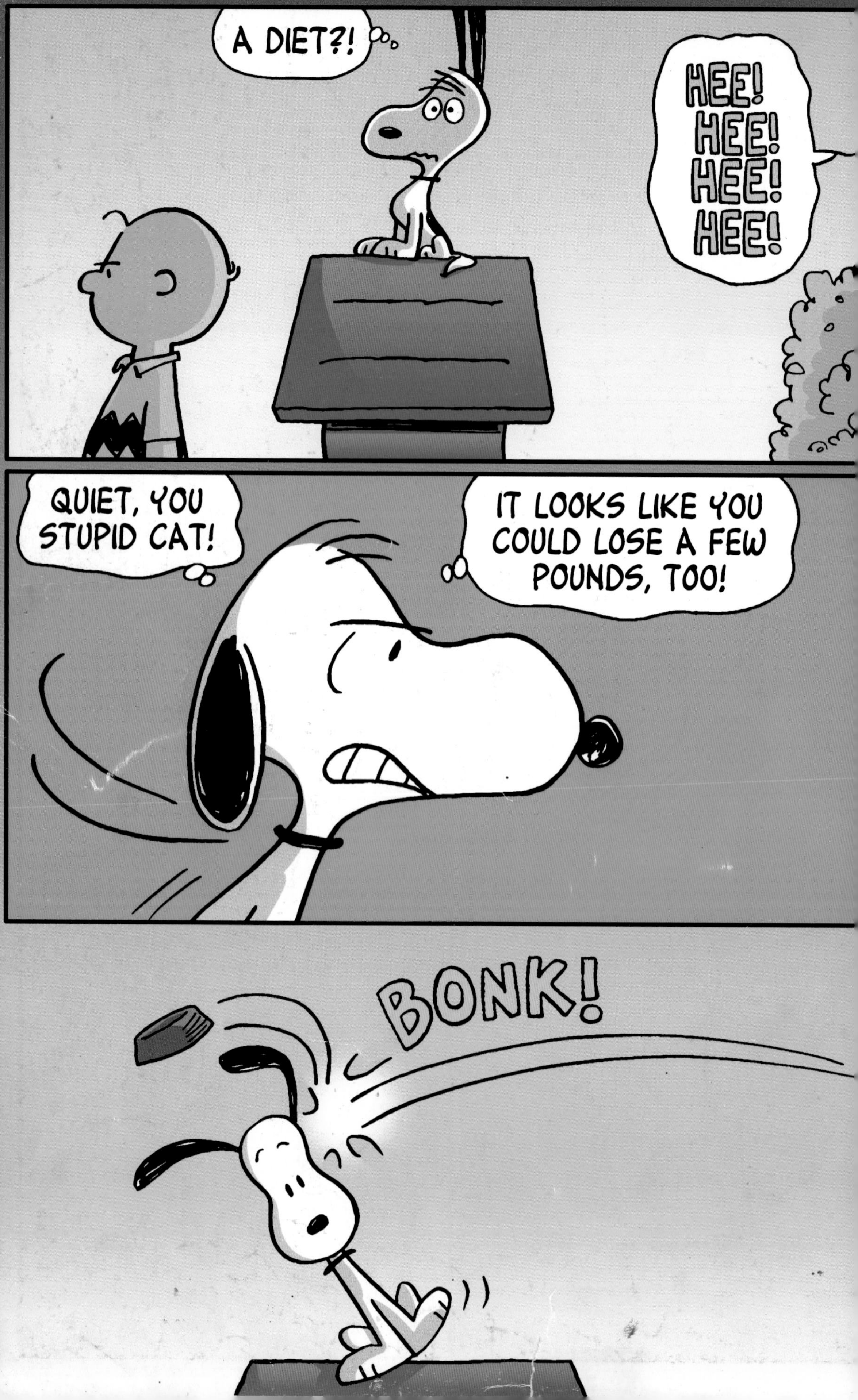
A DIET?!
HEE! HEE! HEE! HEE!
QUIET, YOU STUPID CAT!
IT LOOKS LIKE YOU COULD LOSE A FEW POUNDS, TOO!
BONK!

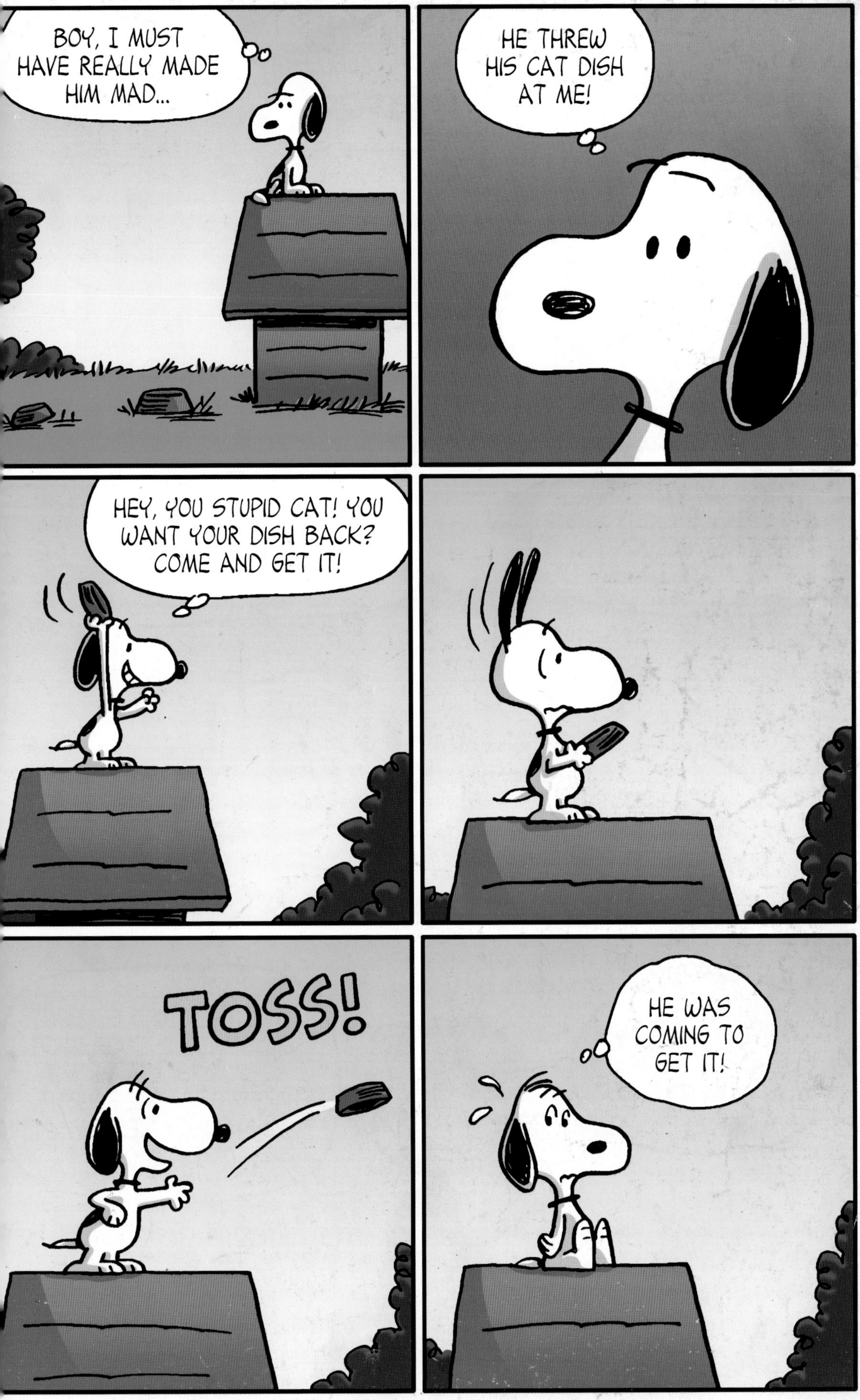
BOY, I MUST HAVE REALLY MADE HIM MAD...
HE THREW HIS CAT DISH AT ME!
HEY, YOU STUPID CAT! YOU WANT YOUR DISH BACK? COME AND GET IT!
TOSS!
HE WAS COMING TO GET IT!

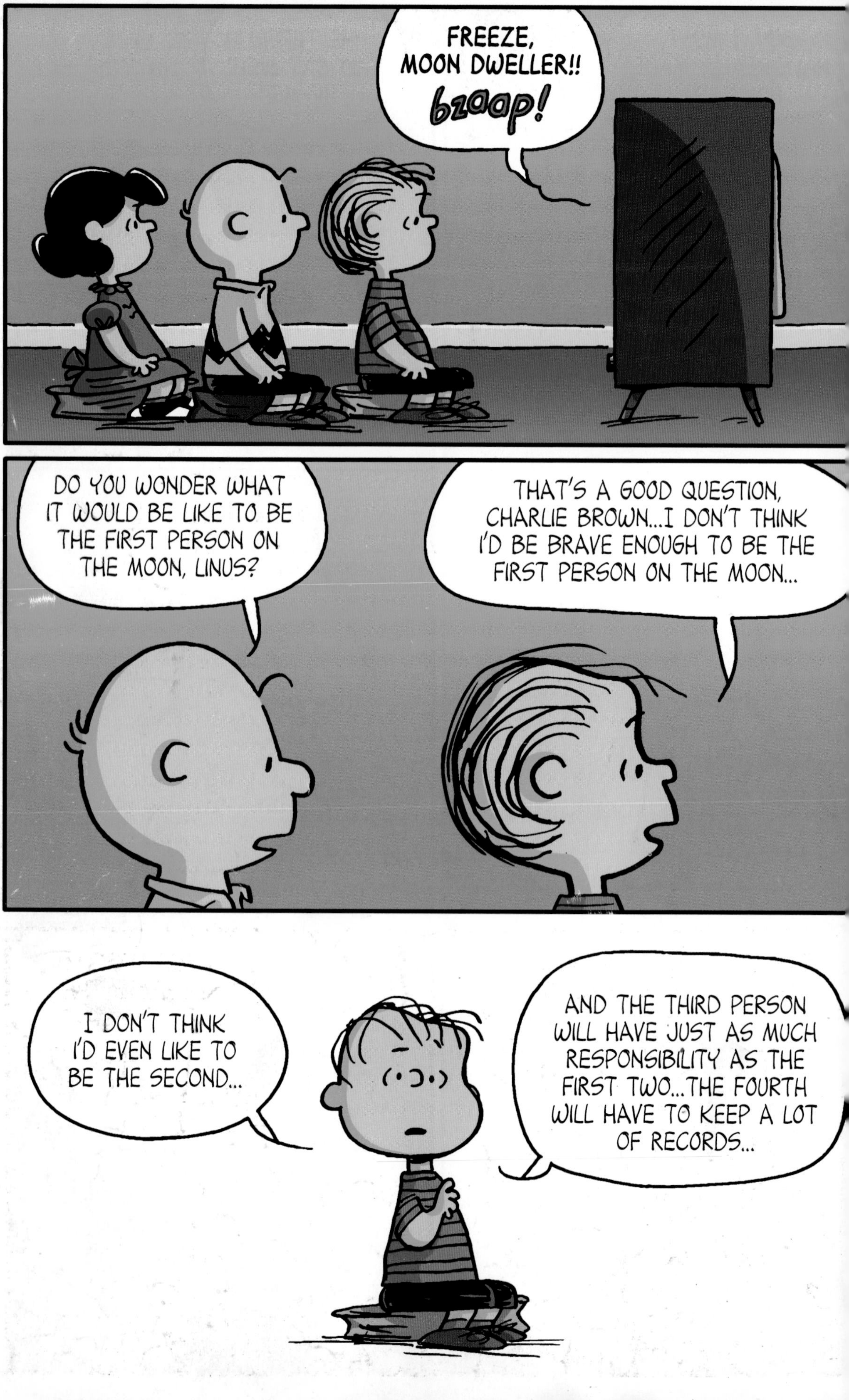
FREEZE, MOON DWELLER!! bzaap!
DO YOU WONDER WHAT IT WOULD BE LIKE TO BE THE FIRST PERSON ON THE MOON, LINUS?
THAT'S A GOOD QUESTION, CHARLIE BROWN...I DON'T THINK I'D BE BRAVE ENOUGH TO BE THE FIRST PERSON ON THE MOON...
I DON'T THINK I'D EVEN LIKE TO BE THE SECOND...
AND THE THIRD PERSON WILL HAVE JUST AS MUCH RESPONSIBILITY AS THE FIRST TWO...THE FOURTH WILL HAVE TO KEEP A LOT OF RECORDS...

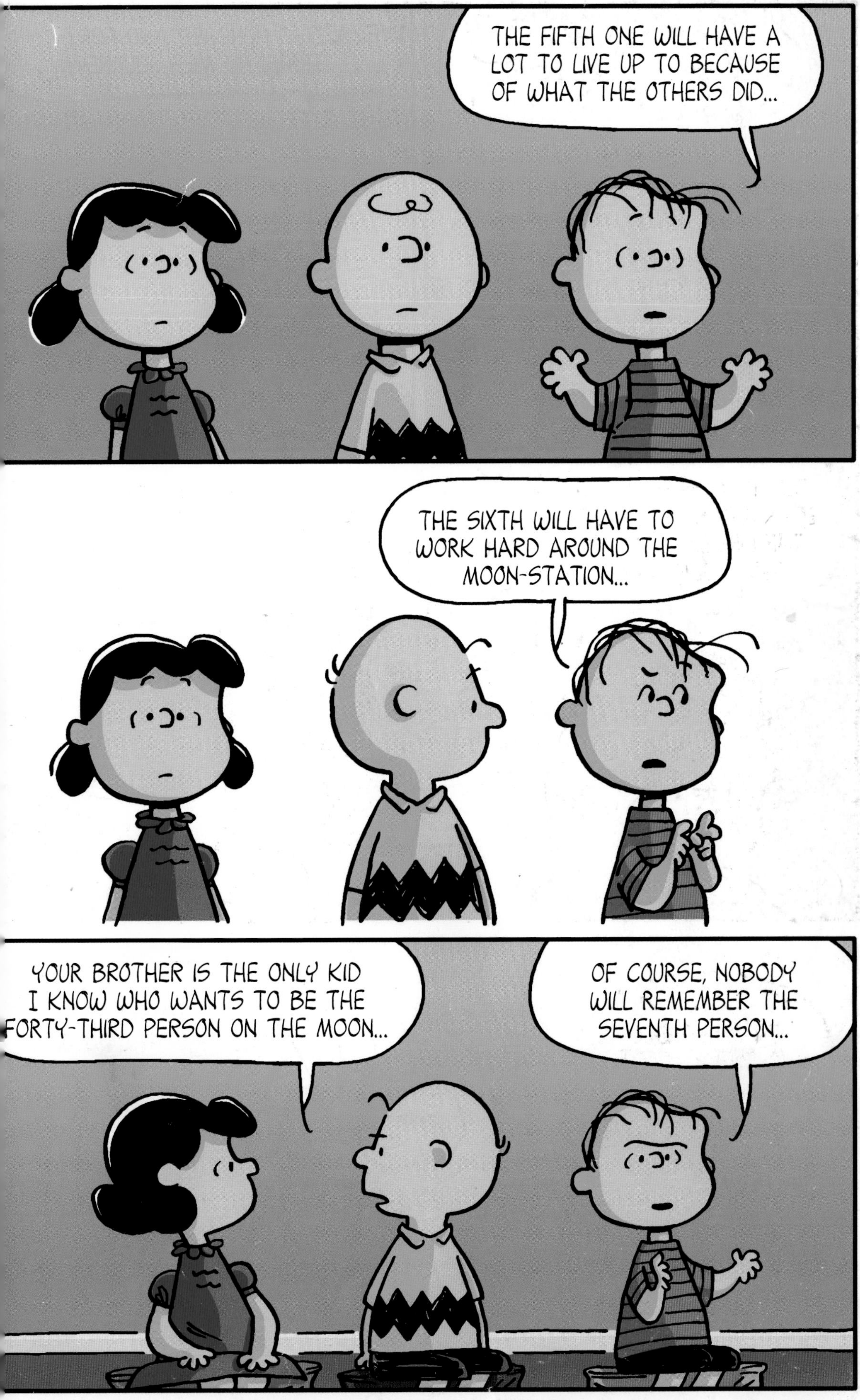
THE FIFTH ONE WILL HAVE A LOT TO LIVE UP TO BECAUSE OF WHAT THE OTHERS DID...
THE SIXTH WILL HAVE TO WORK HARD AROUND THE MOON-STATION...
OF COURSE, NOBODY WILL REMEMBER THE SEVENTH PERSON...
YOUR BROTHER IS THE ONLY KID I KNOW WHO WANTS TO BE THE FORTY-THIRD PERSON ON THE MOON...

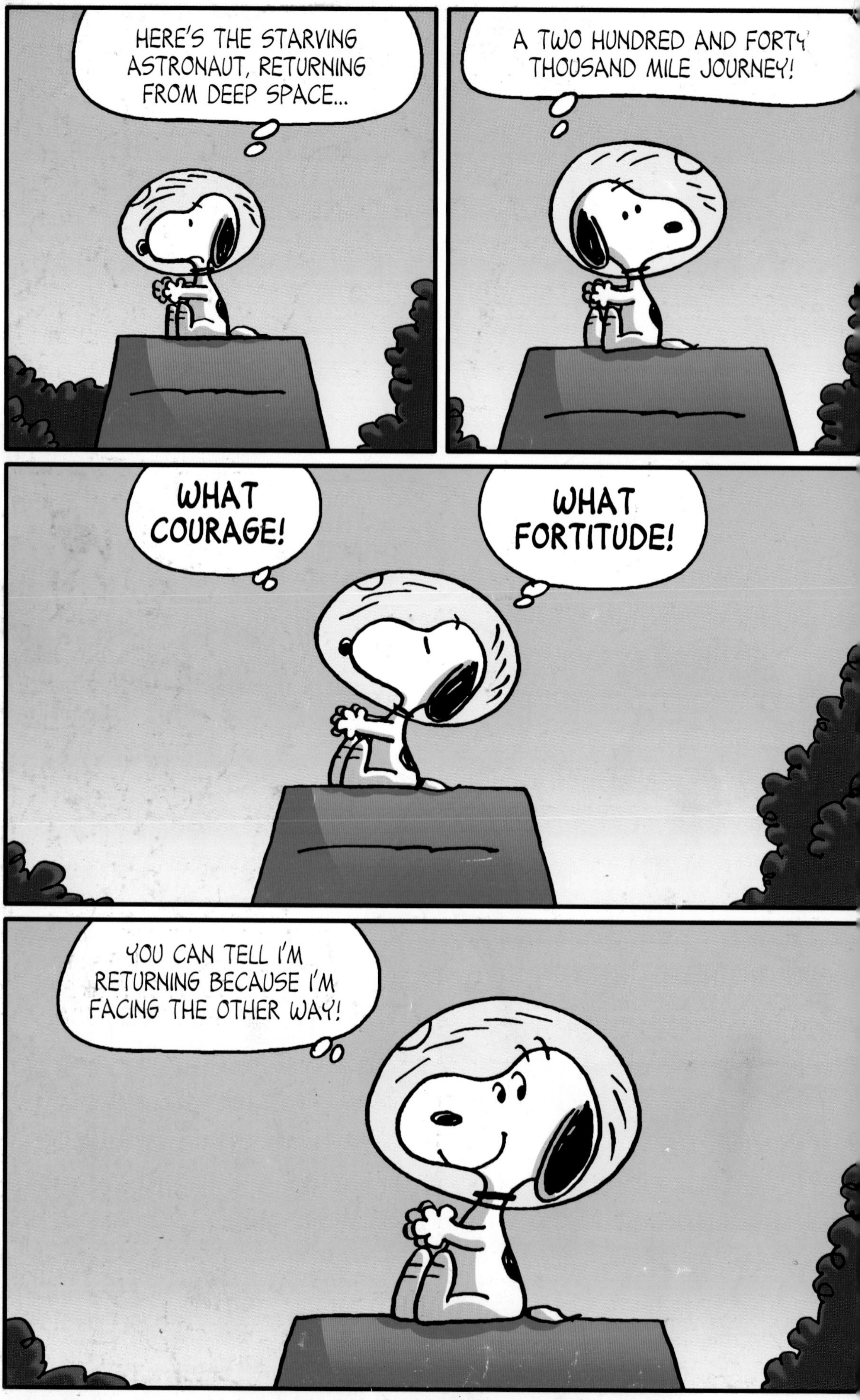
HERE'S THE STARVING ASTRONAUT, RETURNING FROM DEEP SPACE...
A TWO HUNDRED AND FORTY THOUSAND MILE JOURNEY!
WHAT COURAGE!
WHAT FORTITUDE!
YOU CAN TELL I'M RETURNING BECAUSE I'M FACING THE OTHER WAY!

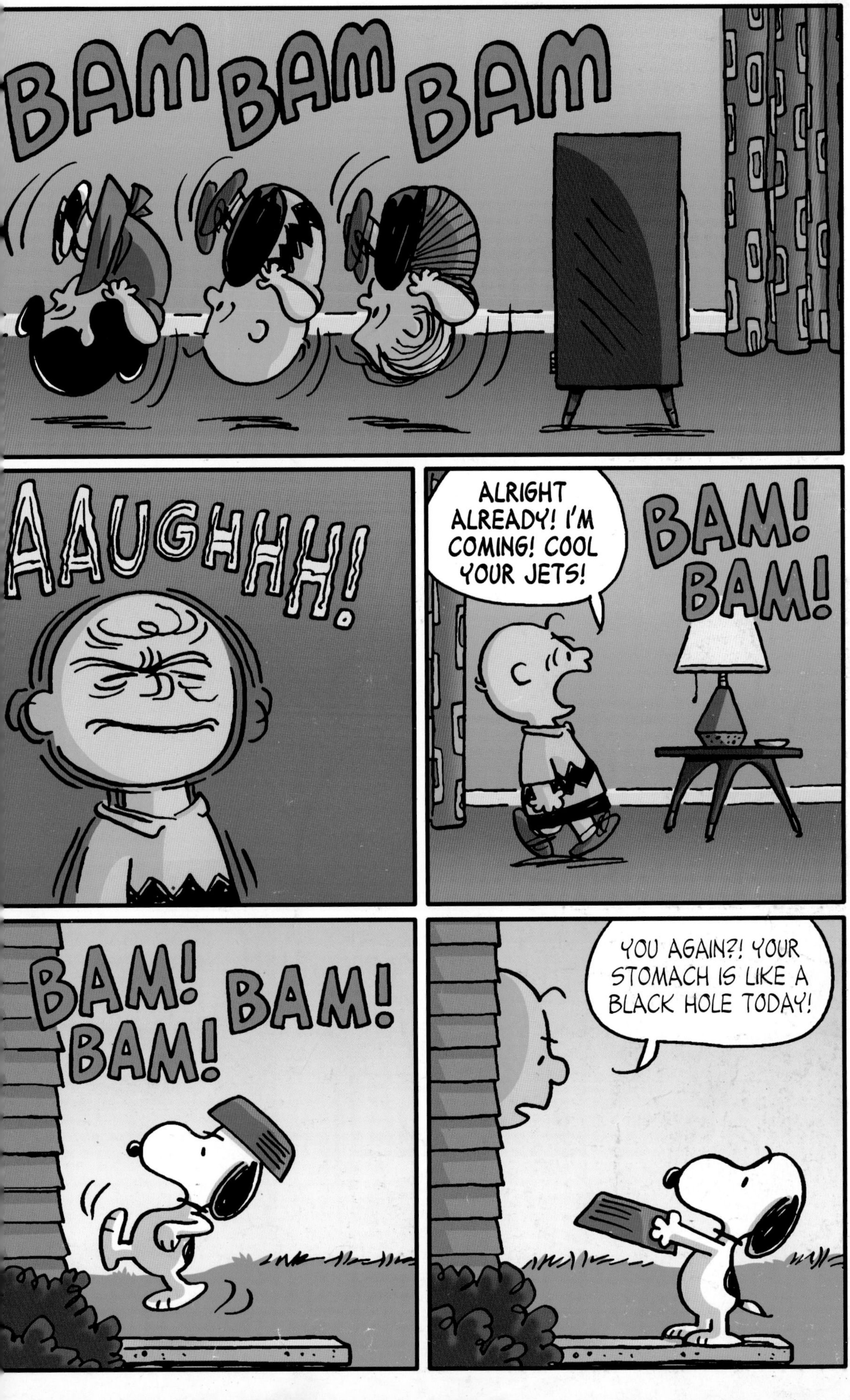
BAM BAM BAM
AAUGHHH!
ALRIGHT ALREADY! I'M COMING! COOL YOUR JETS!
BAM! BAM!
BAM! BAM! BAM!
YOU AGAIN?! YOUR STOMACH IS LIKE A BLACK HOLE TODAY!

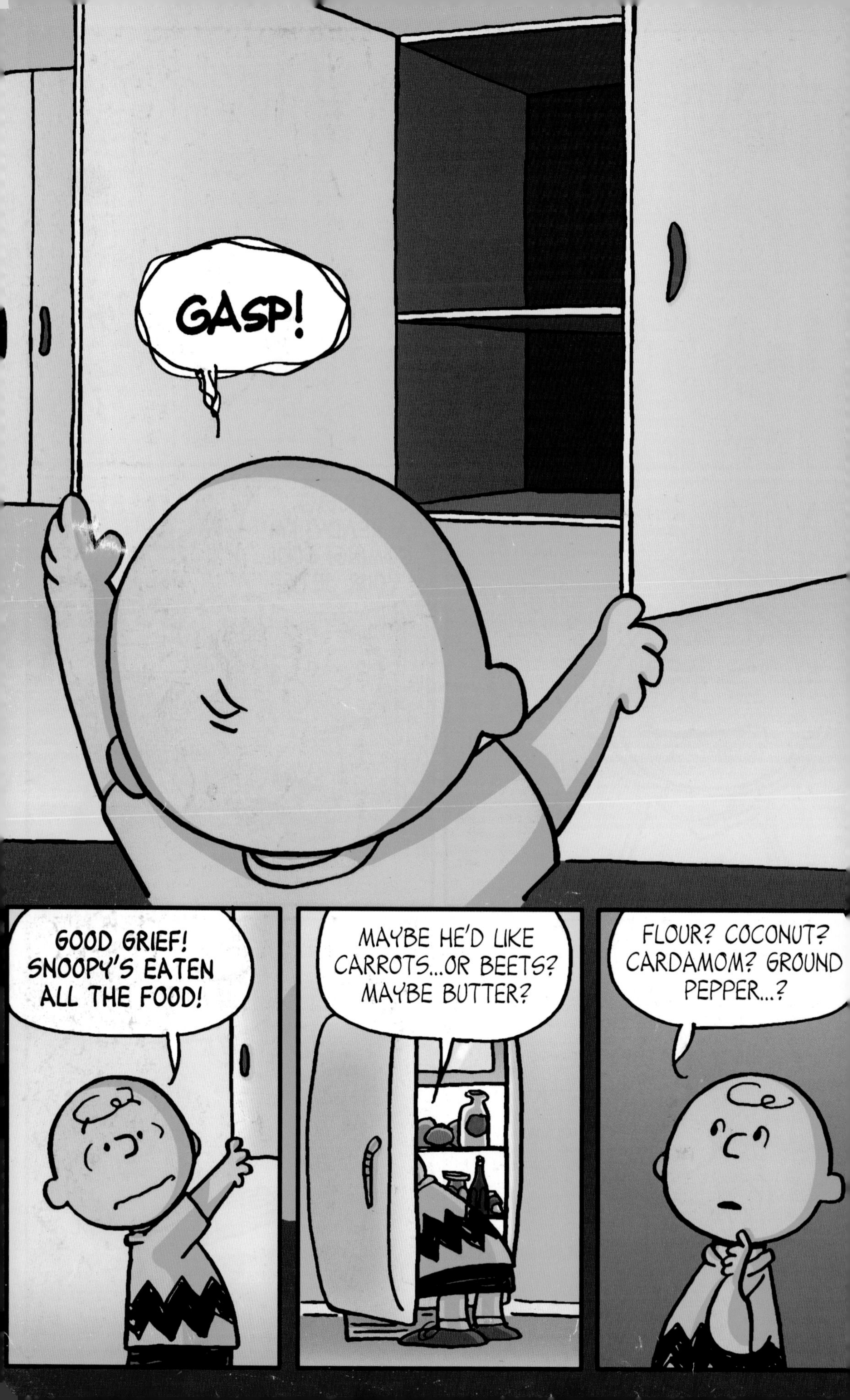
GASP!
GOOD GRIEF! SNOOPY'S EATEN ALL THE FOOD!
MAYBE HE'D LIKE CARROTS...OR BEETS? MAYBE BUTTER?
FLOUR? COCONUT? CARDAMOM? GROUND PEPPER...?

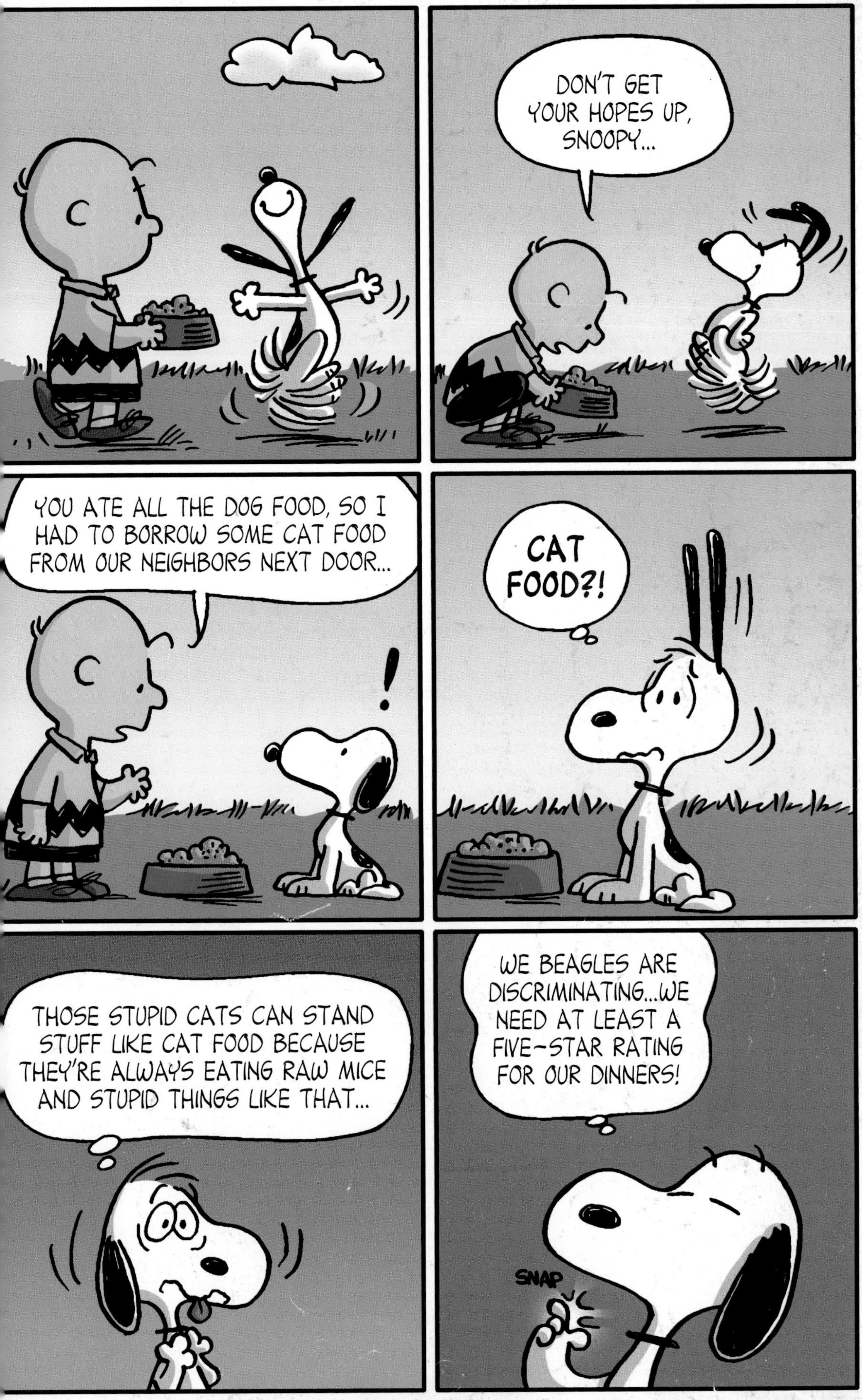
DON'T GET YOUR HOPES UP, SNOOPY...
YOU ATE ALL THE DOG FOOD, SO I HAD TO BORROW SOME CAT FOOD FROM OUR NEIGHBORS NEXT DOOR...
!
CAT FOOD?!
THOSE STUPID CATS CAN STAND STUFF LIKE CAT FOOD BECAUSE THEY'RE ALWAYS EATING RAW MICE AND STUPID THINGS LIKE THAT...
WE BEAGLES ARE DISCRIMINATING...WE NEED AT LEAST A FIVE-STAR RATING FOR OUR DINNERS!
SNAP

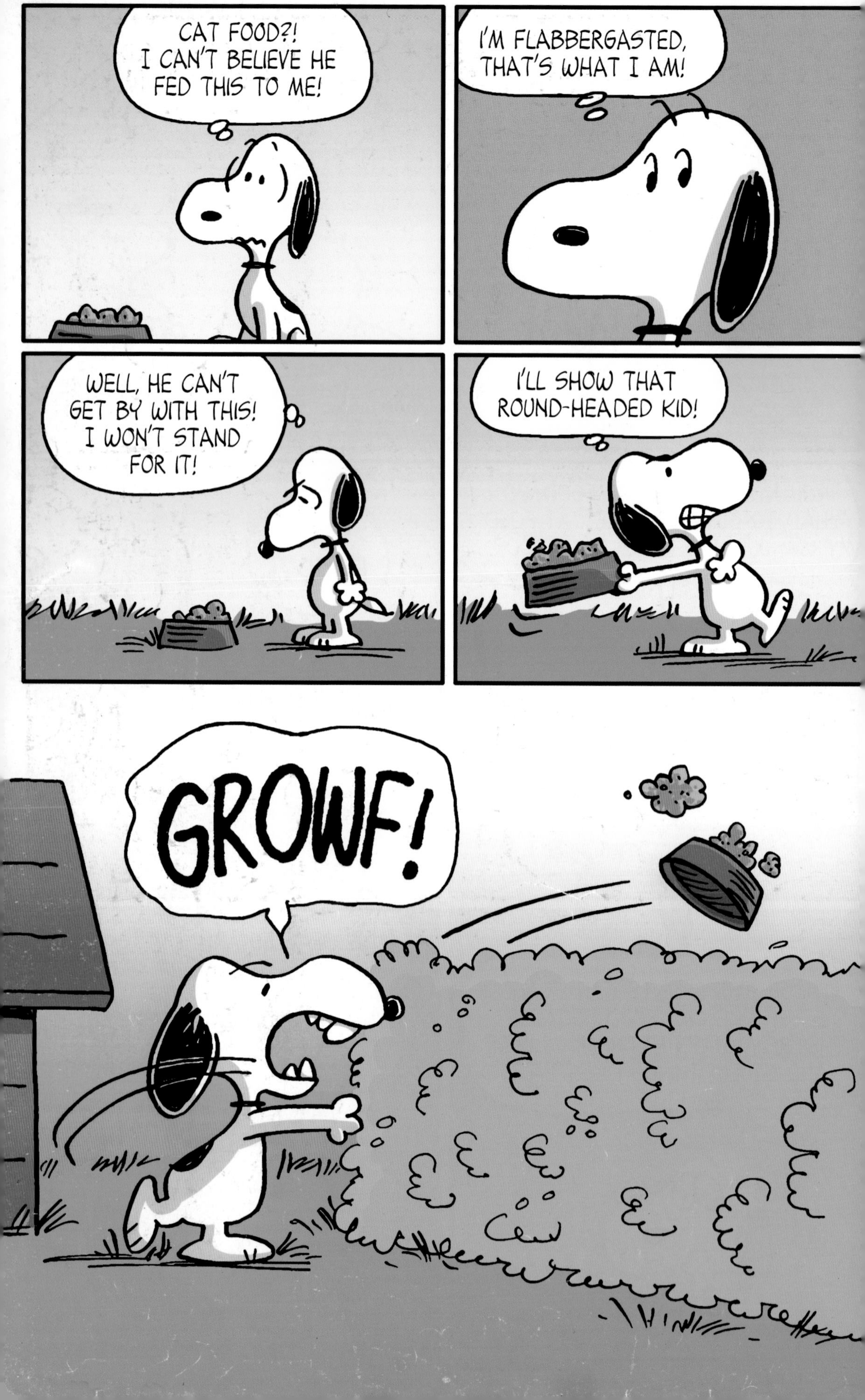
CAT FOOD?! I CAN'T BELIEVE HE FED THIS TO ME!
I'M FLABBERGASTED, THAT'S WHAT I AM!
WELL, HE CAN'T GET BY WITH THIS! I WON'T STAND FOR IT!
I'LL SHOW THAT ROUND-HEADED KID!
GROWF!

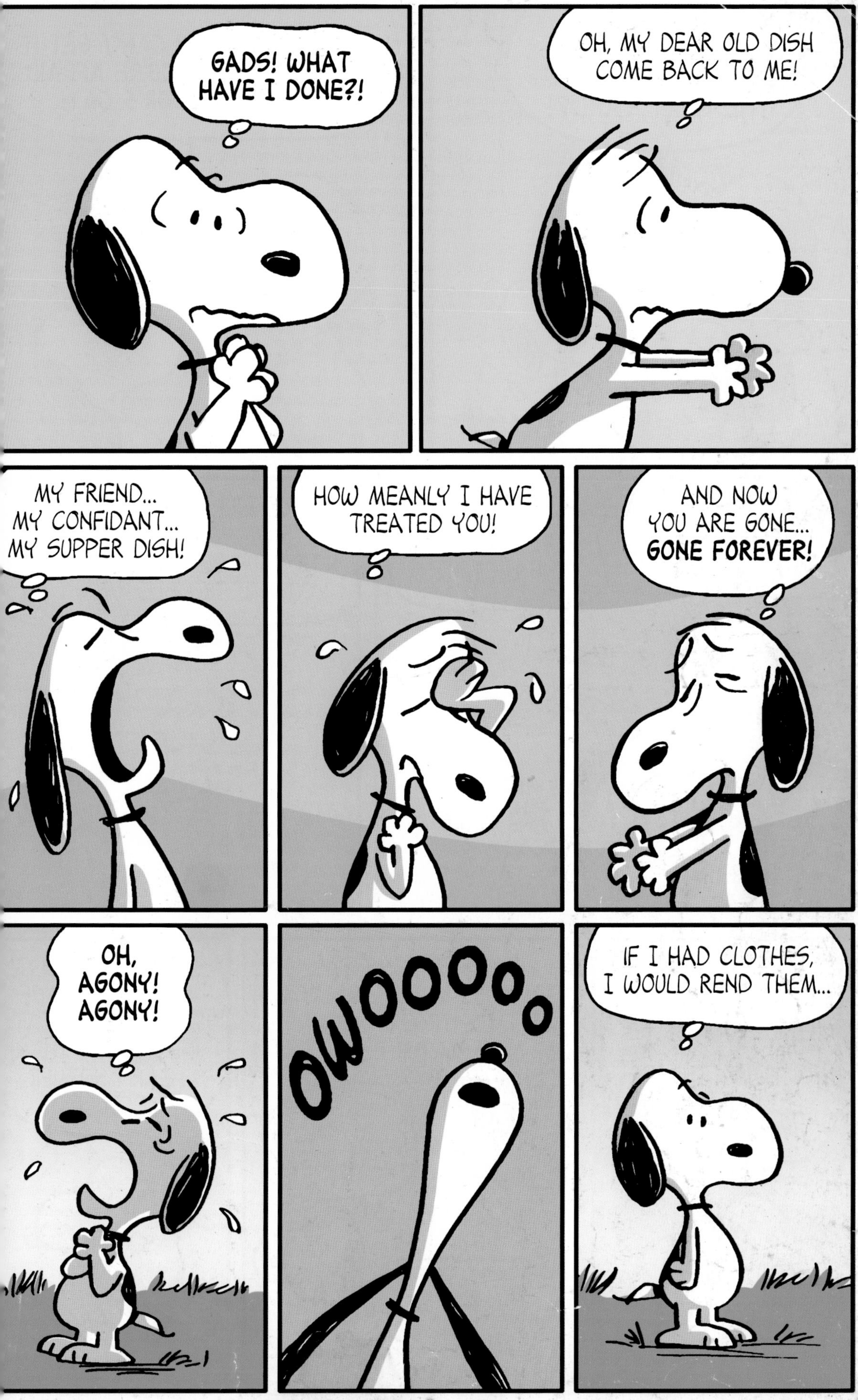
GADS! WHAT HAVE I DONE?!
OH, MY DEAR OLD DISH COME BACK TO ME!
MY FRIEND... MY CONFIDANT... MY SUPPER DISH!
HOW MEANLY I HAVE TREATED YOU!
AND NOW YOU ARE GONE... GONE FOREVER!
OH, AGONY! AGONY!
OWOOOOOO
IF I HAD CLOTHES, I WOULD REND THEM...

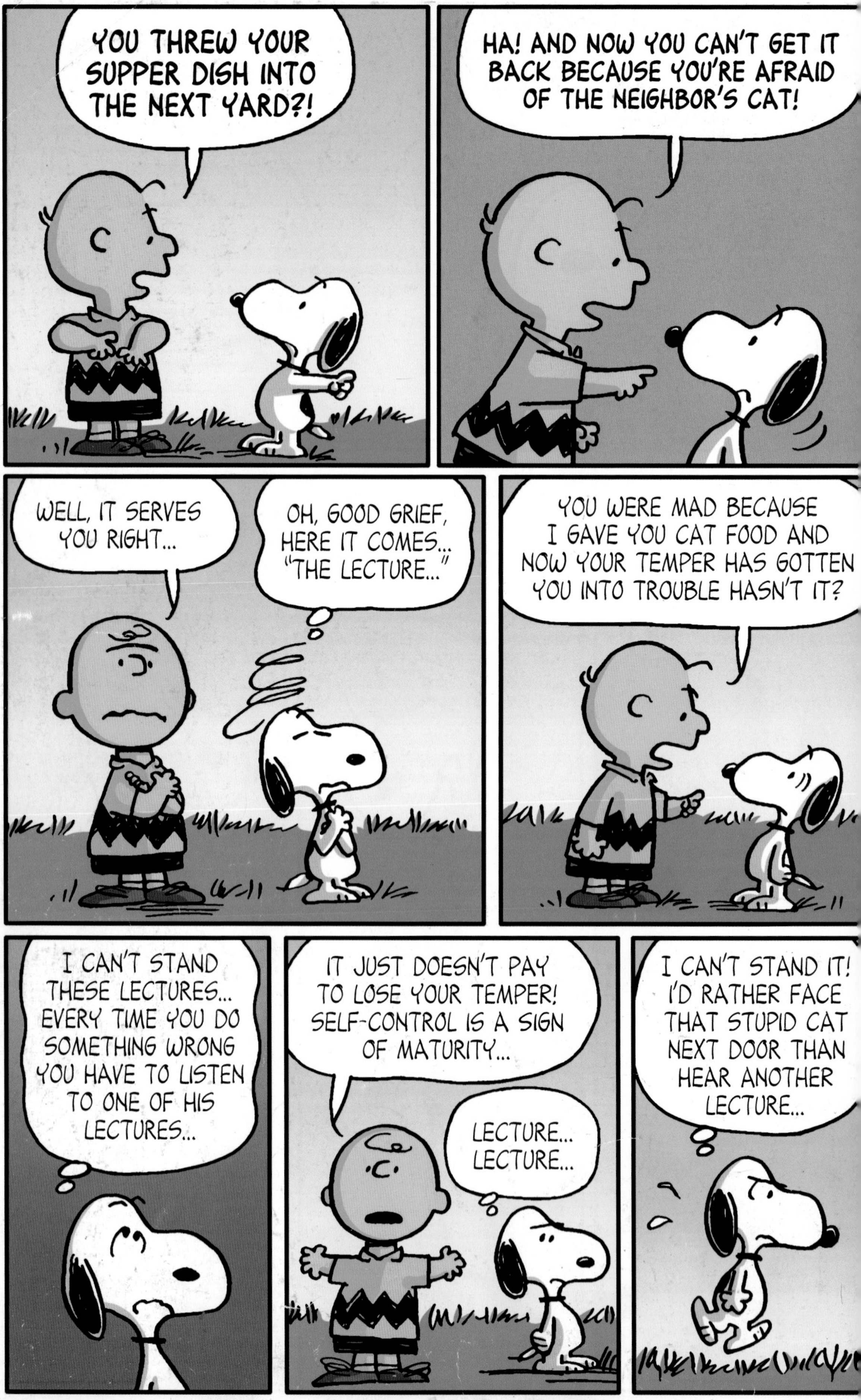
YOU THREW YOUR SUPPER DISH INTO THE NEXT YARD?!
HA! AND NOW YOU CAN'T GET IT BACK BECAUSE YOU'RE AFRAID OF THE NEIGHBOR'S CAT!
WELL, IT SERVES YOU RIGHT...
OH, GOOD GRIEF, HERE IT COMES... "THE LECTURE..."
YOU WERE MAD BECAUSE I GAVE YOU CAT FOOD AND NOW YOUR TEMPER HAS GOTTEN YOU INTO TROUBLE HASN'T IT?
I CAN'T STAND THESE LECTURES... EVERY TIME YOU DO SOMETHING WRONG YOU HAVE TO LISTEN TO ONE OF HIS LECTURES...
IT JUST DOESN'T PAY TO LOSE YOUR TEMPER! SELF-CONTROL IS A SIGN OF MATURITY...
LECTURE... LECTURE...
I CAN'T STAND IT! I'D RATHER FACE THAT STUPID CAT NEXT DOOR THAN HEAR ANOTHER LECTURE...

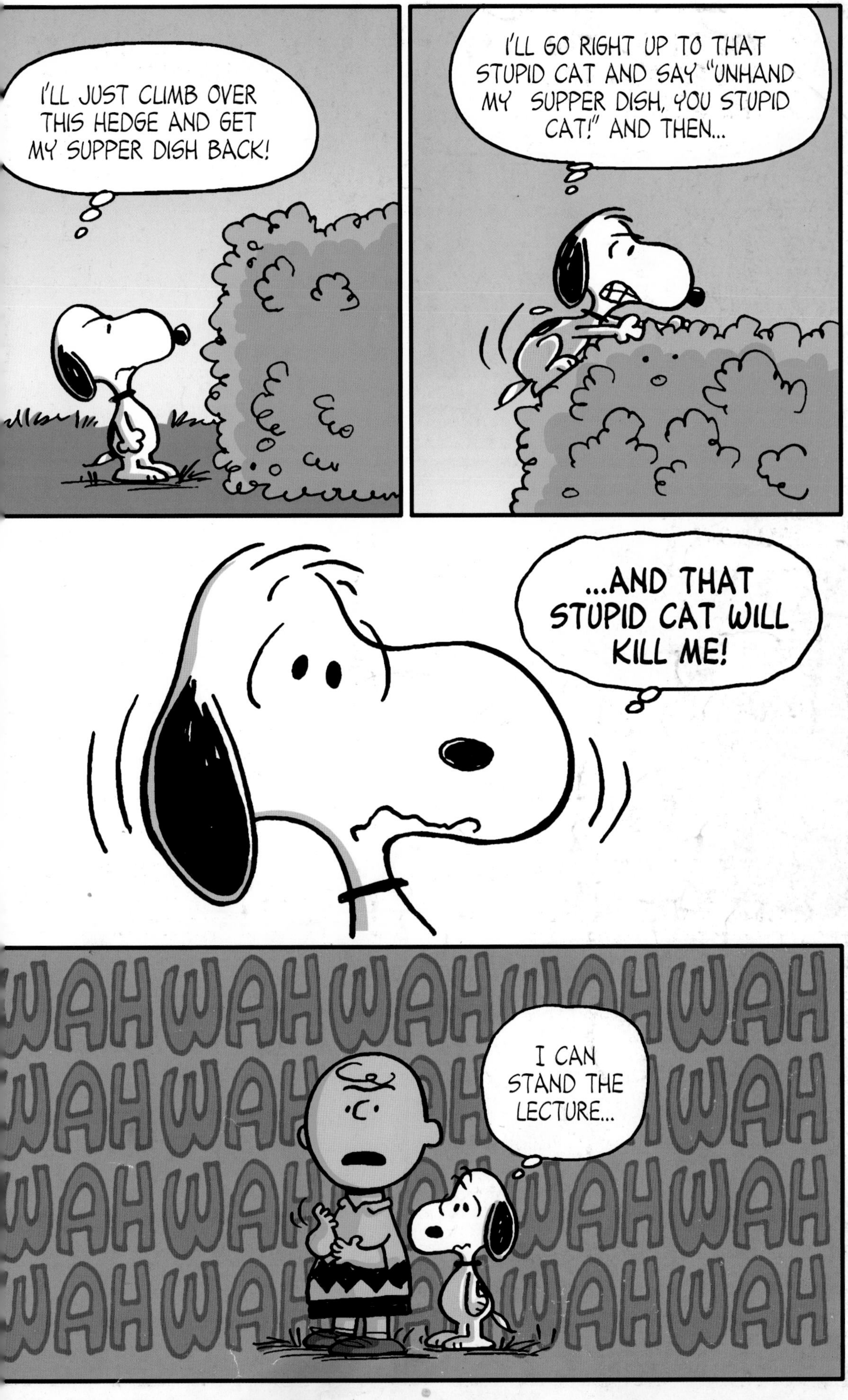
I'LL JUST CLIMB OVER THIS HEDGE AND GET MY SUPPER DISH BACK!
I'LL GO RIGHT UP TO THAT STUPID CAT AND SAY "UNHAND MY SUPPER DISH, YOU STUPID CAT!" AND THEN...
...AND THAT STUPID CAT WILL KILL ME!
WAH WAH WAH WAH WAH WAH
I CAN STAND THE LECTURE...

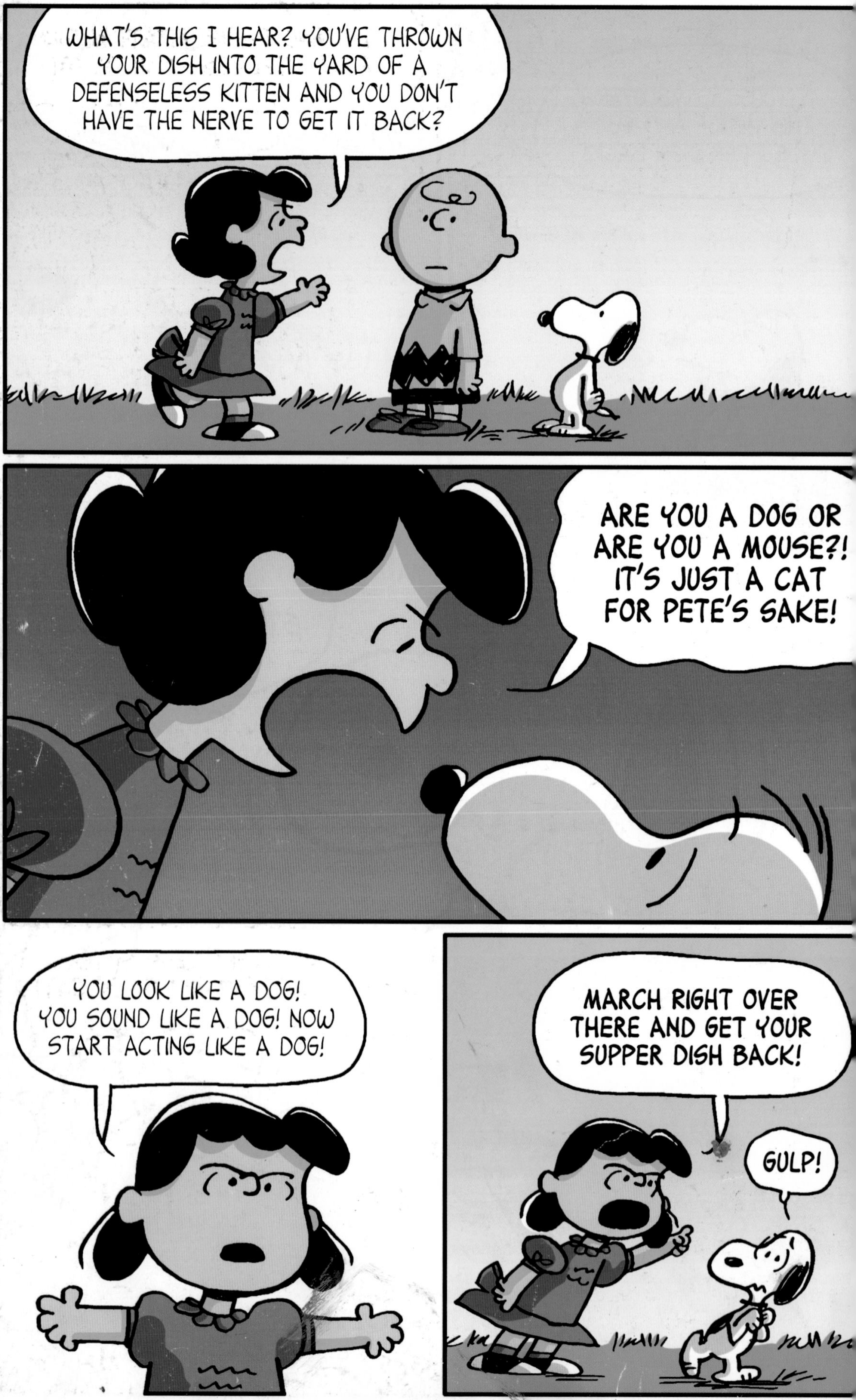
WHAT'S THIS I HEAR? YOU'VE THROWN YOUR DISH INTO THE YARD OF A DEFENSELESS KITTEN AND YOU DON'T HAVE THE NERVE TO GET IT BACK?
ARE YOU A DOG OR ARE YOU A MOUSE?! IT'S JUST A CAT FOR PETE'S SAKE!
YOU LOOK LIKE A DOG! YOU SOUND LIKE A DOG! NOW START ACTING LIKE A DOG!
MARCH RIGHT OVER THERE AND GET YOUR SUPPER DISH BACK!
GULP!

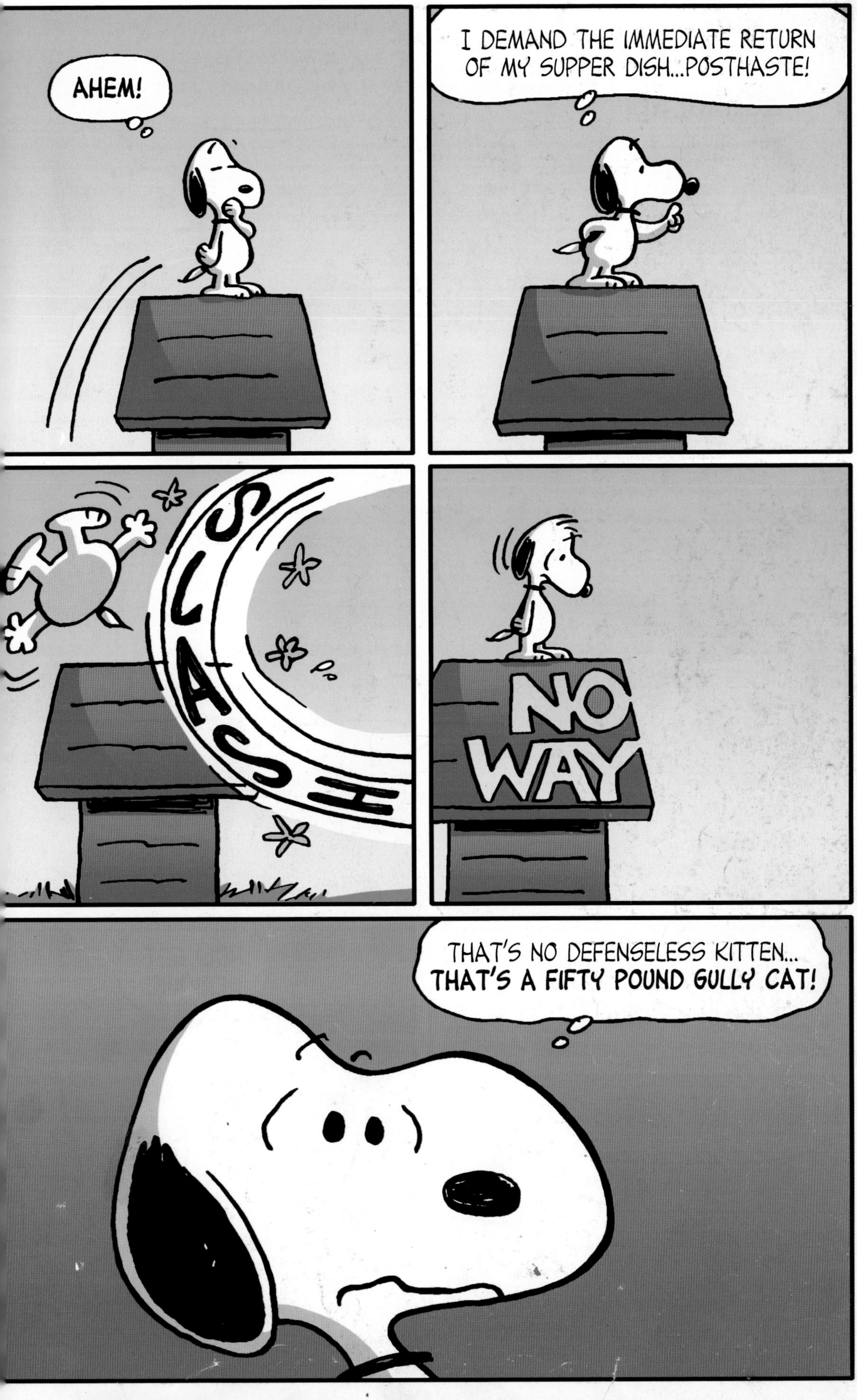
AHEM!
I DEMAND THE IMMEDIATE RETURN OF MY SUPPER DISH...POSTHASTE!
SLASH
NO WAY
THAT'S NO DEFENSELESS KITTEN... THAT'S A FIFTY POUND GULLY CAT!

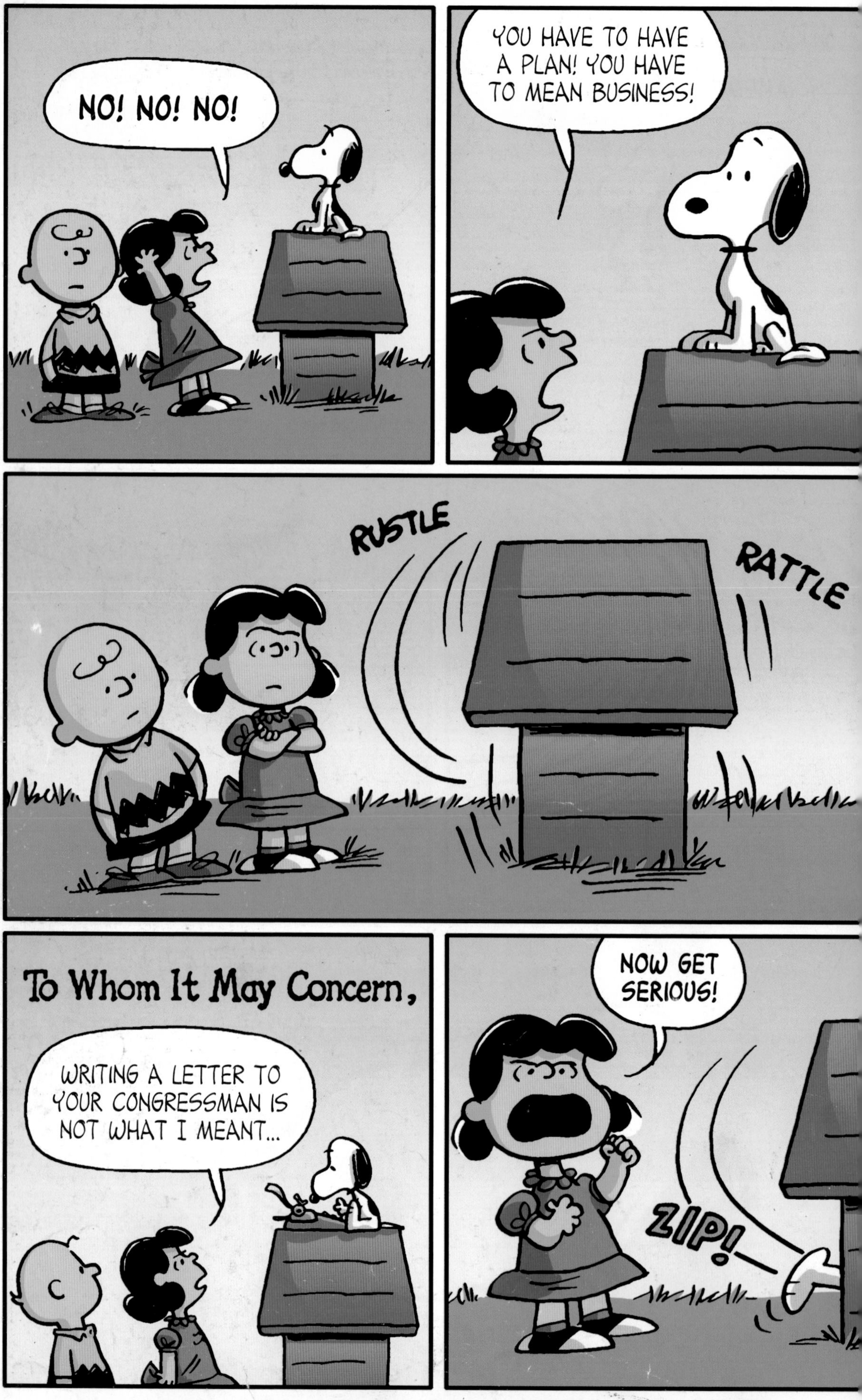
NO! NO! NO!
YOU HAVE TO HAVE A PLAN! YOU HAVE TO MEAN BUSINESS!
RUSTLE
RATTLE
To Whom It May Concern,
WRITING A LETTER TO YOUR CONGRESSMAN IS NOT WHAT I MEANT...
NOW GET SERIOUS!
ZIP!

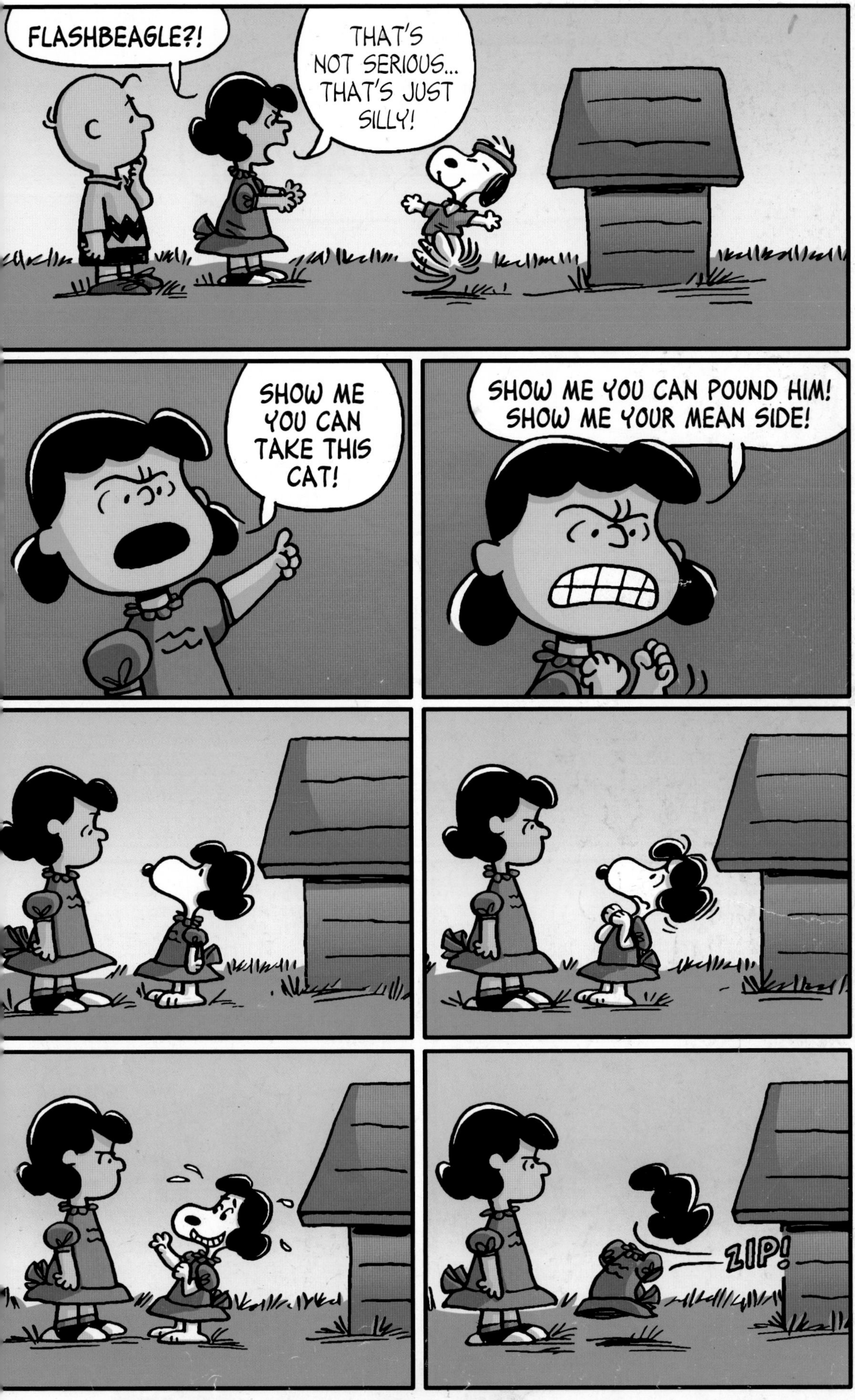
FLASHBEAGLE?!
THAT'S NOT SERIOUS... THAT'S JUST SILLY!
SHOW ME YOU CAN TAKE THIS CAT!
SHOW ME YOU CAN POUND HIM! SHOW ME YOUR MEAN SIDE!
ZIP!

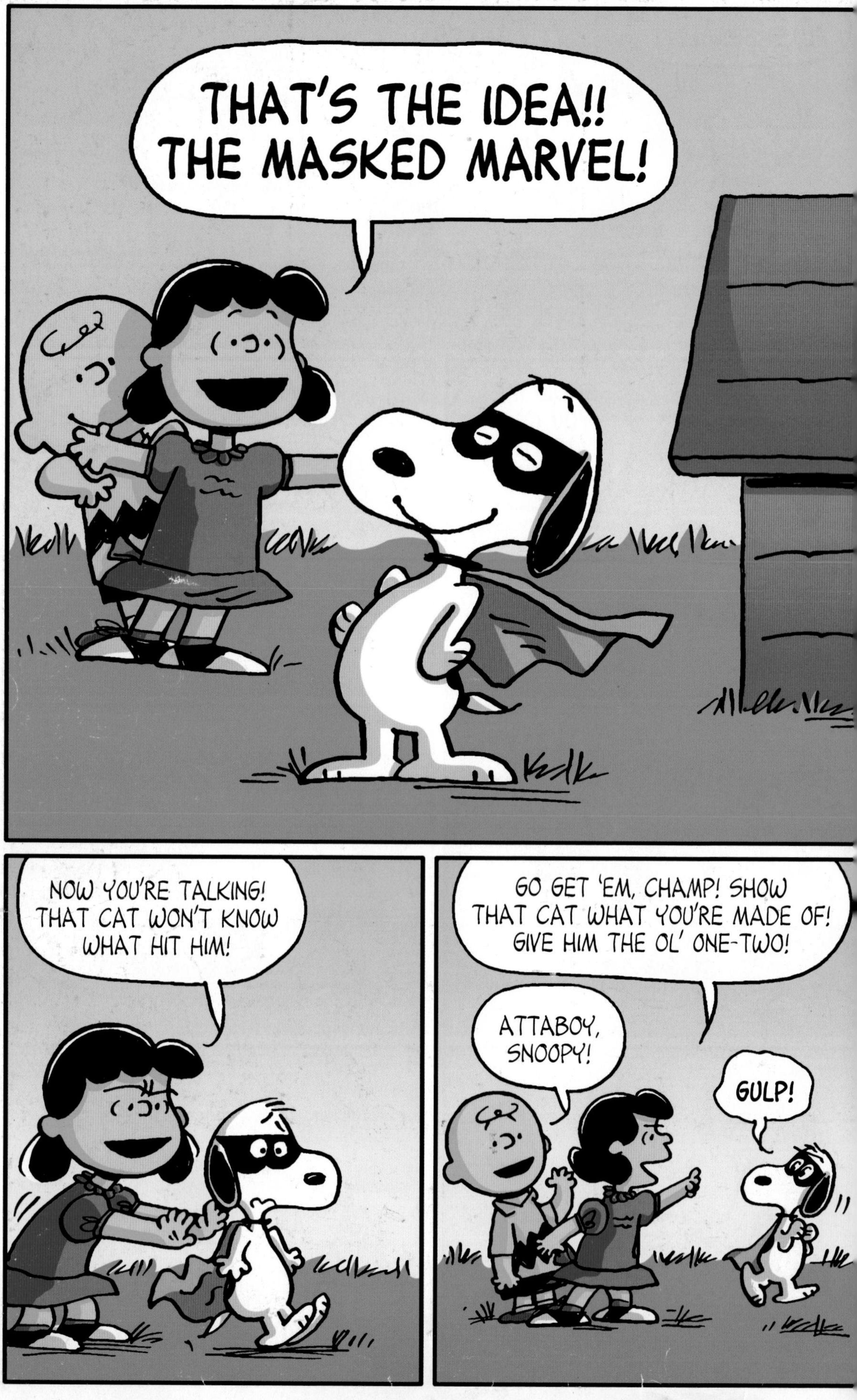
THAT'S THE IDEA!! THE MASKED MARVEL!
NOW YOU'RE TALKING! THAT CAT WON'T KNOW WHAT HIT HIM!
GO GET 'EM, CHAMP! SHOW THAT CAT WHAT YOU'RE MADE OF! GIVE HIM THE OL' ONE-TWO!
ATTABOY, SNOOPY!
GULP!

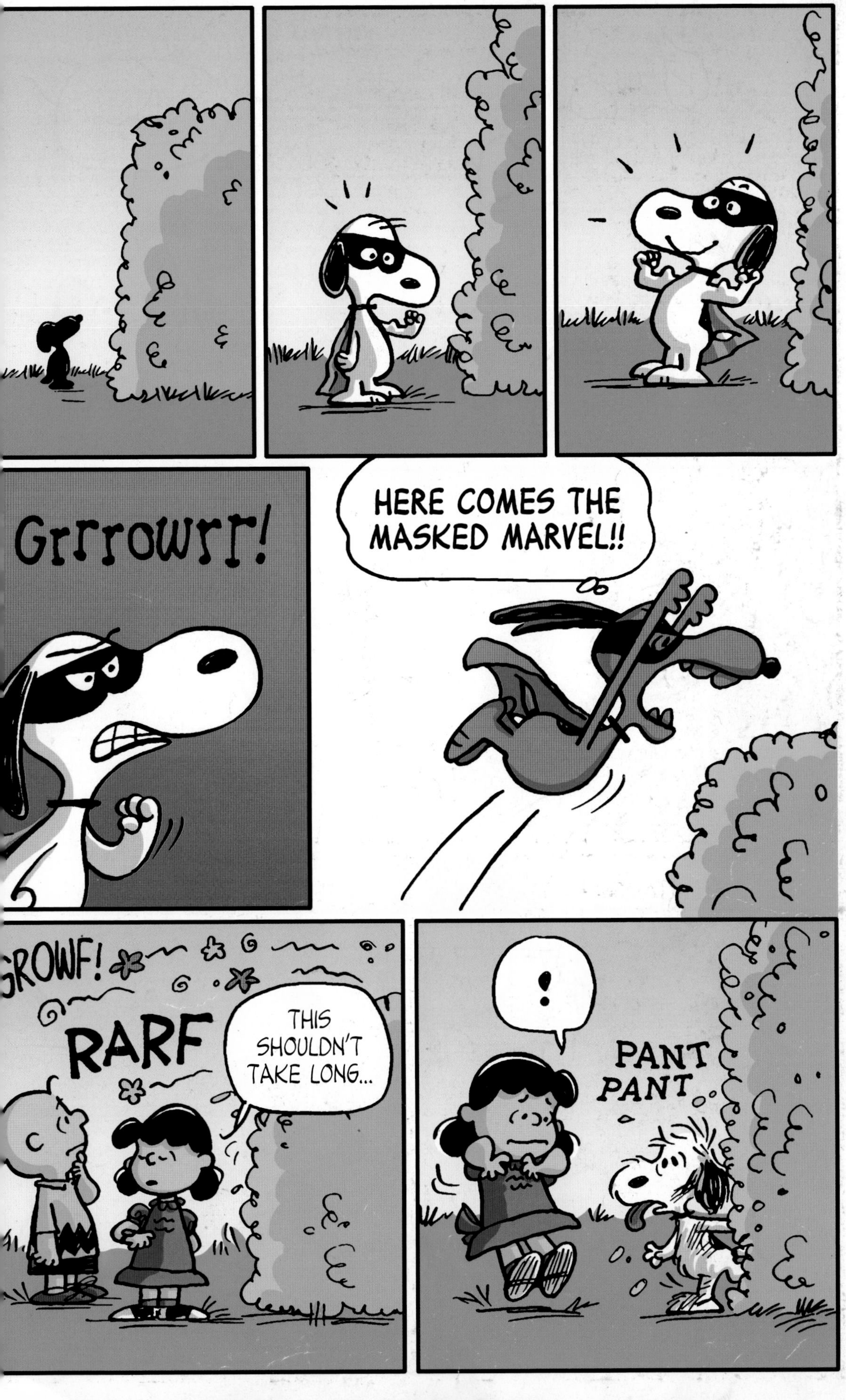

Grrrowrr!
HERE COMES THE MASKED MARVEL!!
GROWF!
RARF
THIS SHOULDN'T TAKE LONG...
!
PANT PANT

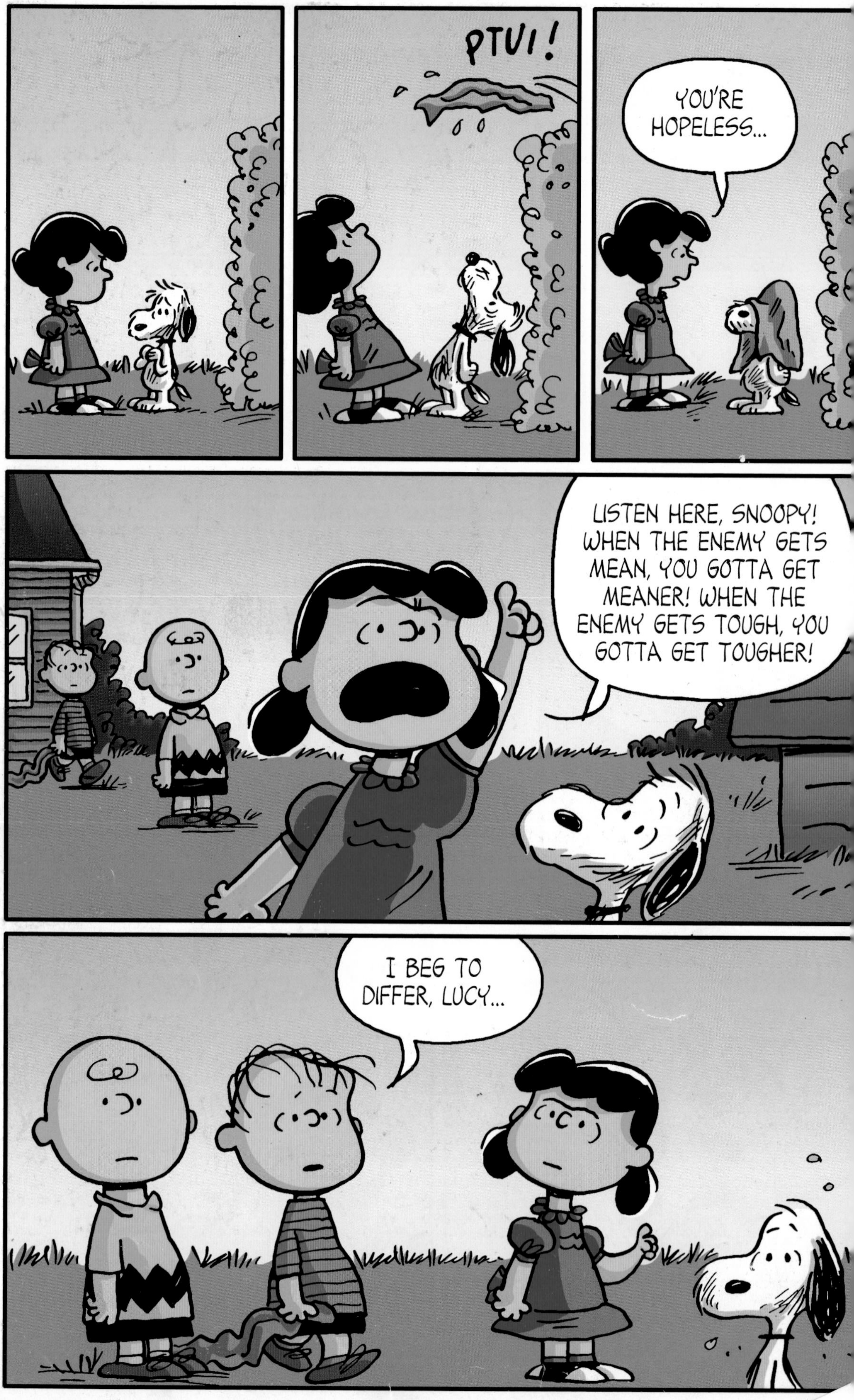
PTUI!
YOU'RE HOPELESS...
LISTEN HERE, SNOOPY! WHEN THE ENEMY GETS MEAN, YOU GOTTA GET MEANER! WHEN THE ENEMY GETS TOUGH, YOU GOTTA GET TOUGHER!
I BEG TO DIFFER, LUCY...

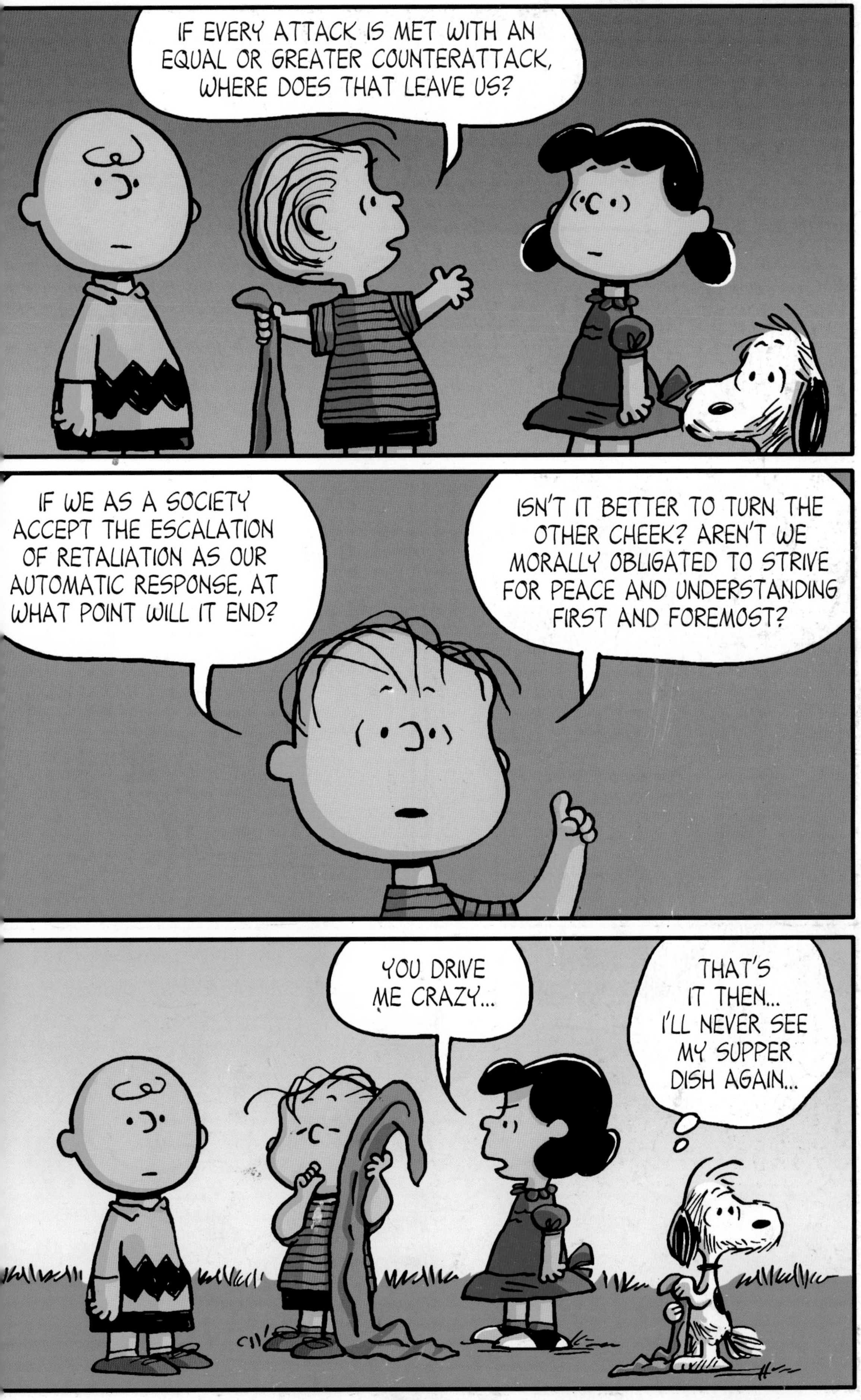
IF EVERY ATTACK IS MET WITH AN EQUAL OR GREATER COUNTERATTACK, WHERE DOES THAT LEAVE US?
IF WE AS A SOCIETY ACCEPT THE ESCALATION OF RETALIATION AS OUR AUTOMATIC RESPONSE, AT WHAT POINT WILL IT END?
ISN'T IT BETTER TO TURN THE OTHER CHEEK? AREN'T WE MORALLY OBLIGATED TO STRIVE FOR PEACE AND UNDERSTANDING FIRST AND FOREMOST?
YOU DRIVE ME CRAZY...
THAT'S IT THEN... I'LL NEVER SEE MY SUPPER DISH AGAIN...

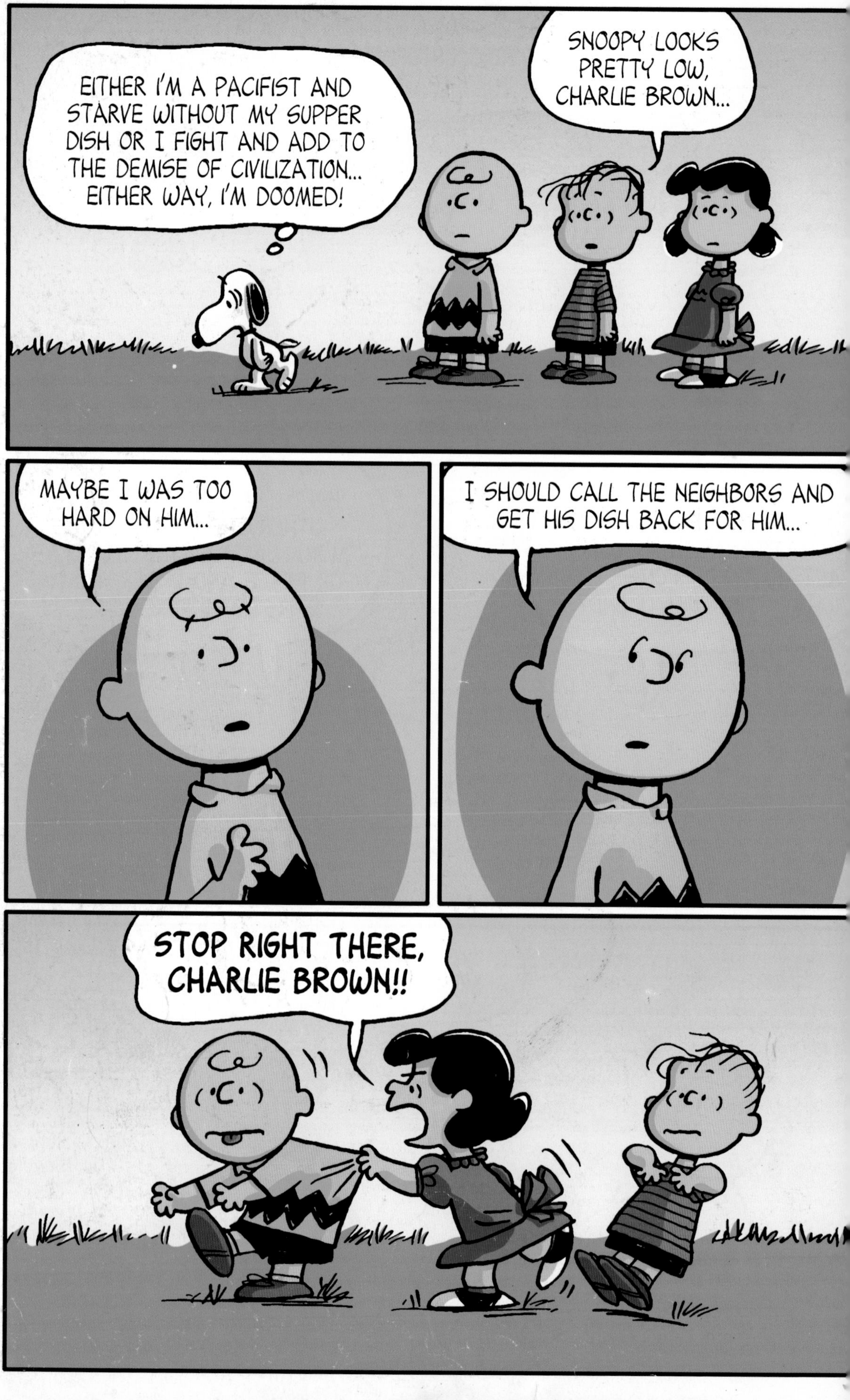
EITHER I'M A PACIFIST AND STARVE WITHOUT MY SUPPER DISH OR I FIGHT AND ADD TO THE DEMISE OF CIVILIZATION... EITHER WAY, I'M DOOMED!
SNOOPY LOOKS PRETTY LOW, CHARLIE BROWN...
MAYBE I WAS TOO HARD ON HIM...
I SHOULD CALL THE NEIGHBORS AND GET HIS DISH BACK FOR HIM...
STOP RIGHT THERE, CHARLIE BROWN!!

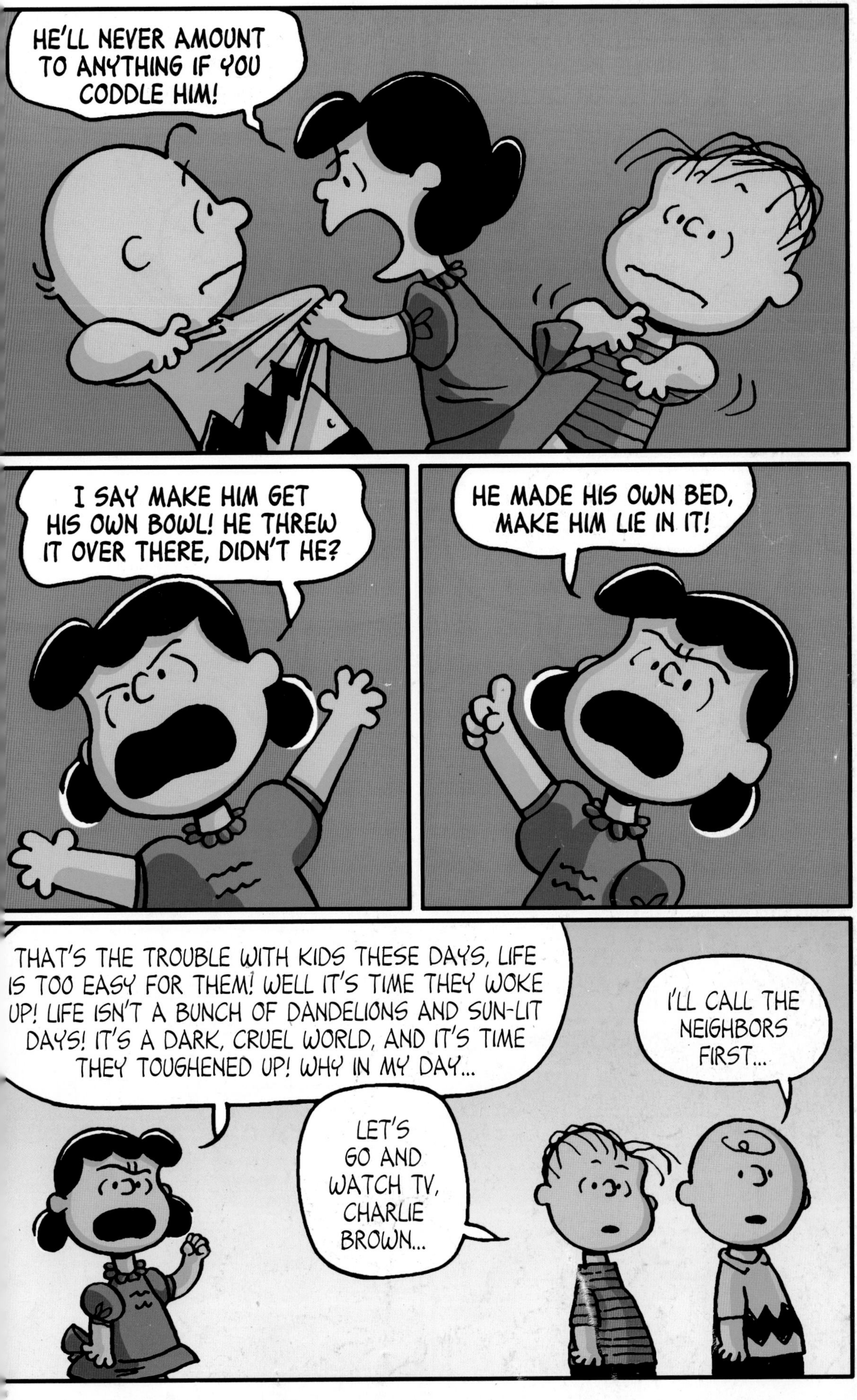
HE'LL NEVER AMOUNT TO ANYTHING IF YOU CODDLE HIM!
I SAY MAKE HIM GET HIS OWN BOWL! HE THREW IT OVER THERE, DIDN'T HE?
HE MADE HIS OWN BED, MAKE HIM LIE IN IT!
THAT'S THE TROUBLE WITH KIDS THESE DAYS, LIFE IS TOO EASY FOR THEM! WELL IT'S TIME THEY WOKE UP! LIFE ISN'T A BUNCH OF DANDELIONS AND SUN-LIT DAYS! IT'S A DARK, CRUEL WORLD, AND IT'S TIME THEY TOUGHENED UP! WHY IN MY DAY...
I'LL CALL THE NEIGHBORS FIRST...
LET'S GO AND WATCH TV, CHARLIE BROWN...

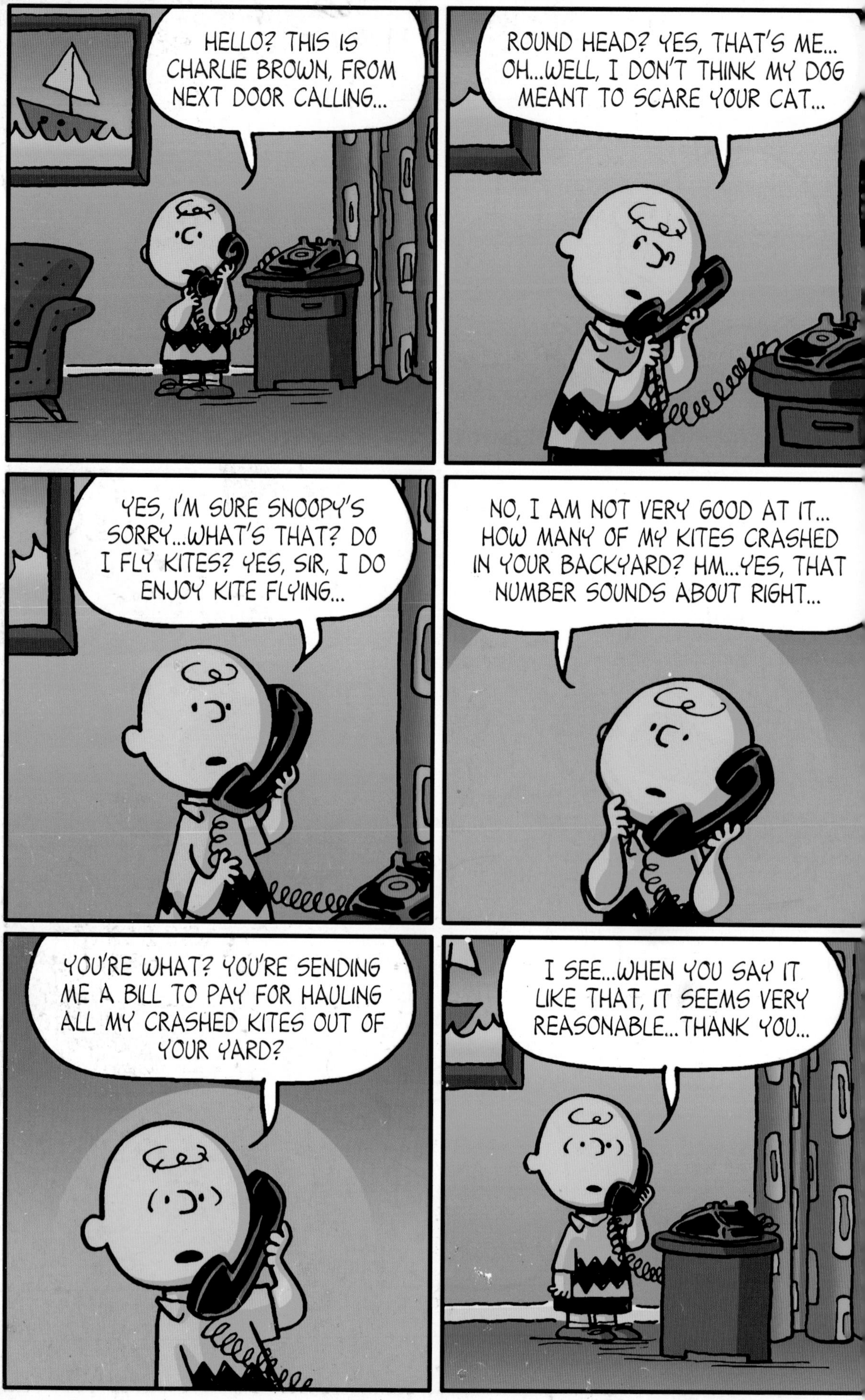
HELLO? THIS IS CHARLIE BROWN, FROM NEXT DOOR CALLING...
ROUND HEAD? YES, THAT'S ME... OH...WELL, I DON'T THINK MY DOG MEANT TO SCARE YOUR CAT...
YES, I'M SURE SNOOPY'S SORRY...WHAT'S THAT? DO I FLY KITES? YES, SIR, I DO ENJOY KITE FLYING...
NO, I AM NOT VERY GOOD AT IT... HOW MANY OF MY KITES CRASHED IN YOUR BACKYARD? HM...YES, THAT NUMBER SOUNDS ABOUT RIGHT...
YOU'RE WHAT? YOU'RE SENDING ME A BILL TO PAY FOR HAULING ALL MY CRASHED KITES OUT OF YOUR YARD?
I SEE...WHEN YOU SAY IT LIKE THAT, IT SEEMS VERY REASONABLE...THANK YOU...

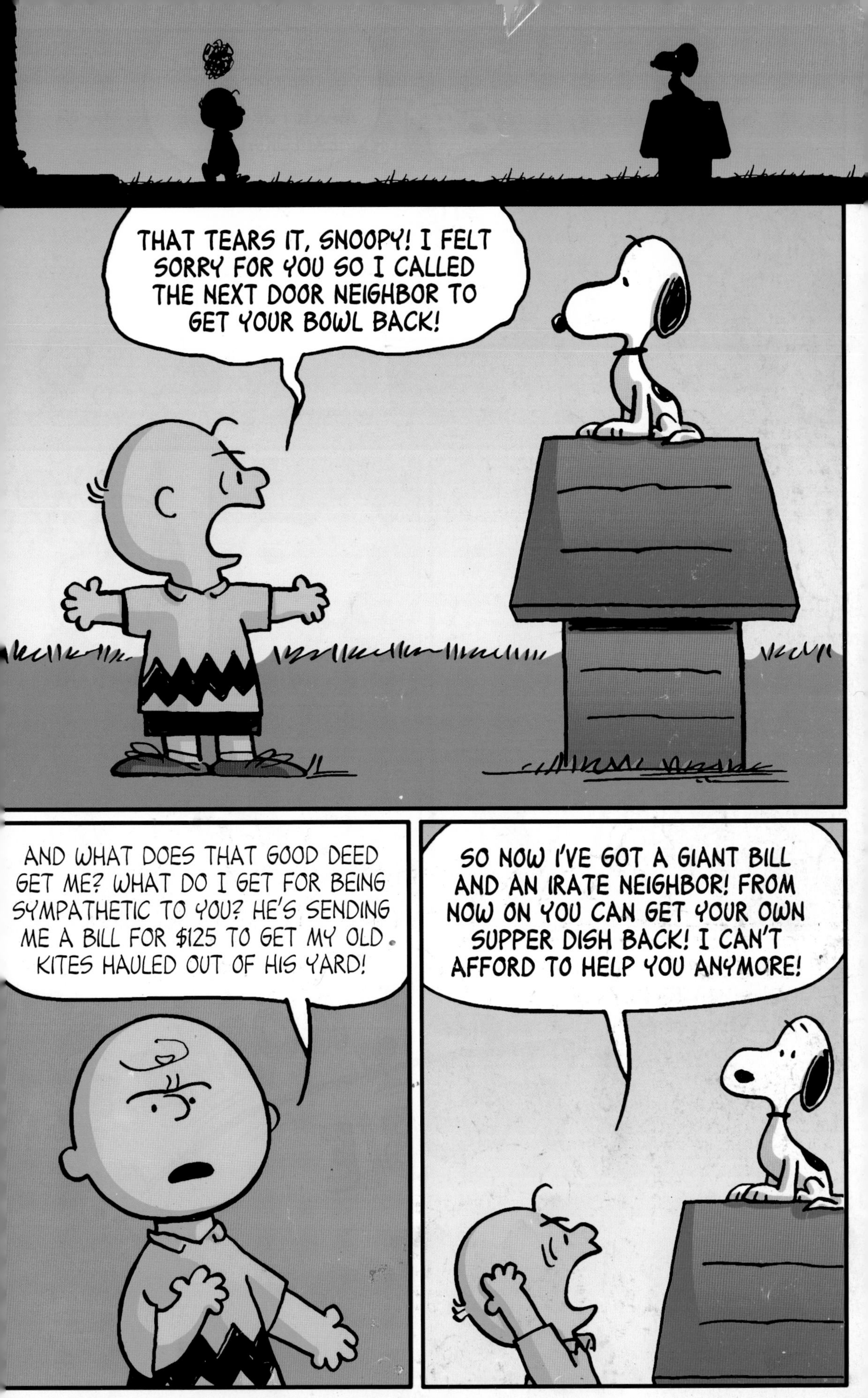
THAT TEARS IT, SNOOPY! I FELT SORRY FOR YOU SO I CALLED THE NEXT DOOR NEIGHBOR TO GET YOUR BOWL BACK!
AND WHAT DOES THAT GOOD DEED GET ME? WHAT DO I GET FOR BEING SYMPATHETIC TO YOU? HE'S SENDING ME A BILL FOR $125 TO GET MY OLD KITES HAULED OUT OF HIS YARD!
SO NOW I'VE GOT A GIANT BILL AND AN IRATE NEIGHBOR! FROM NOW ON YOU CAN GET YOUR OWN SUPPER DISH BACK! I CAN'T AFFORD TO HELP YOU ANYMORE!

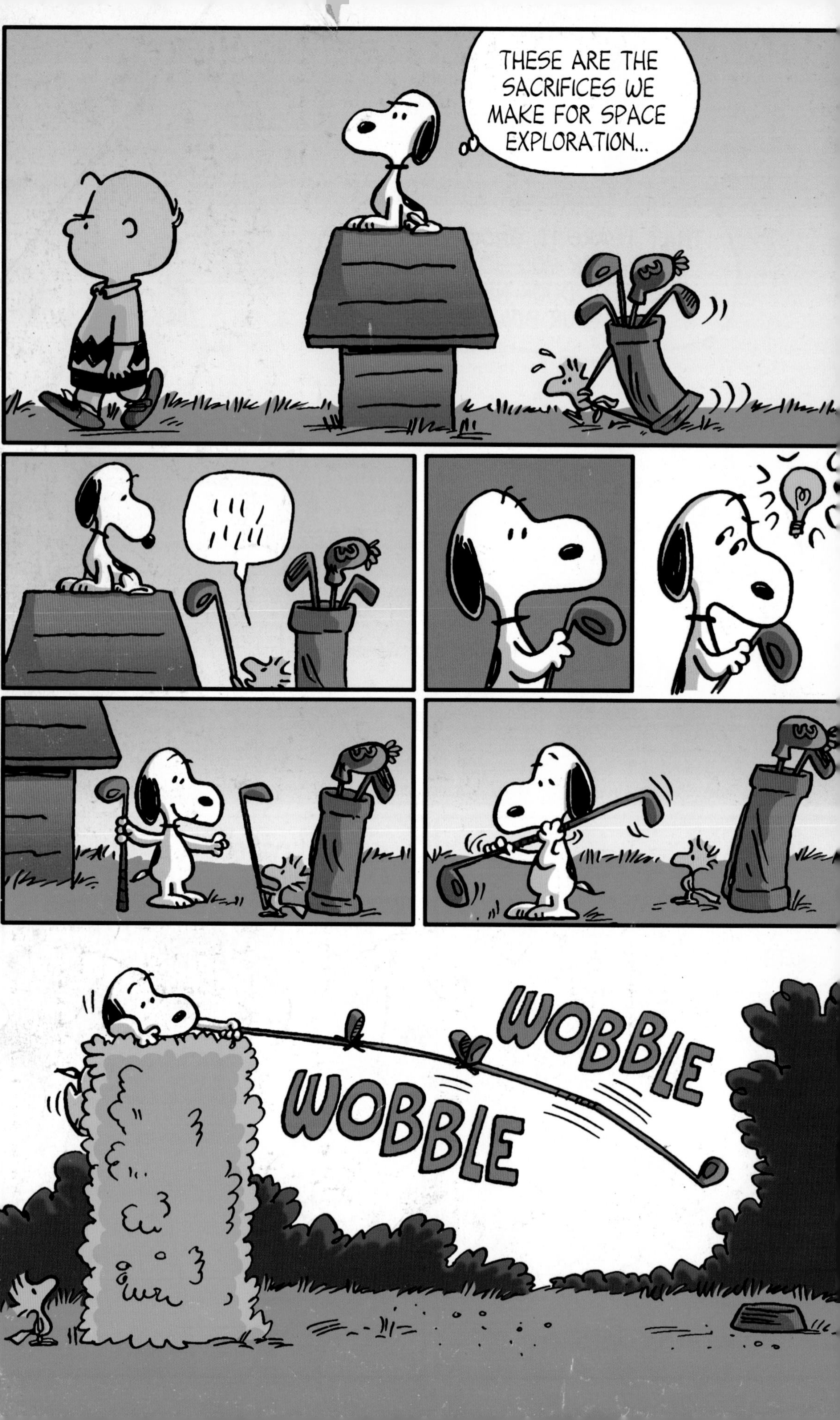
THESE ARE THE SACRIFICES WE MAKE FOR SPACE EXPLORATION...
WOBBLE
WOBBLE

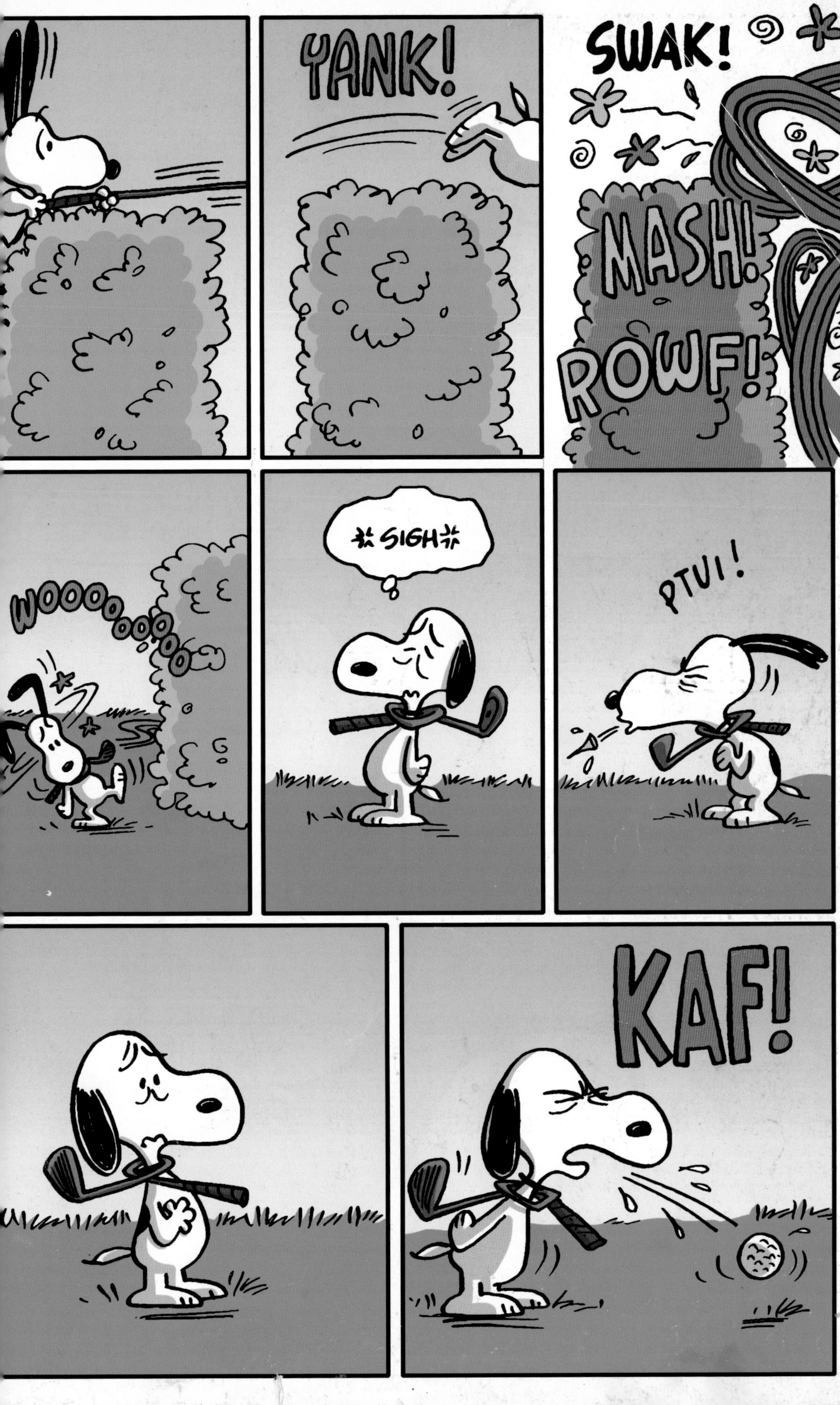
YANK!
SWAK!
MASH!
ROWF!
WOOOOOOOOOO
SIGH
PTUI!
KAF!

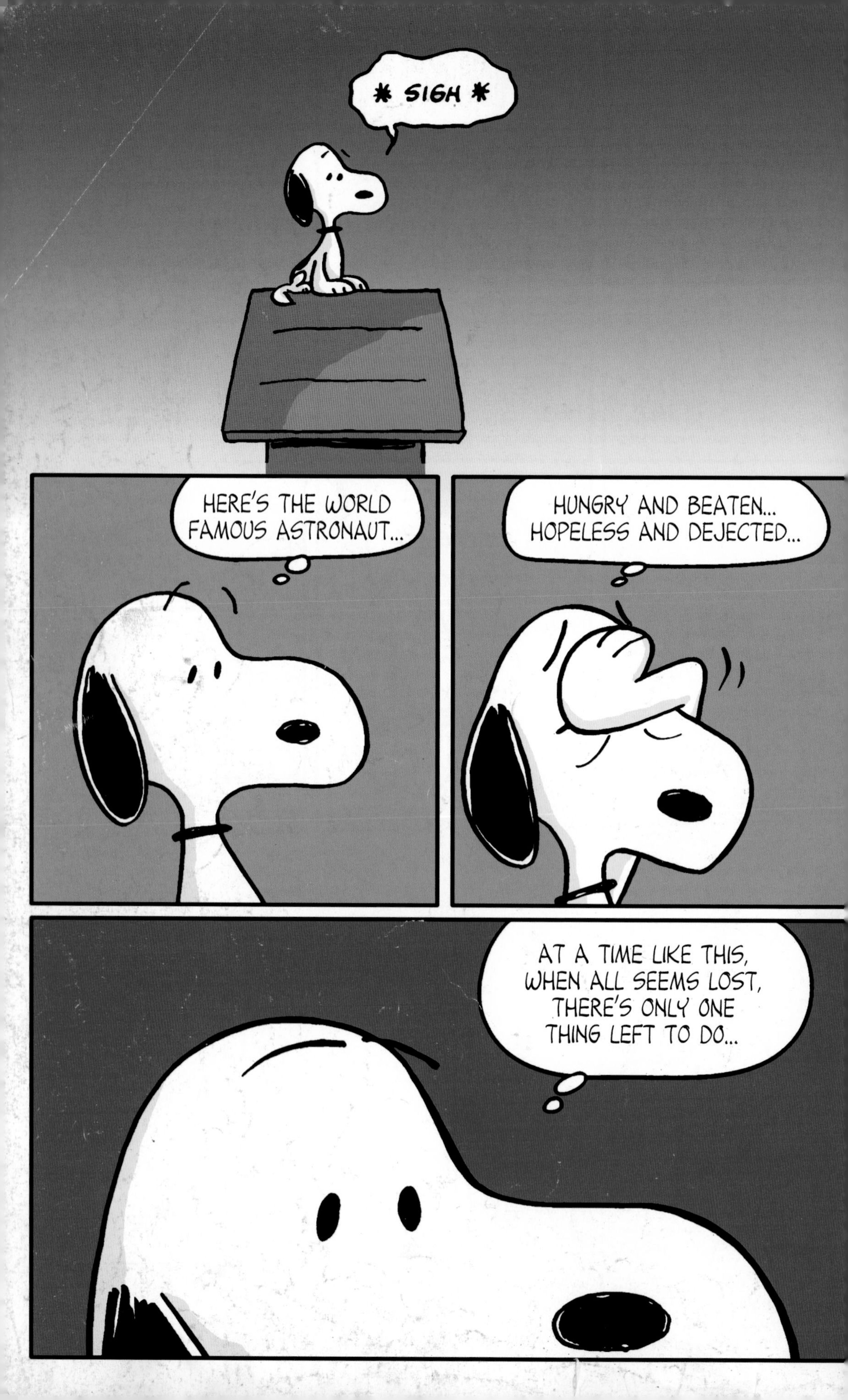
* SIGH *
HERE'S THE WORLD FAMOUS ASTRONAUT...
HUNGRY AND BEATEN... HOPELESS AND DEJECTED...
AT A TIME LIKE THIS, WHEN ALL SEEMS LOST, THERE'S ONLY ONE THING LEFT TO DO...

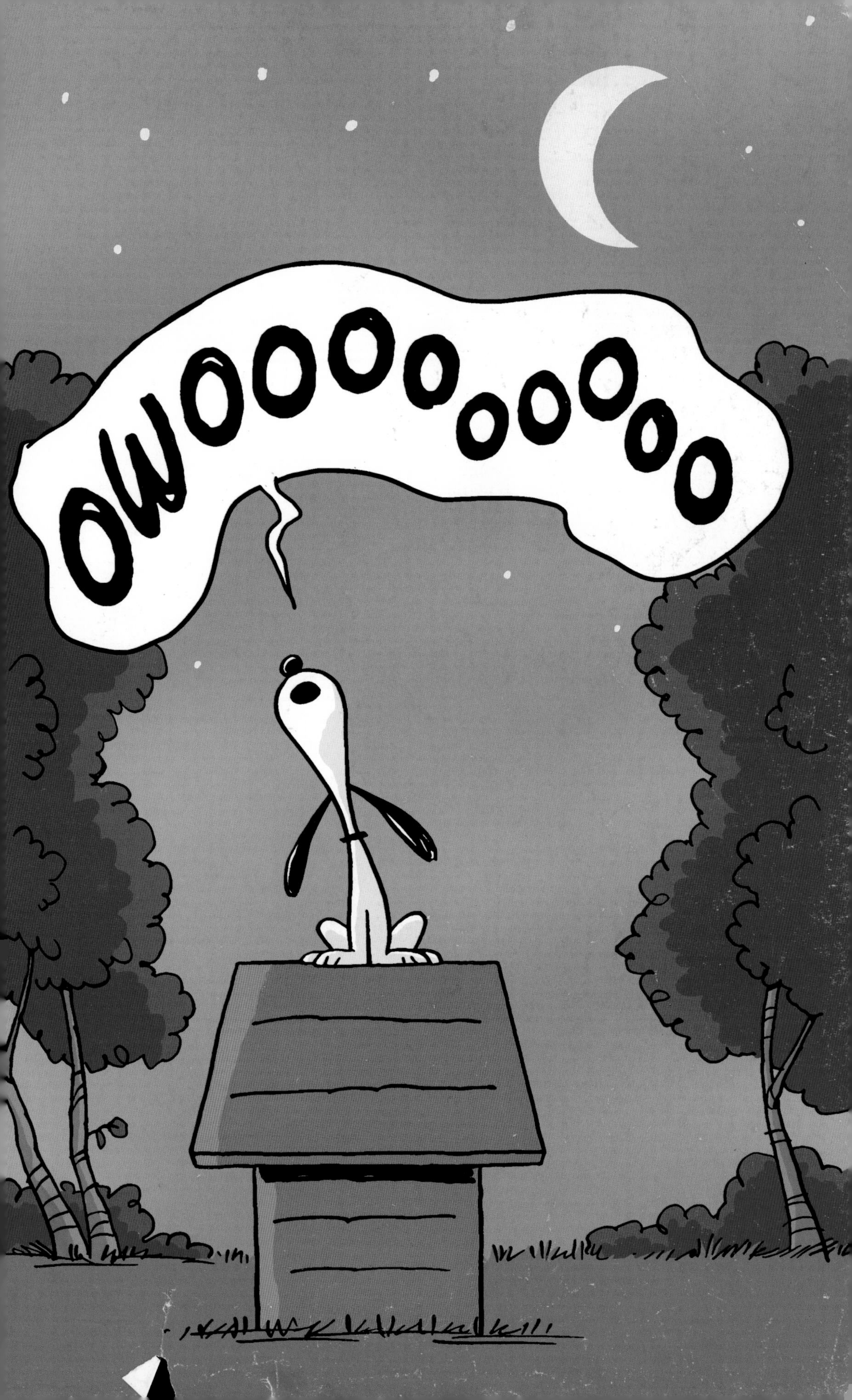
OWOOOOOOOOO

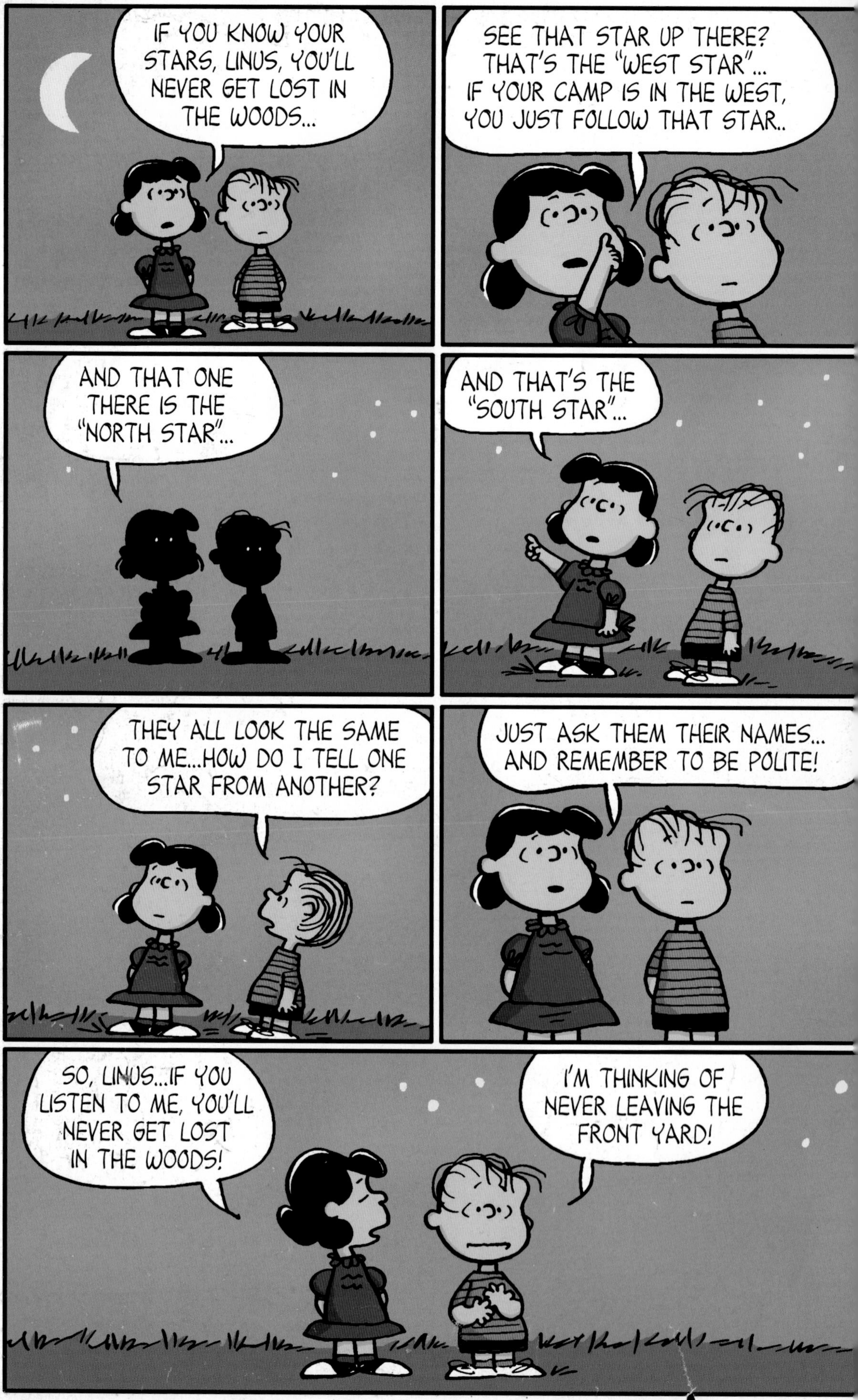
IF YOU KNOW YOUR STARS, LINUS, YOU'LL NEVER GET LOST IN THE WOODS...
SEE THAT STAR UP THERE? THAT'S THE "WEST STAR"... IF YOUR CAMP IS IN THE WEST, YOU JUST FOLLOW THAT STAR..
AND THAT ONE THERE IS THE "NORTH STAR"...
AND THAT'S THE "SOUTH STAR"...
THEY ALL LOOK THE SAME TO ME...HOW DO I TELL ONE STAR FROM ANOTHER?
JUST ASK THEM THEIR NAMES... AND REMEMBER TO BE POLITE!
SO, LINUS...IF YOU LISTEN TO ME, YOU'LL NEVER GET LOST IN THE WOODS!
I'M THINKING OF NEVER LEAVING THE FRONT YARD!

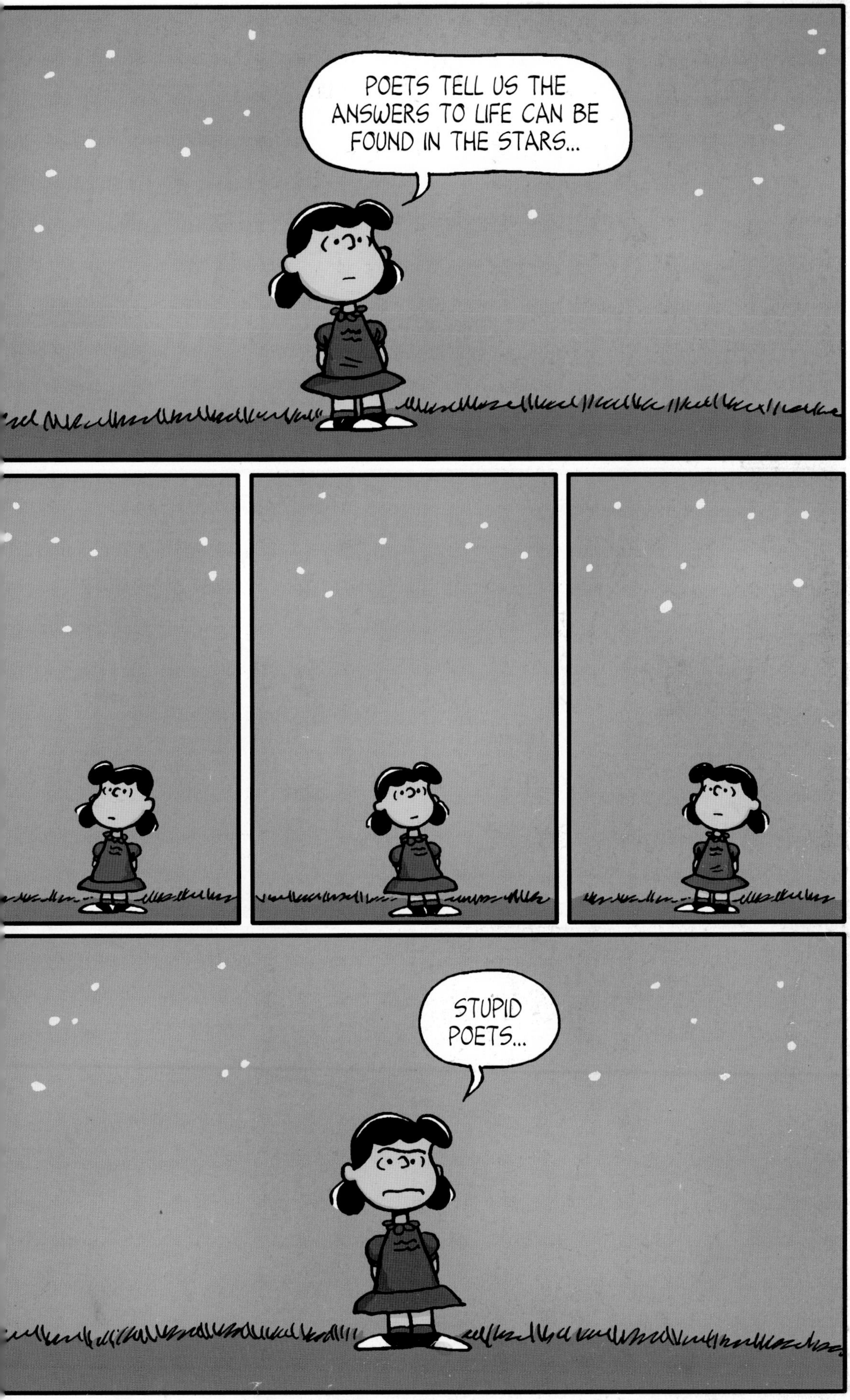
POETS TELL US THE ANSWERS TO LIFE CAN BE FOUND IN THE STARS...
STUPID POETS...

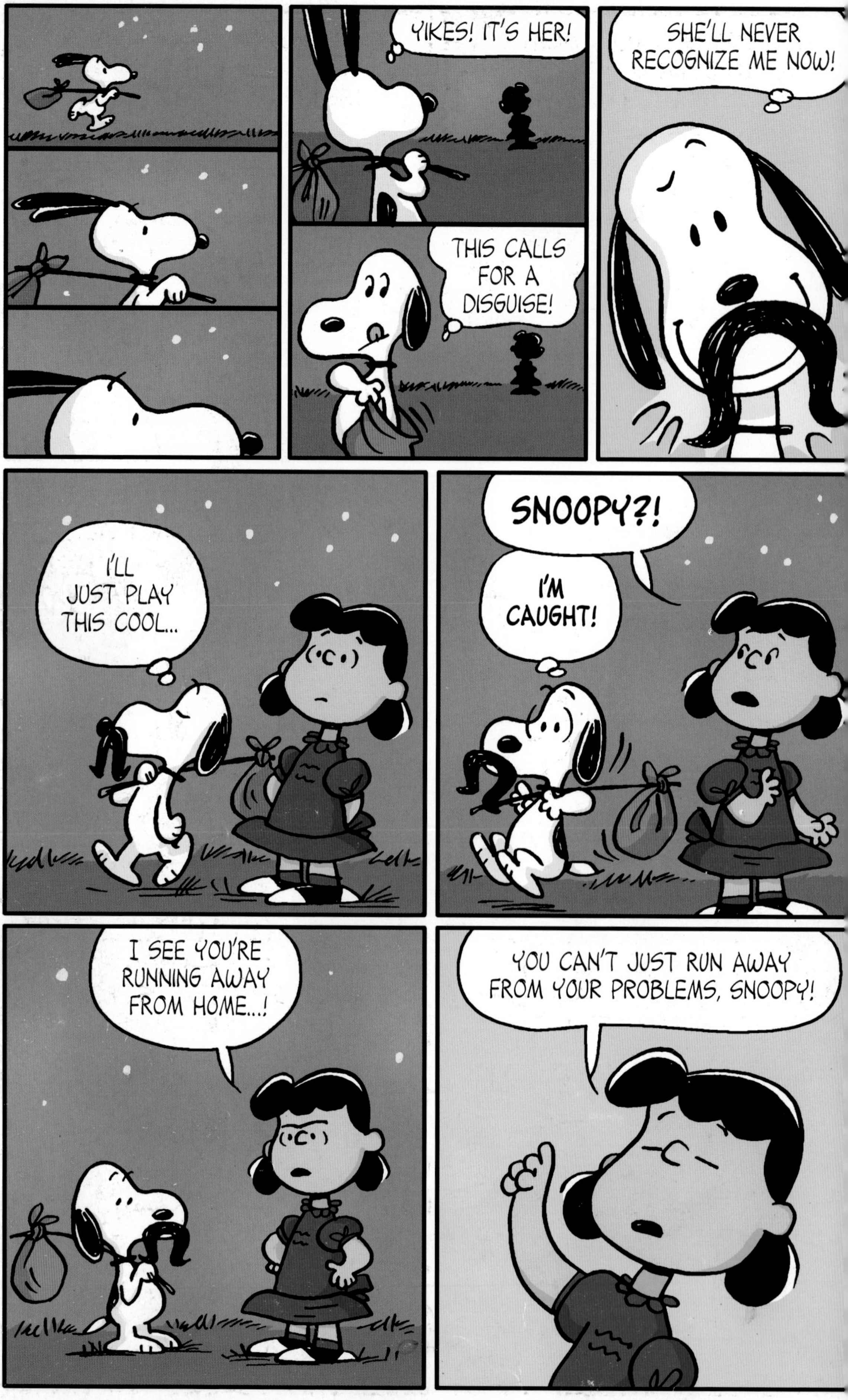
YIKES! IT'S HER!
THIS CALLS FOR A DISGUISE!
SHE'LL NEVER RECOGNIZE ME NOW!
I'LL JUST PLAY THIS COOL...
SNOOPY?!
I'M CAUGHT!
I SEE YOU'RE RUNNING AWAY FROM HOME...!
YOU CAN'T JUST RUN AWAY FROM YOUR PROBLEMS, SNOOPY!

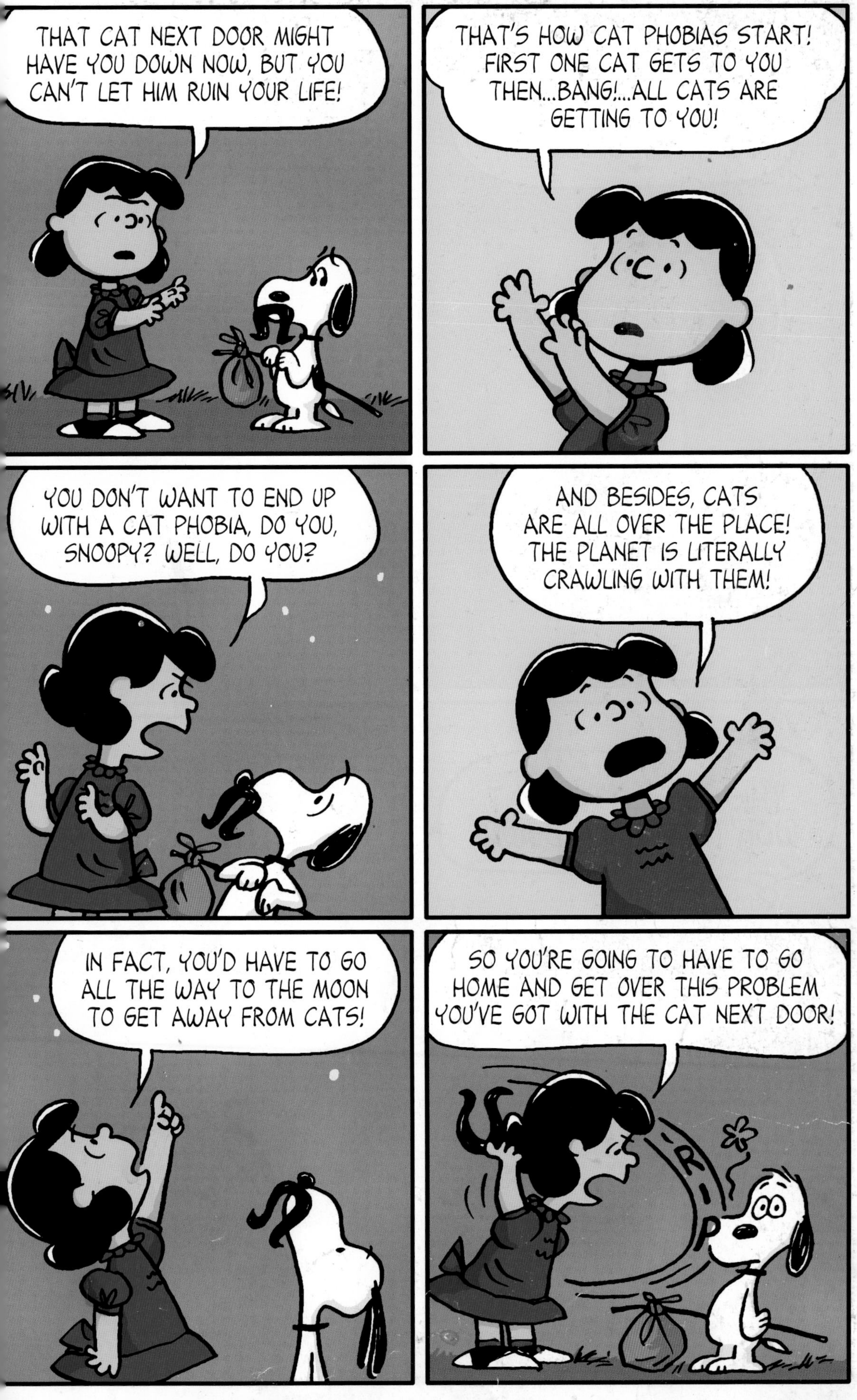
THAT CAT NEXT DOOR MIGHT HAVE YOU DOWN NOW, BUT YOU CAN'T LET HIM RUIN YOUR LIFE!
THAT'S HOW CAT PHOBIAS START! FIRST ONE CAT GETS TO YOU THEN...BANG!...ALL CATS ARE GETTING TO YOU!
YOU DON'T WANT TO END UP WITH A CAT PHOBIA, DO YOU, SNOOPY? WELL, DO YOU?
AND BESIDES, CATS ARE ALL OVER THE PLACE! THE PLANET IS LITERALLY CRAWLING WITH THEM!
IN FACT, YOU'D HAVE TO GO ALL THE WAY TO THE MOON TO GET AWAY FROM CATS!
SO YOU'RE GOING TO HAVE TO GO HOME AND GET OVER THIS PROBLEM YOU'VE GOT WITH THE CAT NEXT DOOR!
-R-I-P

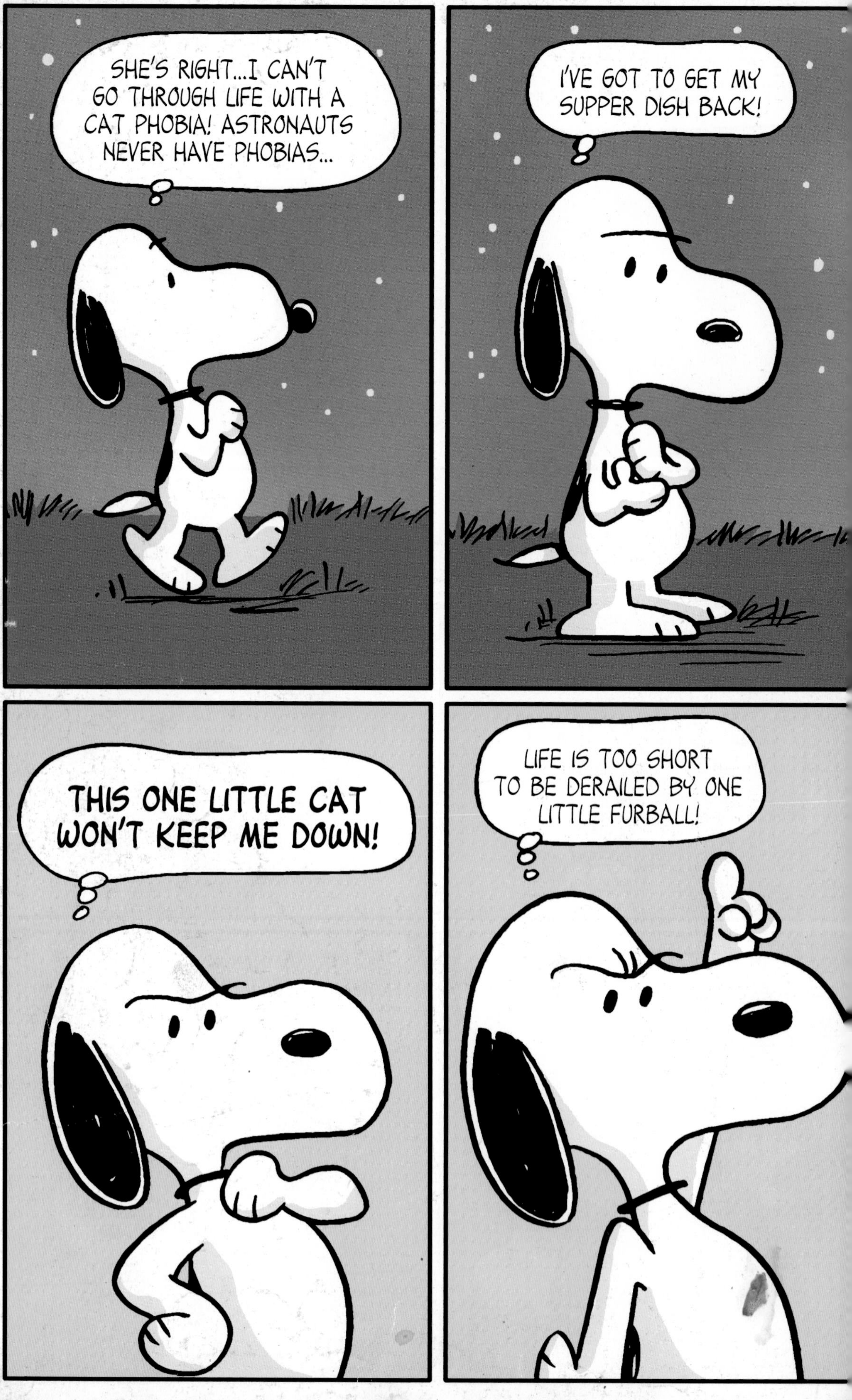
SHE'S RIGHT...I CAN'T GO THROUGH LIFE WITH A CAT PHOBIA! ASTRONAUTS NEVER HAVE PHOBIAS...
I'VE GOT TO GET MY SUPPER DISH BACK!
THIS ONE LITTLE CAT WON'T KEEP ME DOWN!
LIFE IS TOO SHORT TO BE DERAILED BY ONE LITTLE FURBALL!

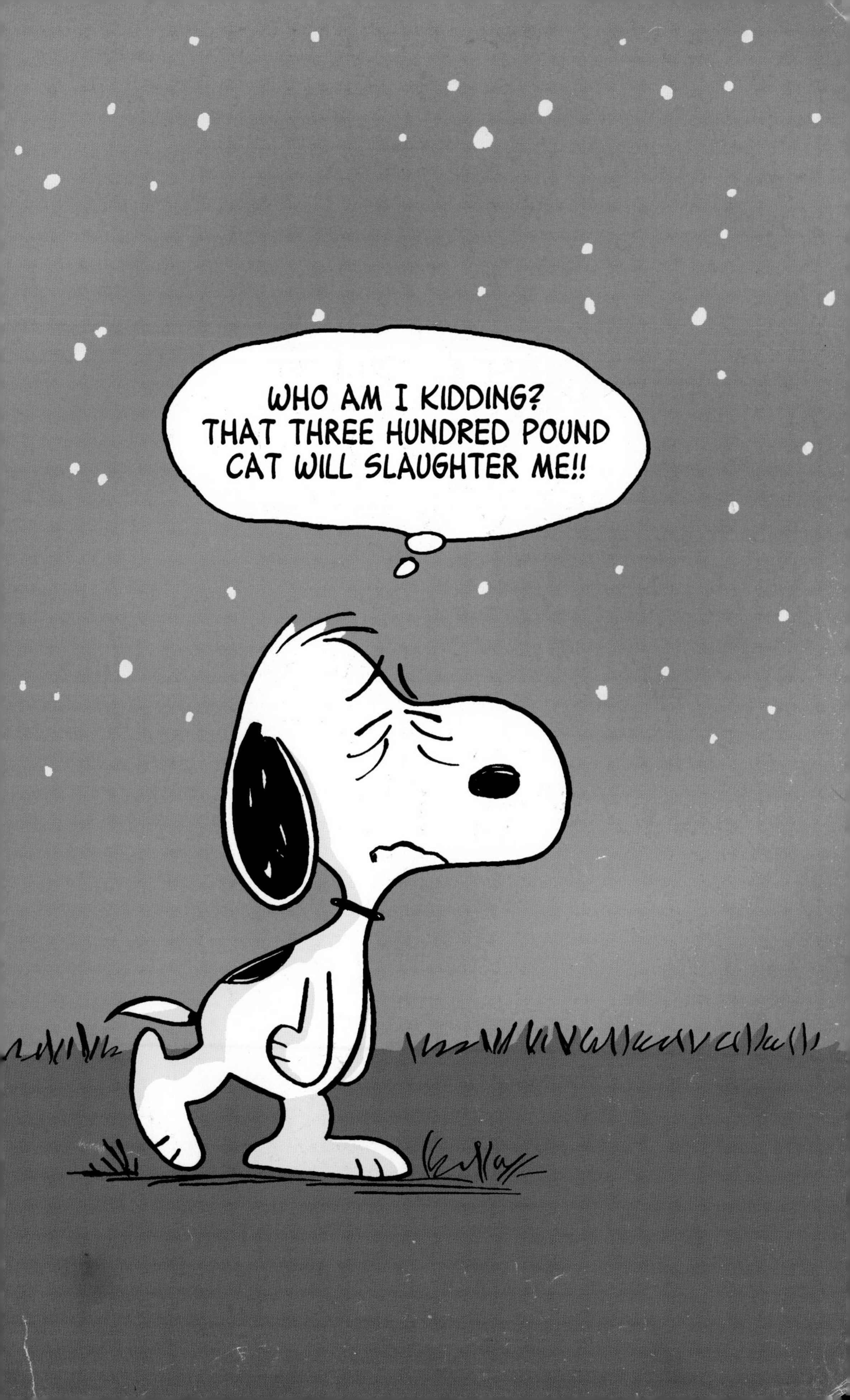
WHO AM I KIDDING? THAT THREE HUNDRED POUND CAT WILL SLAUGHTER ME!!

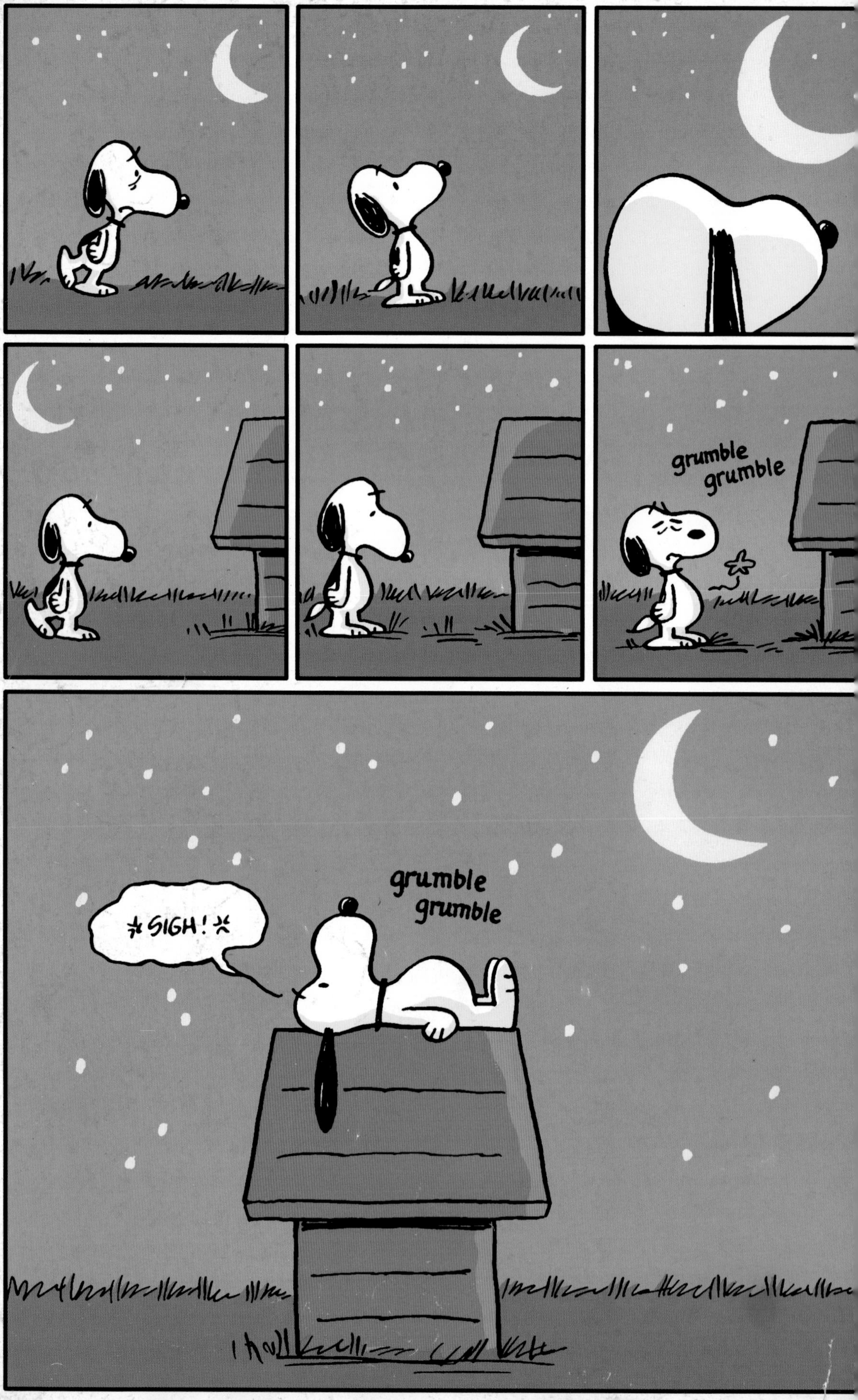
grumble grumble
SIGH!
grumble grumble

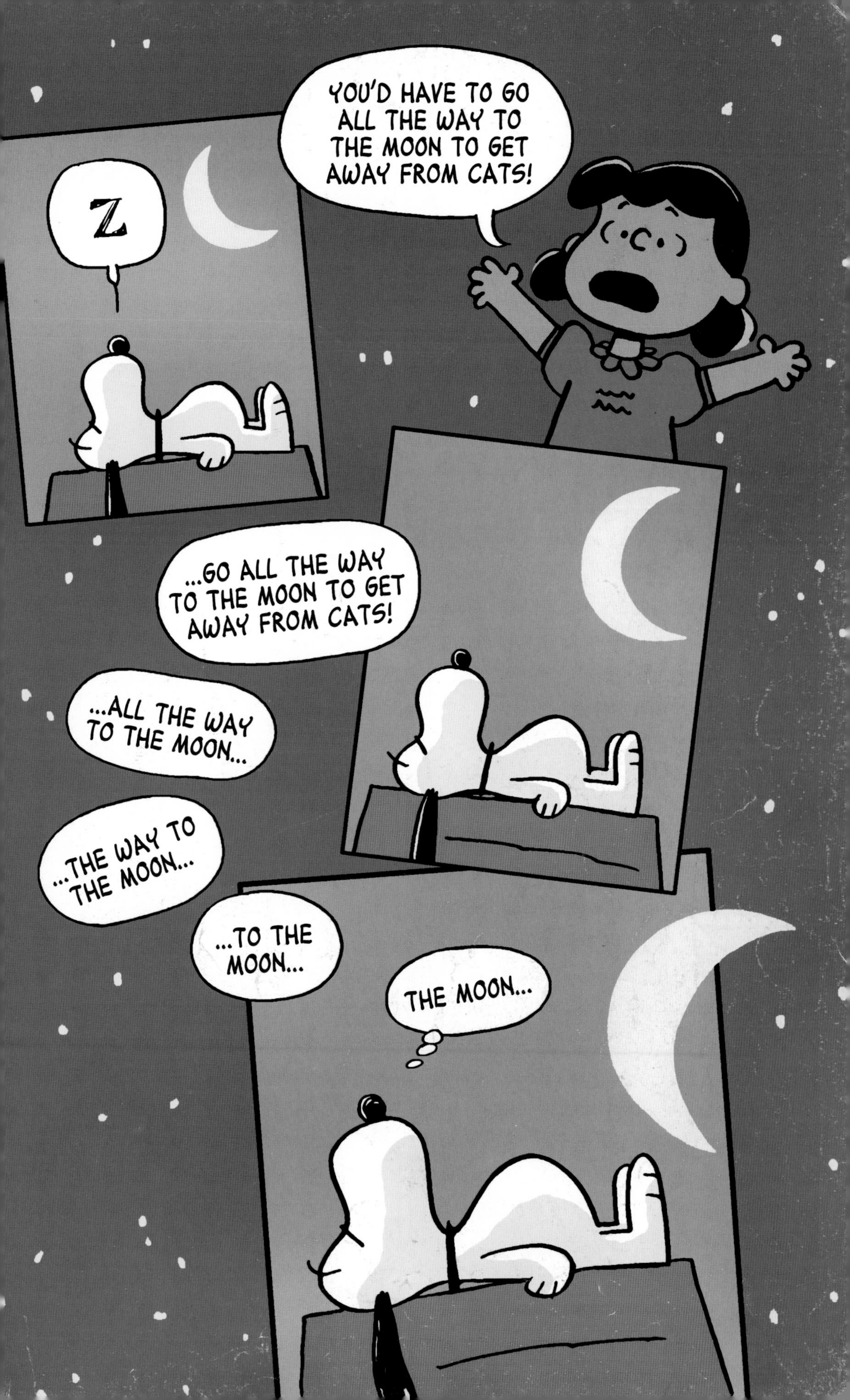
Z
YOU'D HAVE TO GO ALL THE WAY TO THE MOON TO GET AWAY FROM CATS!
...GO ALL THE WAY TO THE MOON TO GET AWAY FROM CATS!
...ALL THE WAY TO THE MOON...
...THE WAY TO THE MOON...
...TO THE MOON...
THE MOON...

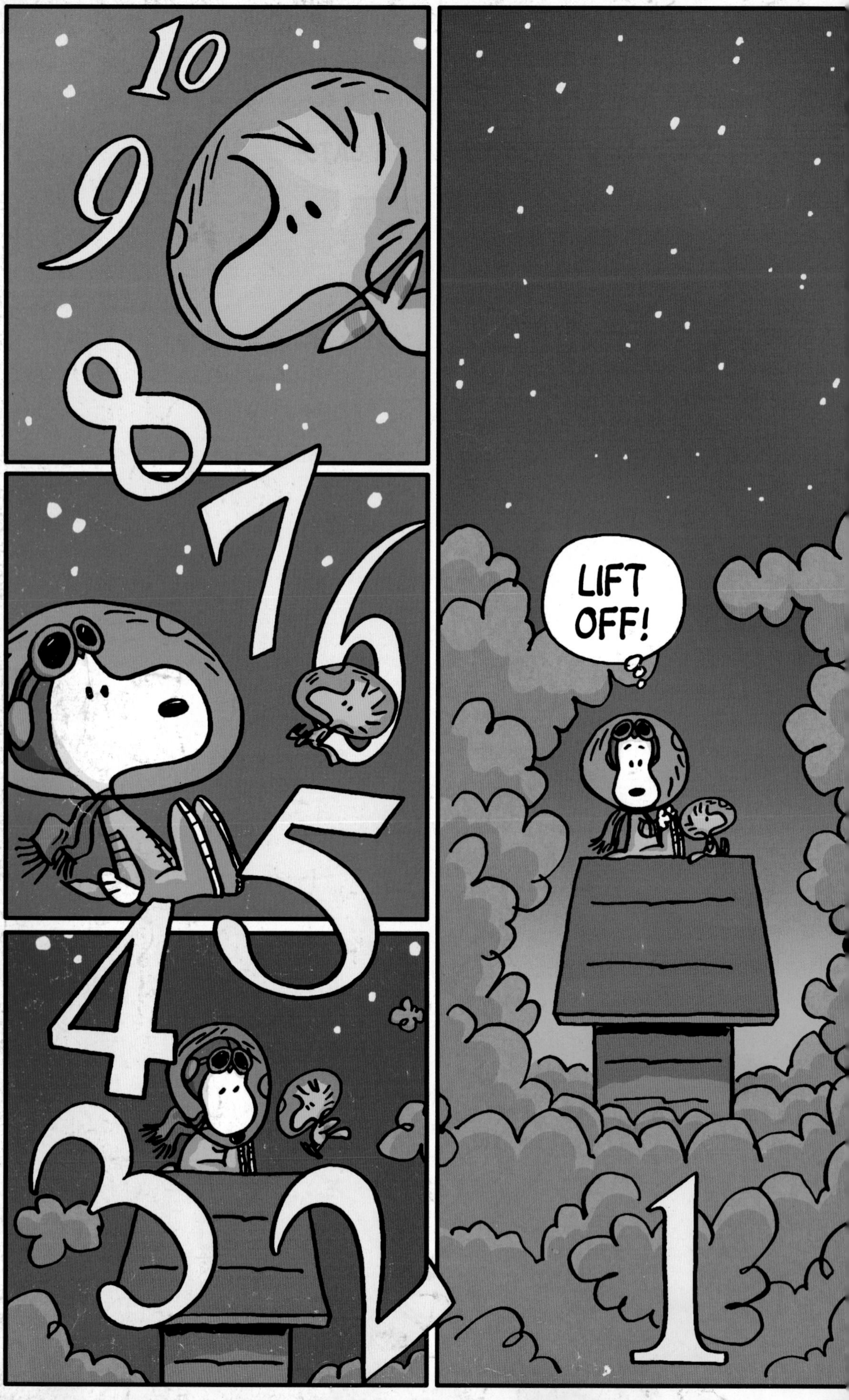
10
9
8
7
6
5
4
3
2
1
LIFT OFF!

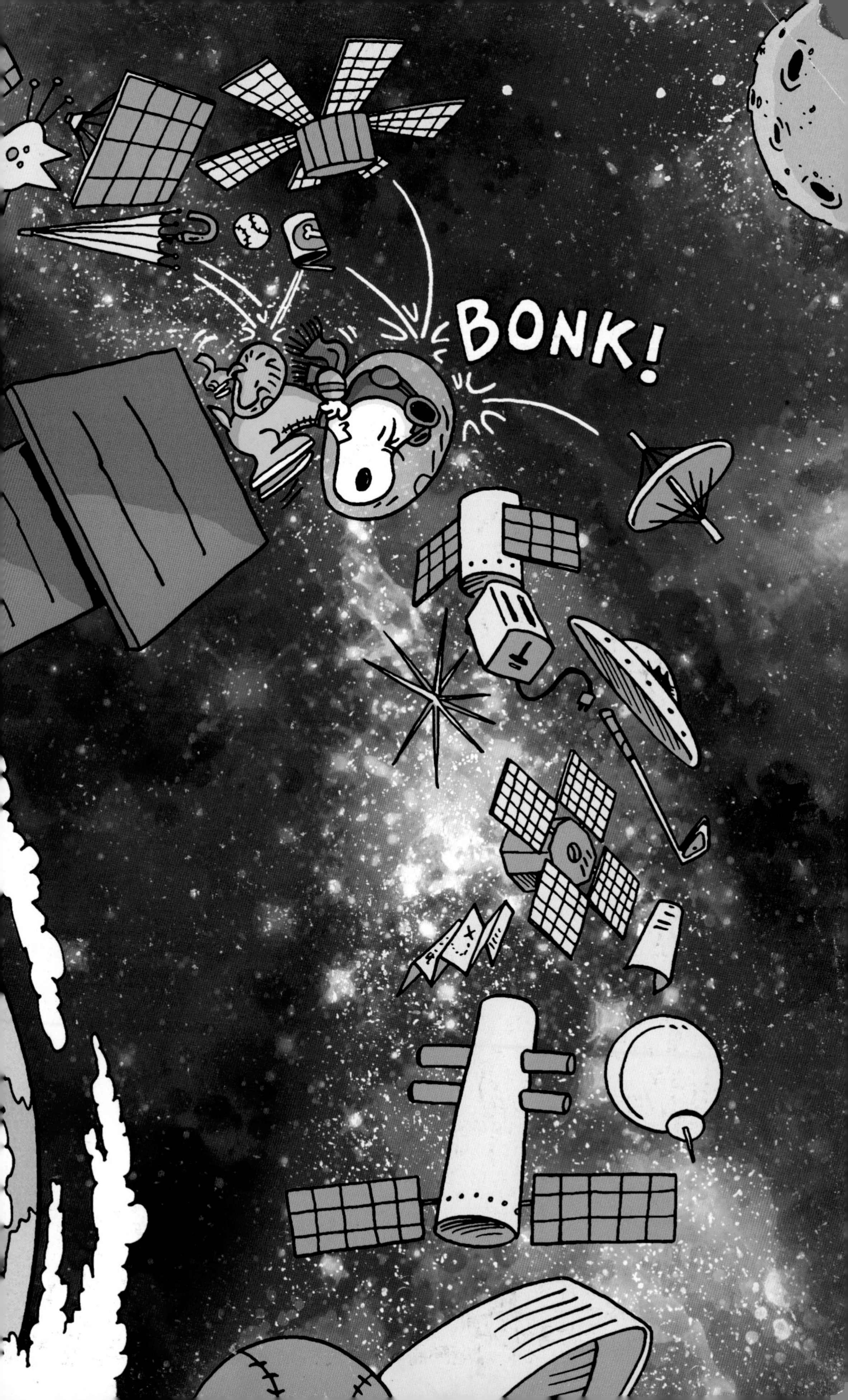
BONK!

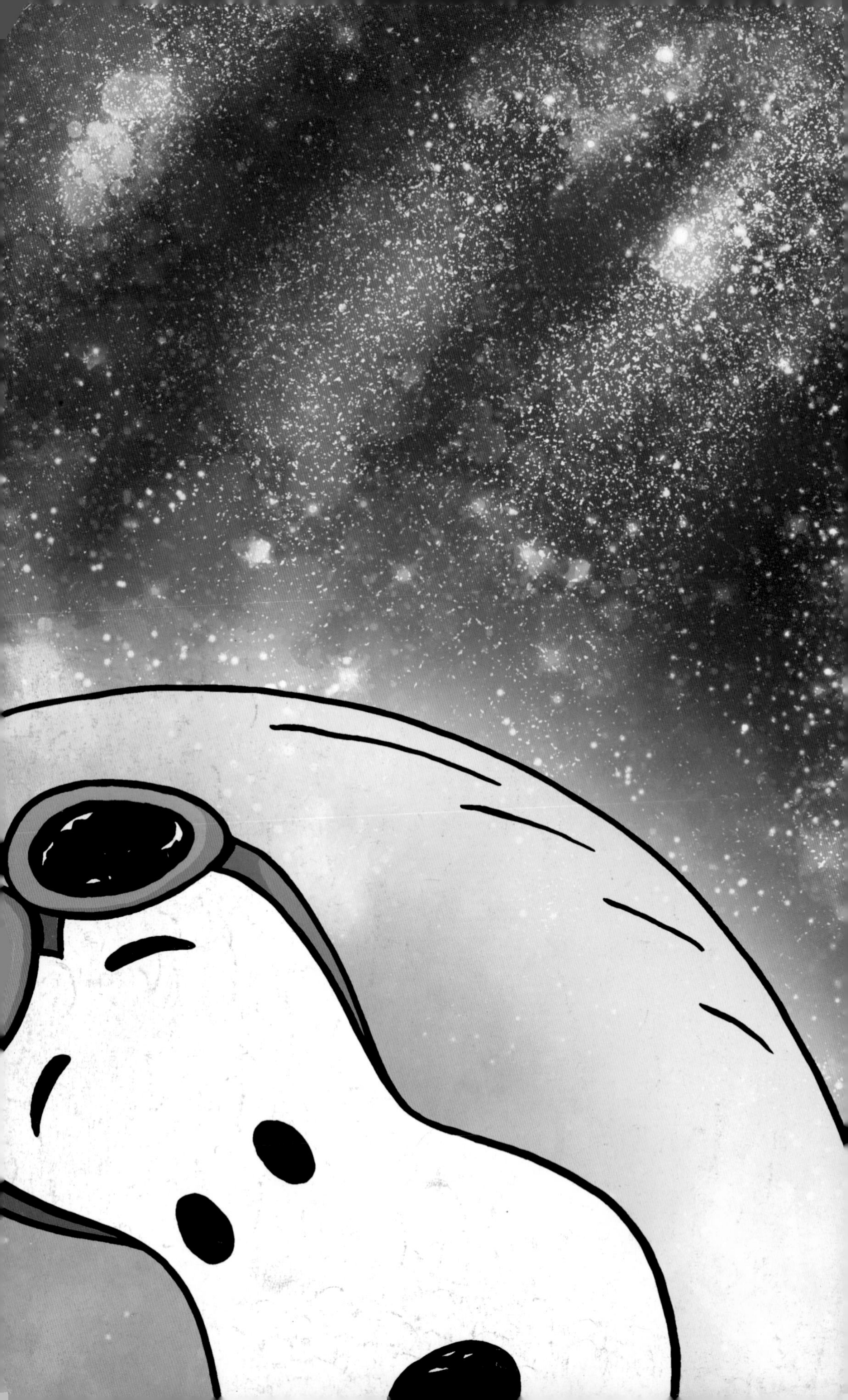

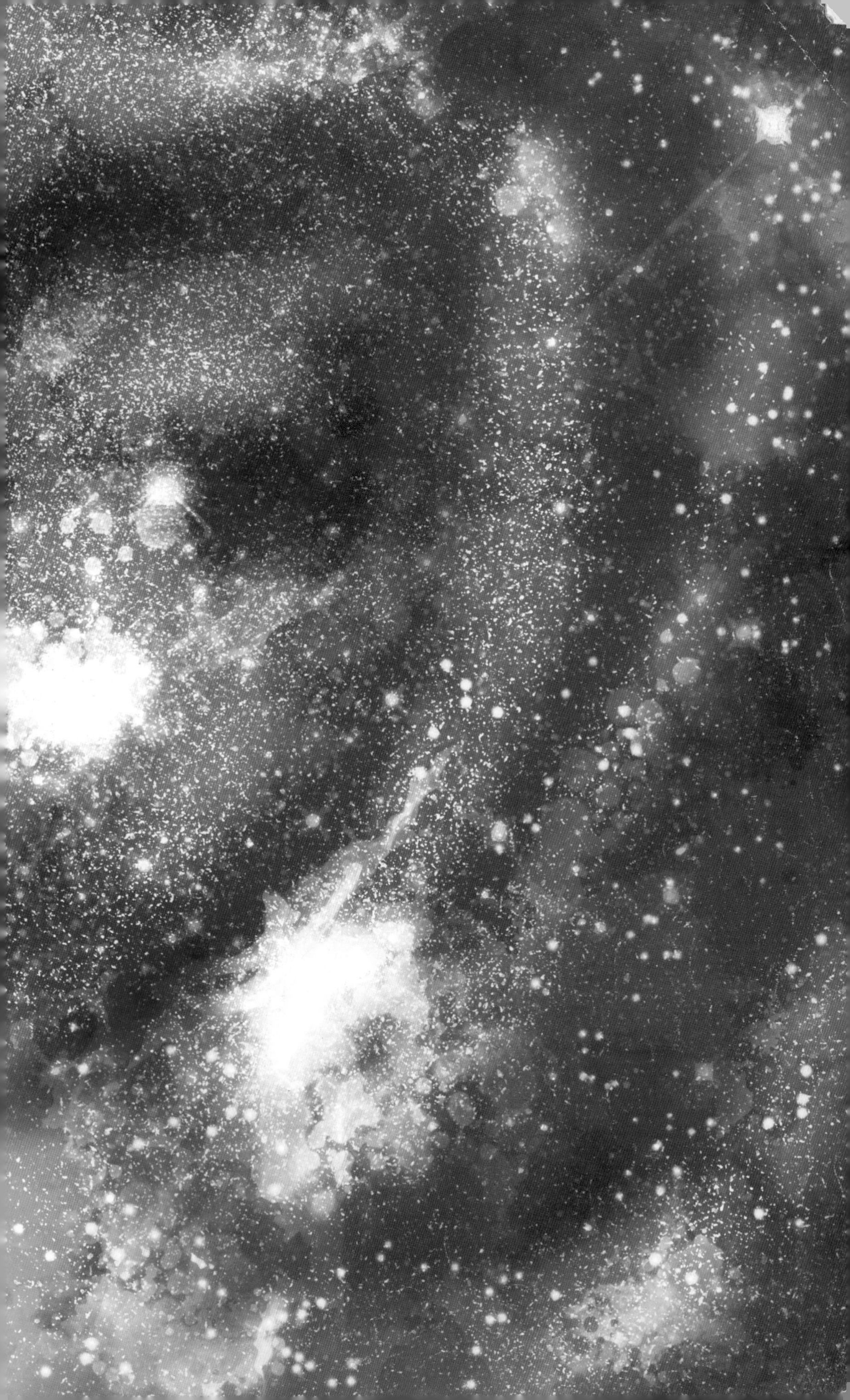

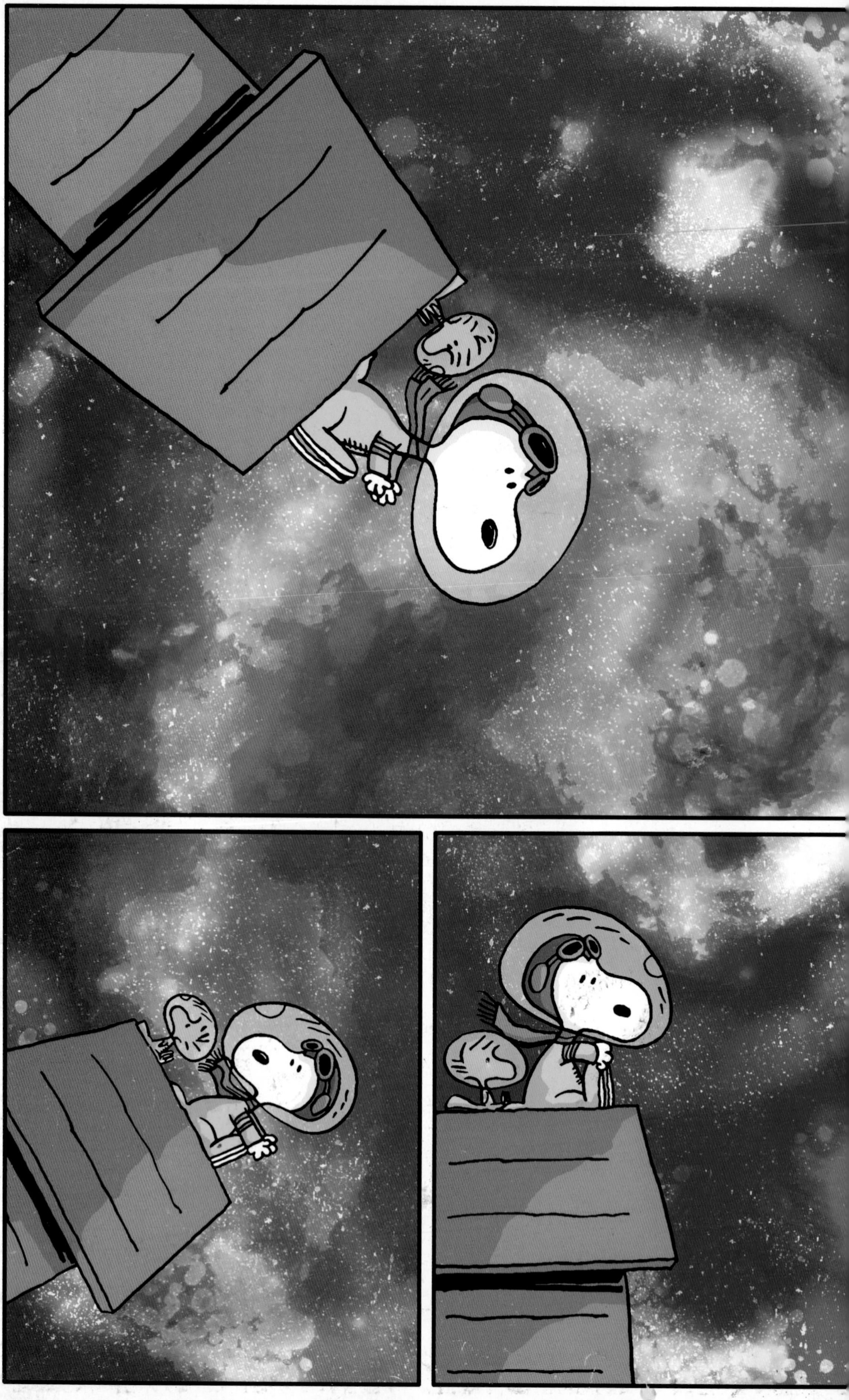

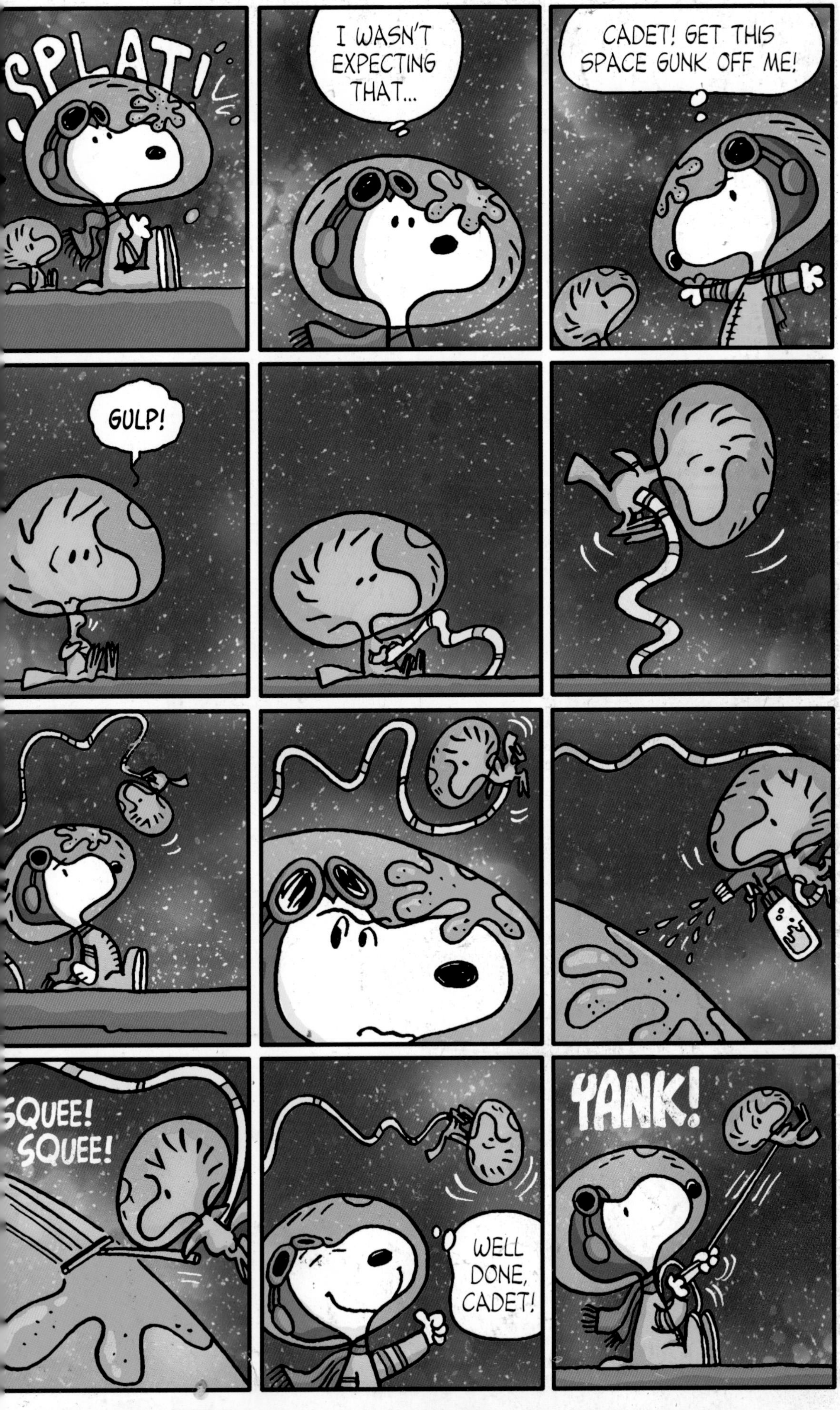

SPLAT!
I WASN'T EXPECTING THAT...
CADET! GET THIS SPACE GUNK OFF ME!
GULP!
SQUEE! SQUEE!
WELL DONE, CADET!
YANK!

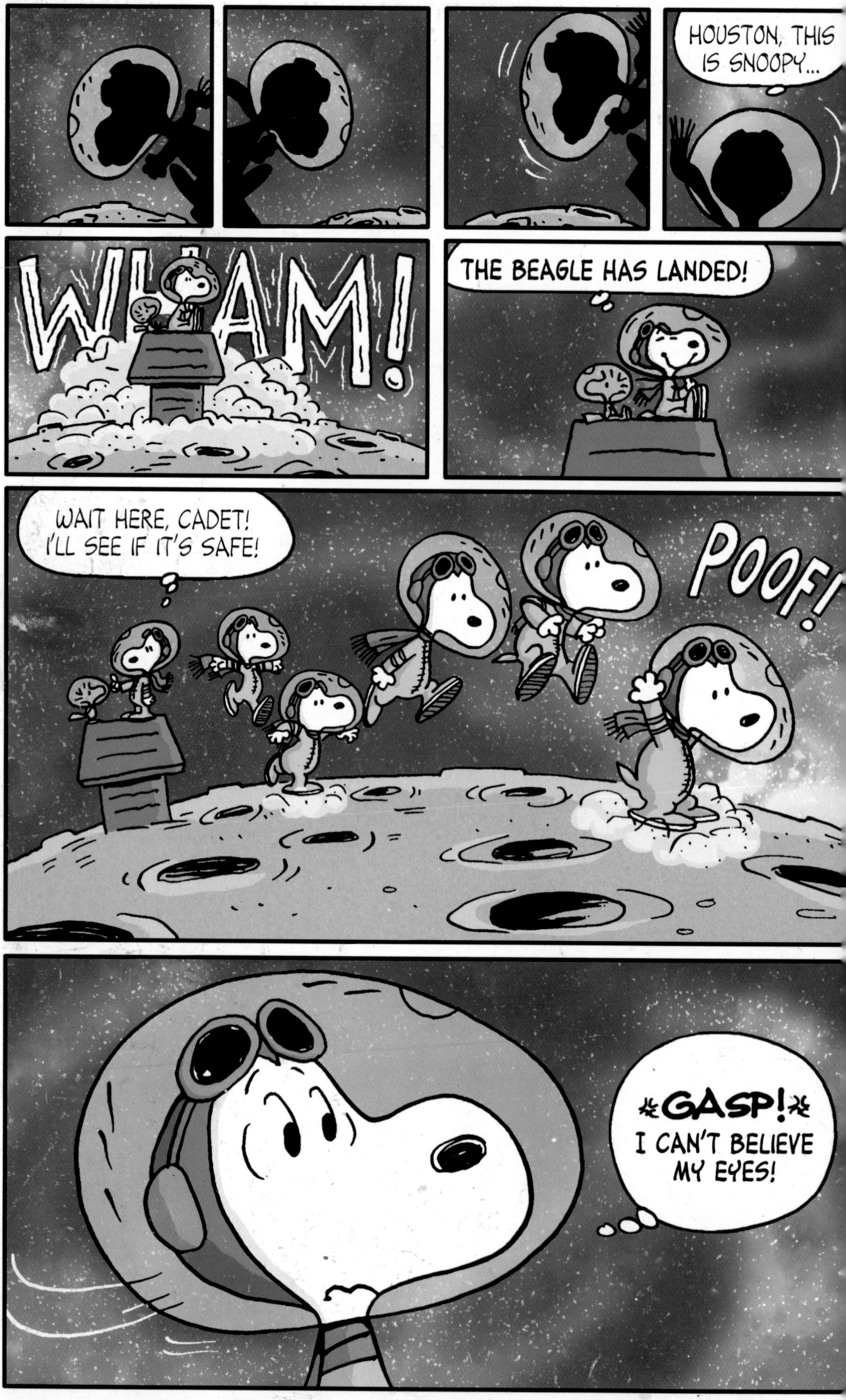
HOUSTON, THIS IS SNOOPY...
WHAM!
THE BEAGLE HAS LANDED!
WAIT HERE, CADET! I'LL SEE IF IT'S SAFE!
POOF!
GASP! I CAN'T BELIEVE MY EYES!

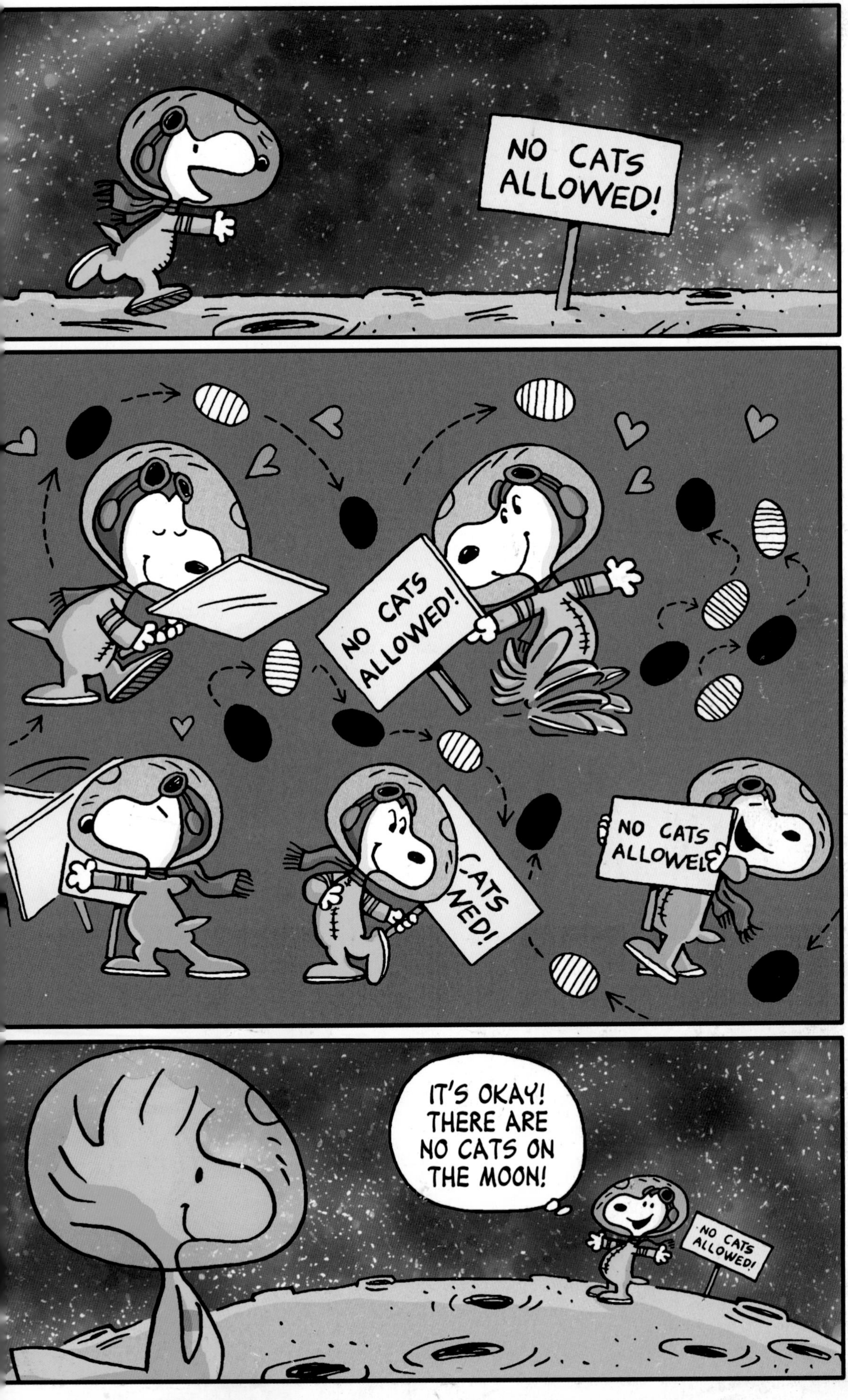
NO CATS ALLOWED!
NO CATS ALLOWED!
IT'S OKAY! THERE ARE NO CATS ON THE MOON!
NO CATS ALLOWED!

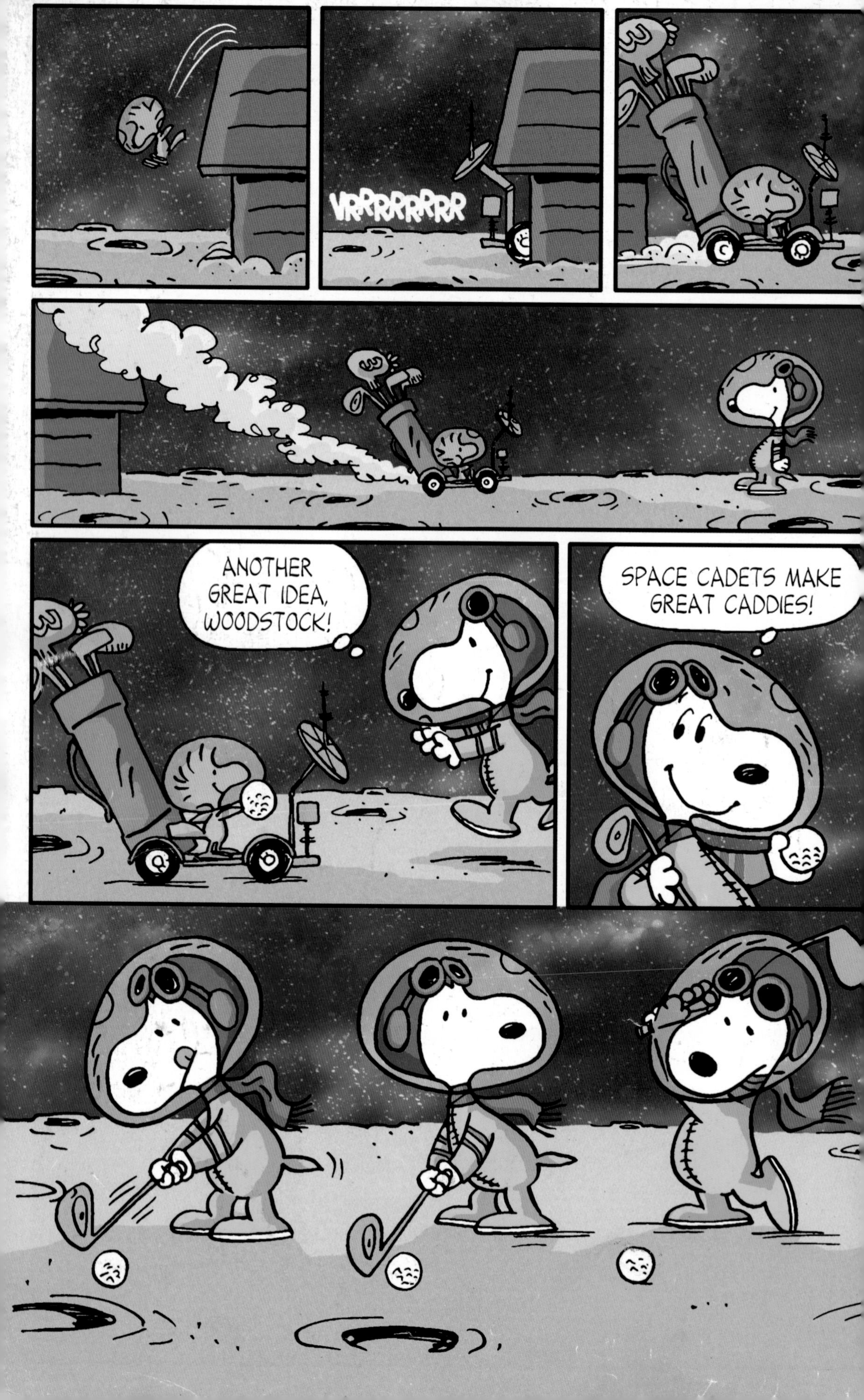
VRRRRRRRRR
ANOTHER GREAT IDEA, WOODSTOCK!
SPACE CADETS MAKE GREAT CADDIES!

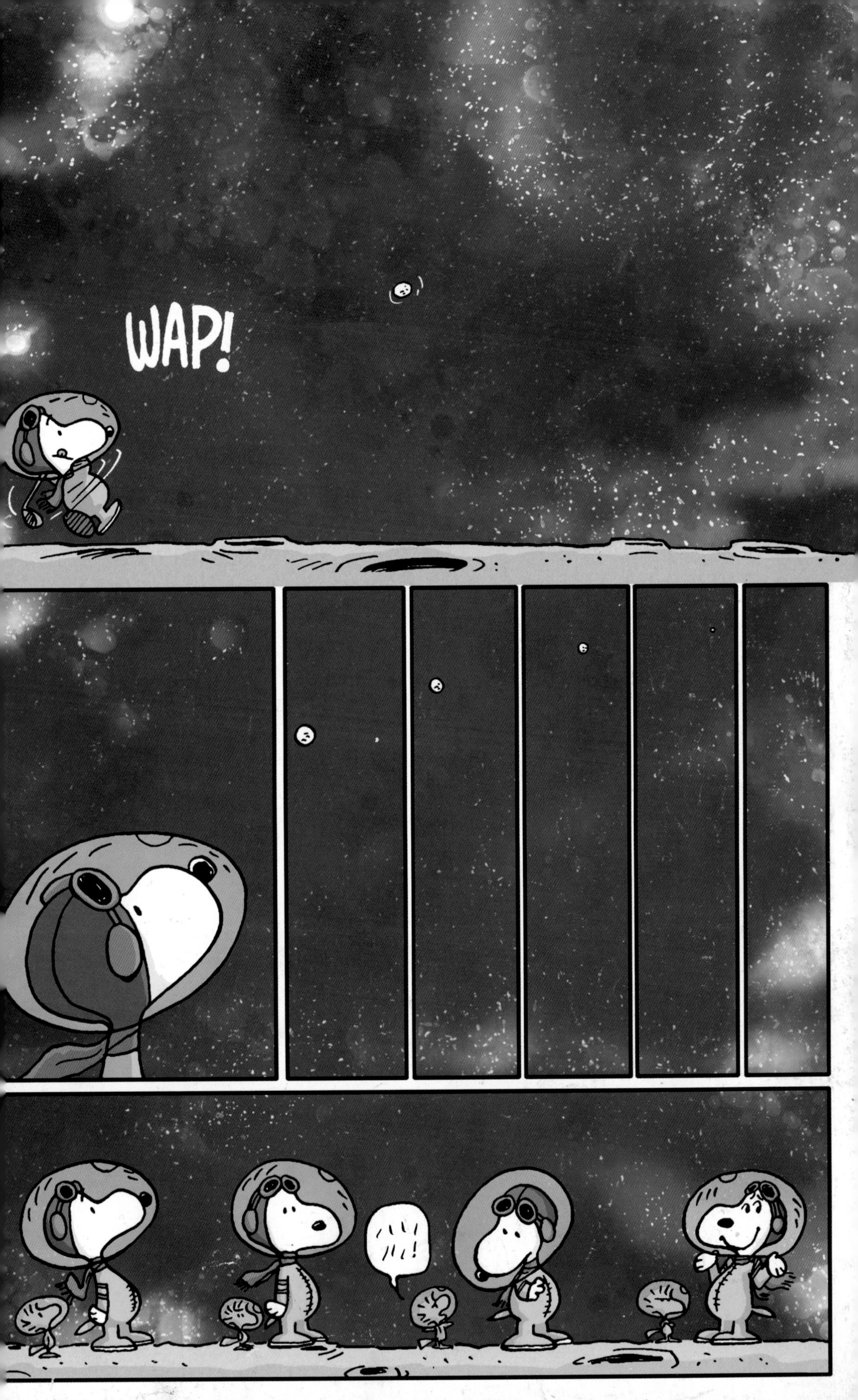
WAP!

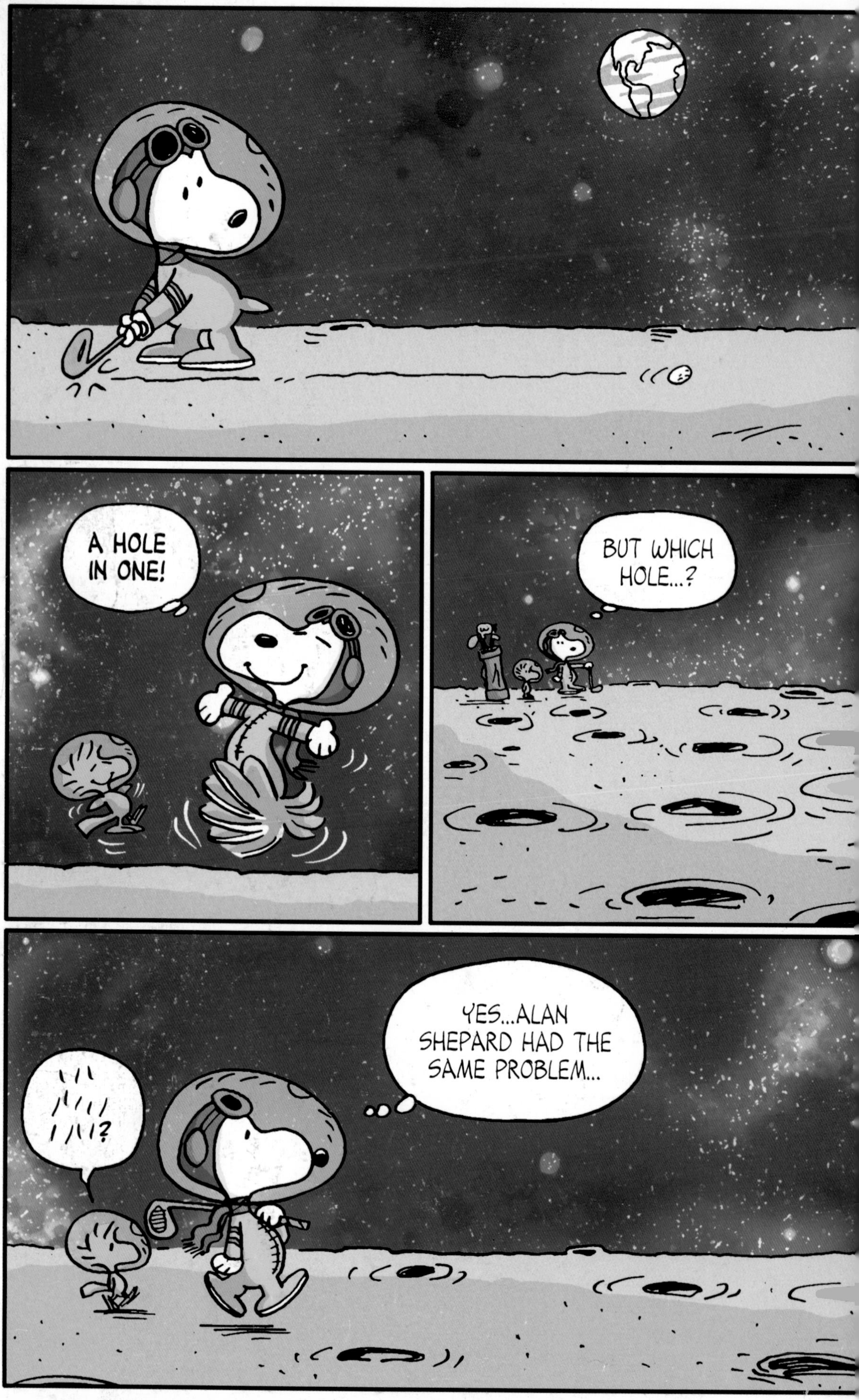
A HOLE IN ONE!
BUT WHICH HOLE...?
YES...ALAN SHEPARD HAD THE SAME PROBLEM...

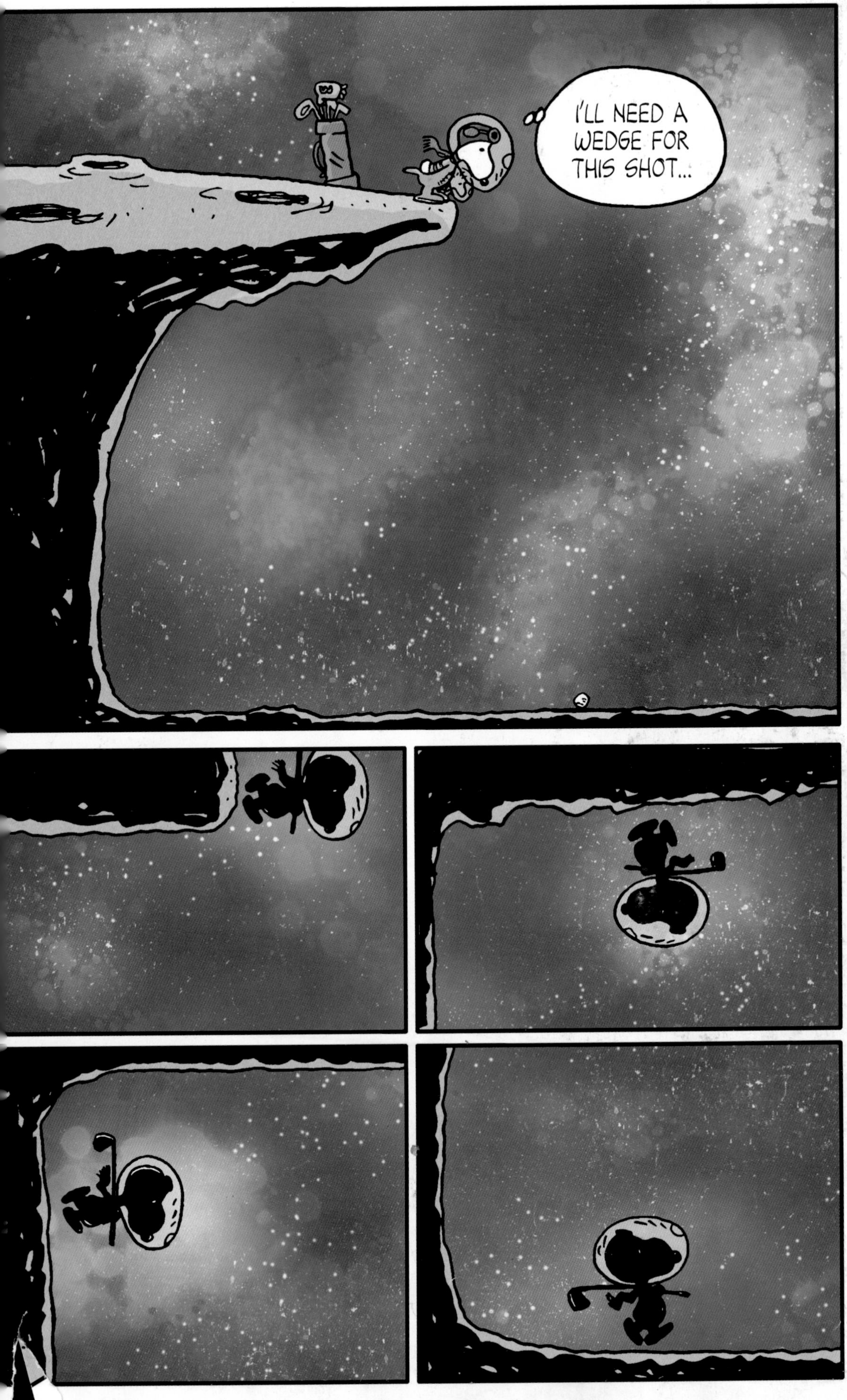
I'LL NEED A WEDGE FOR THIS SHOT...

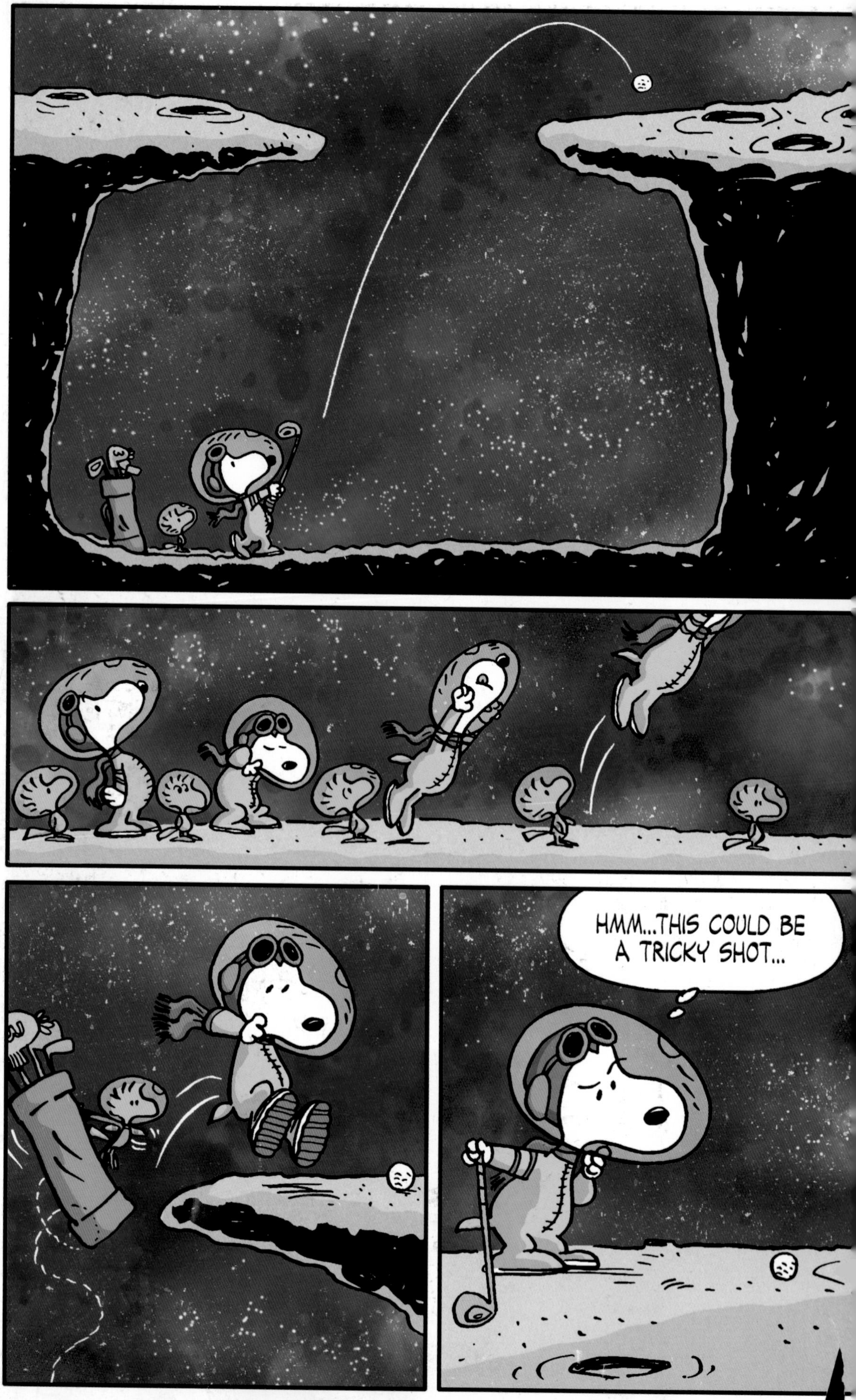
HMM...THIS COULD BE A TRICKY SHOT...

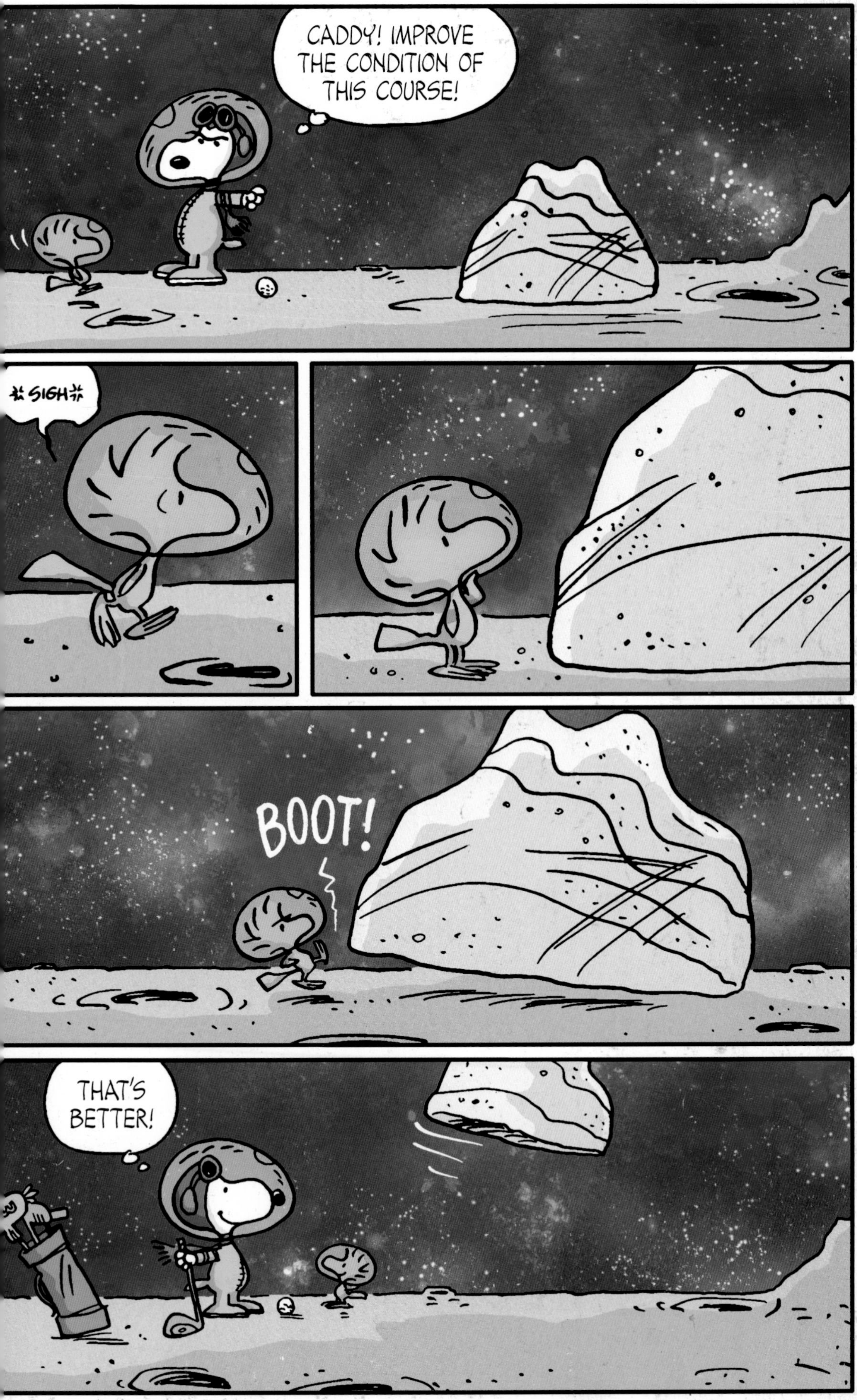
CADDY! IMPROVE THE CONDITION OF THIS COURSE!
SIGH
BOOT!
THAT'S BETTER!

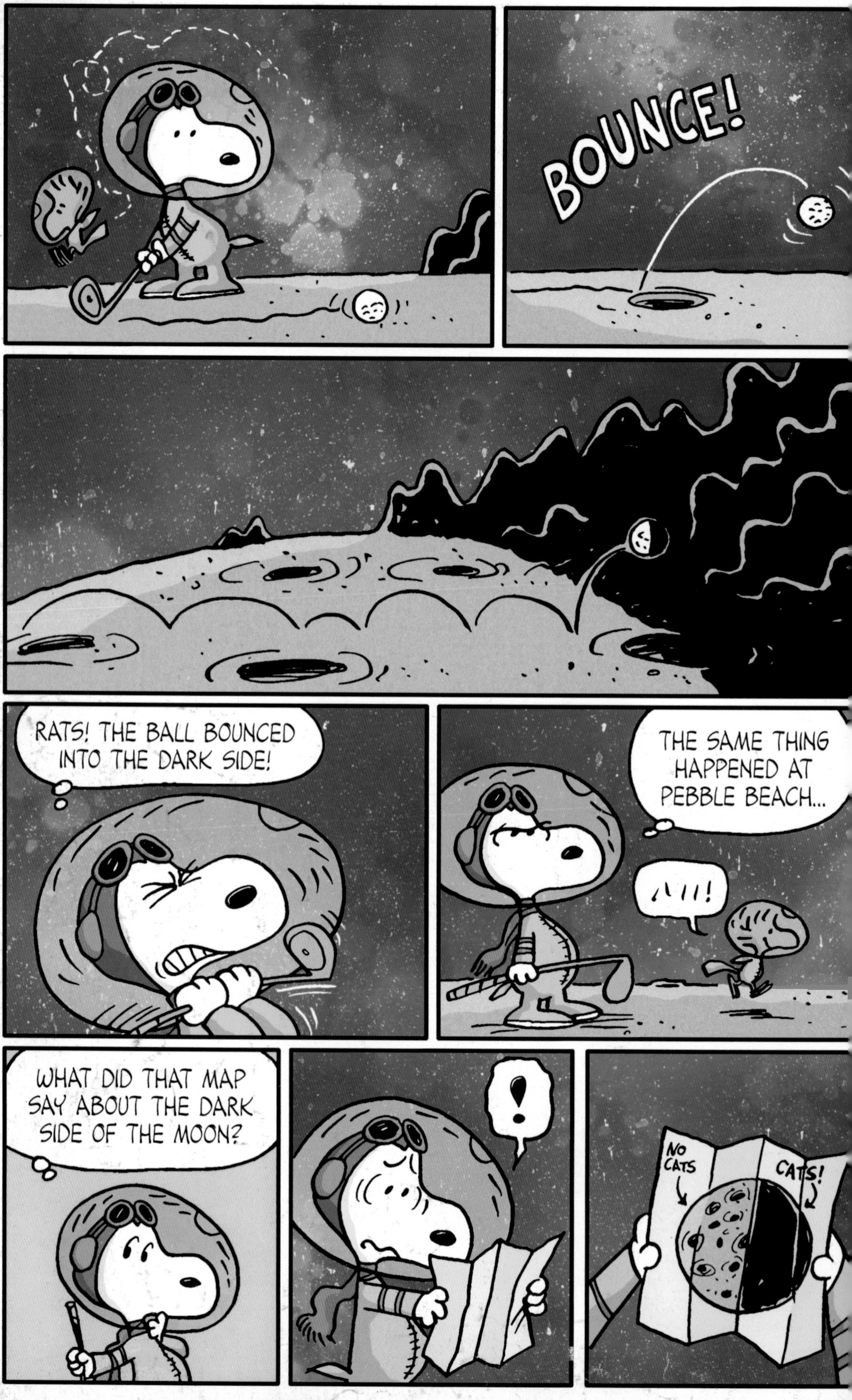
BOUNCE!
RATS! THE BALL BOUNCED INTO THE DARK SIDE!
THE SAME THING HAPPENED AT PEBBLE BEACH...
WHAT DID THAT MAP SAY ABOUT THE DARK SIDE OF THE MOON?
!
NO CATS
CATS!

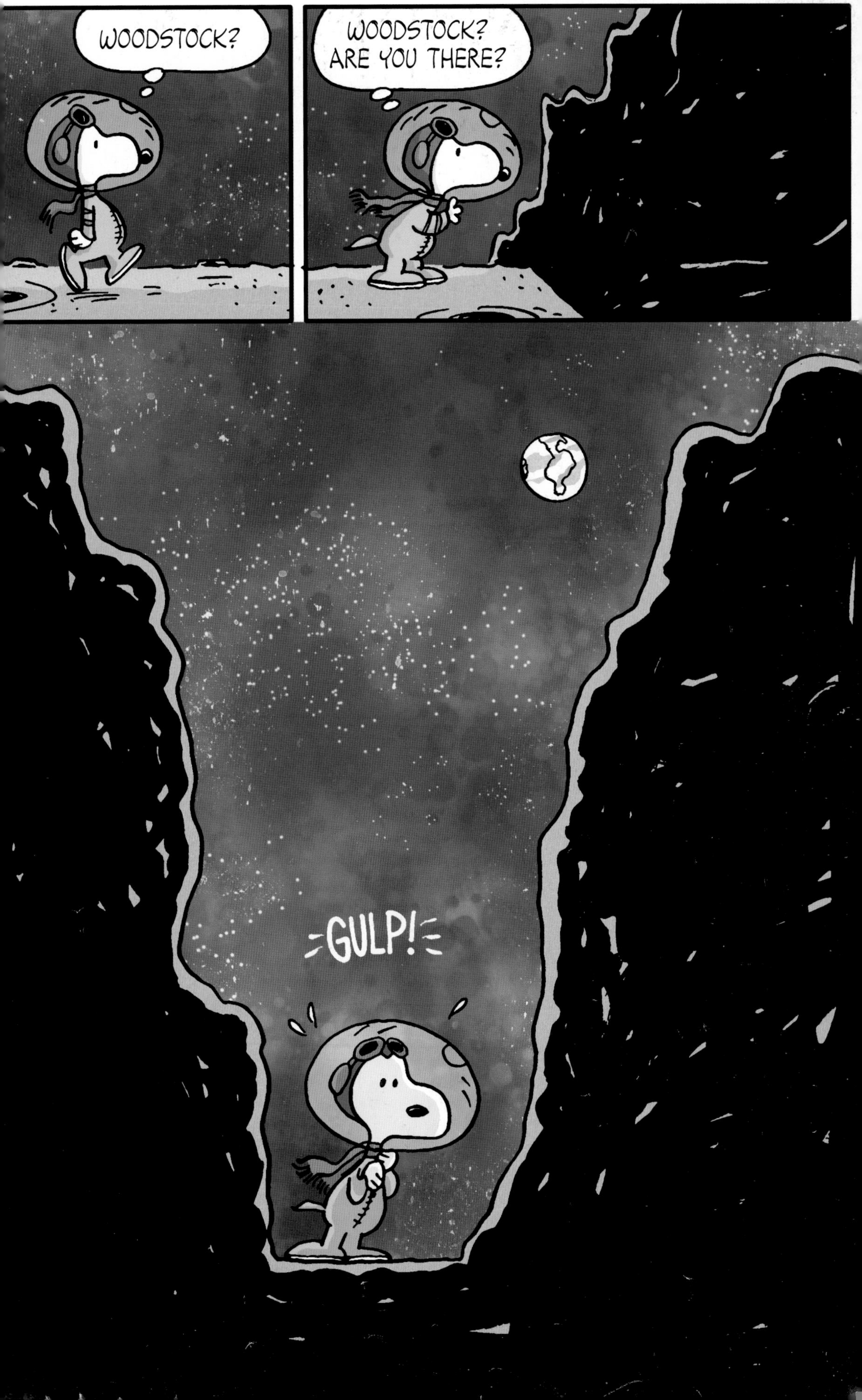
WOODSTOCK?
WOODSTOCK? ARE YOU THERE?
GULP!

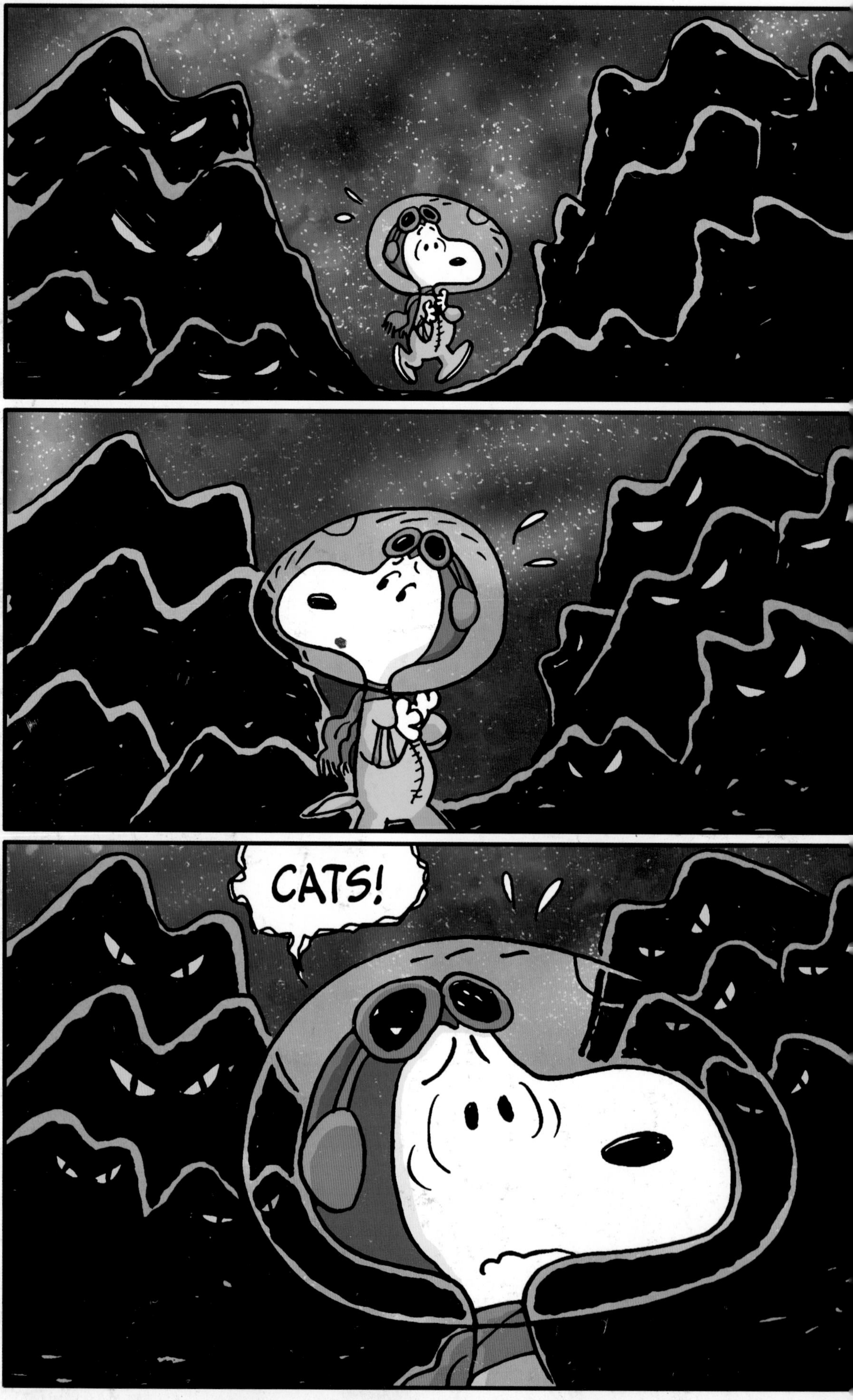
CATS!

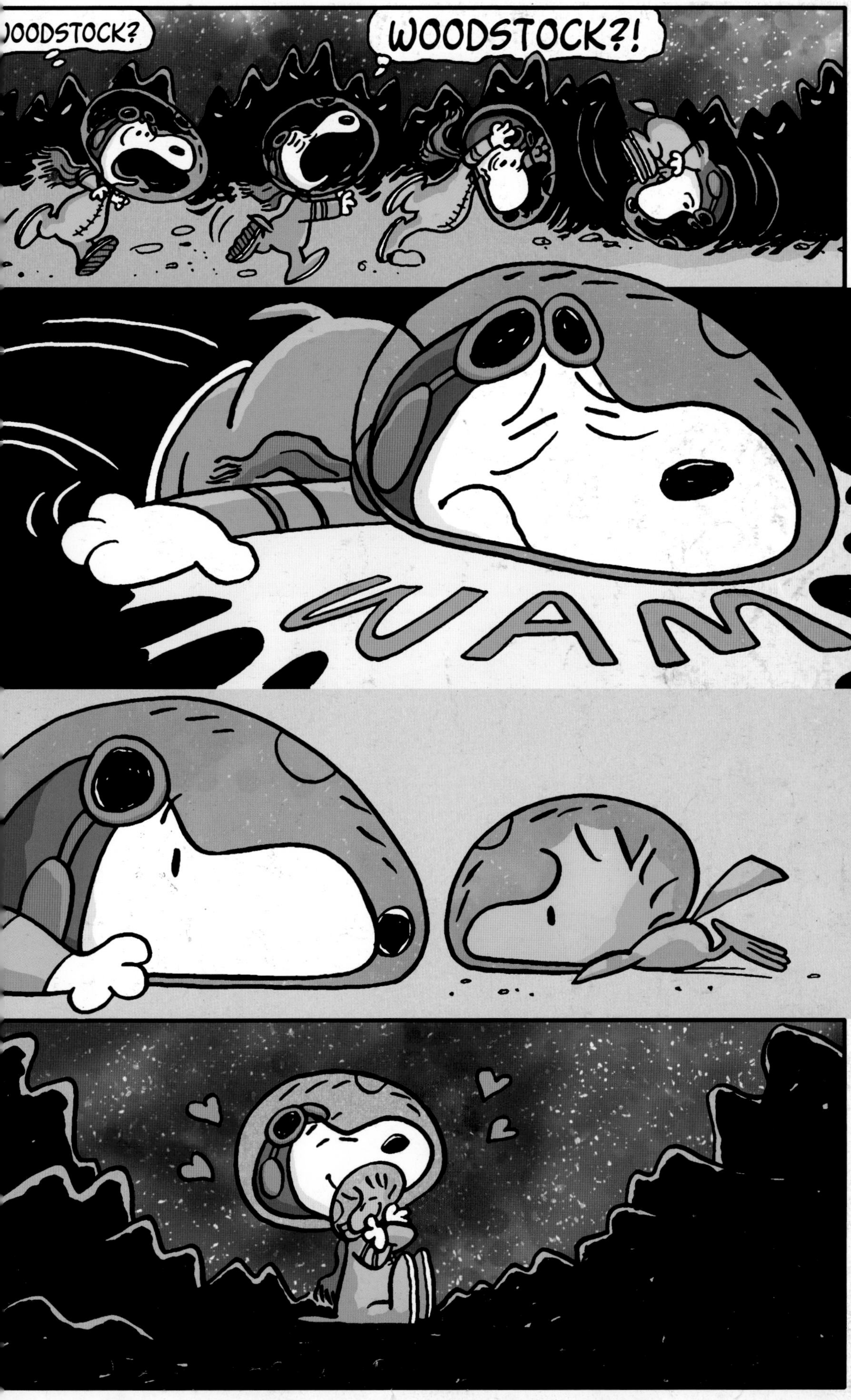

WOODSTOCK?
WOODSTOCK?!
WAM

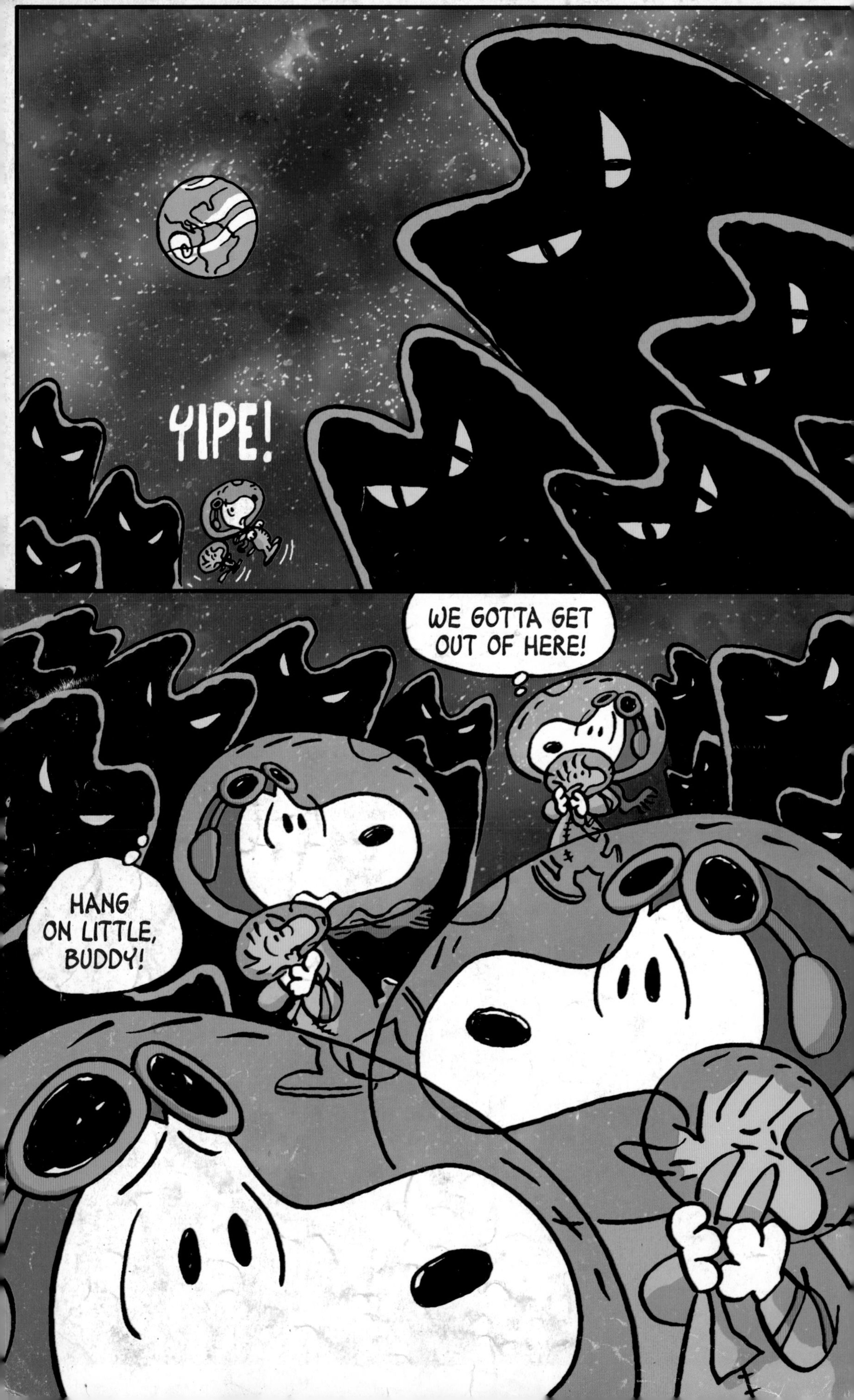
YIPE!
WE GOTTA GET OUT OF HERE!
HANG ON LITTLE, BUDDY!

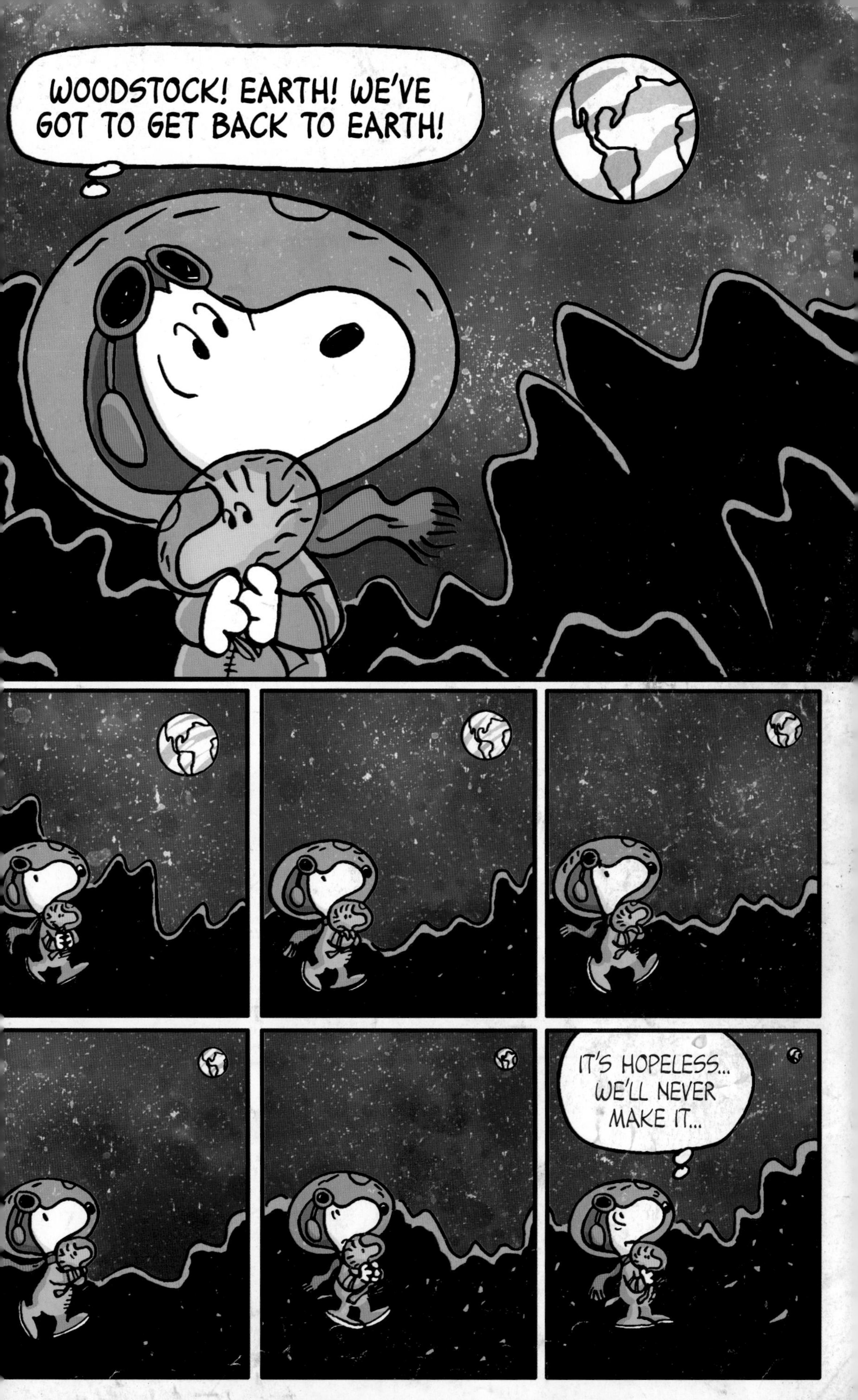
WOODSTOCK! EARTH! WE'VE GOT TO GET BACK TO EARTH!
IT'S HOPELESS... WE'LL NEVER MAKE IT...

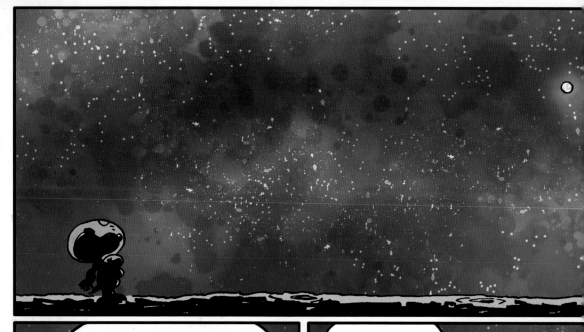

WE'RE STRANDED, WOODSTOCK...SURROUNDED BY NOTHING BUT SPACE....

RUMBLE! RUMBLE!

AND CATS!! AND THEY SOUND HUNGRY!

RUMBLE RUMBLE

WE HAVE COME ALL THE WAY TO THE MOON...

JUST TO END UP AS CAT FOOD!

RUMBLE RUMBLE! RUMBLE!

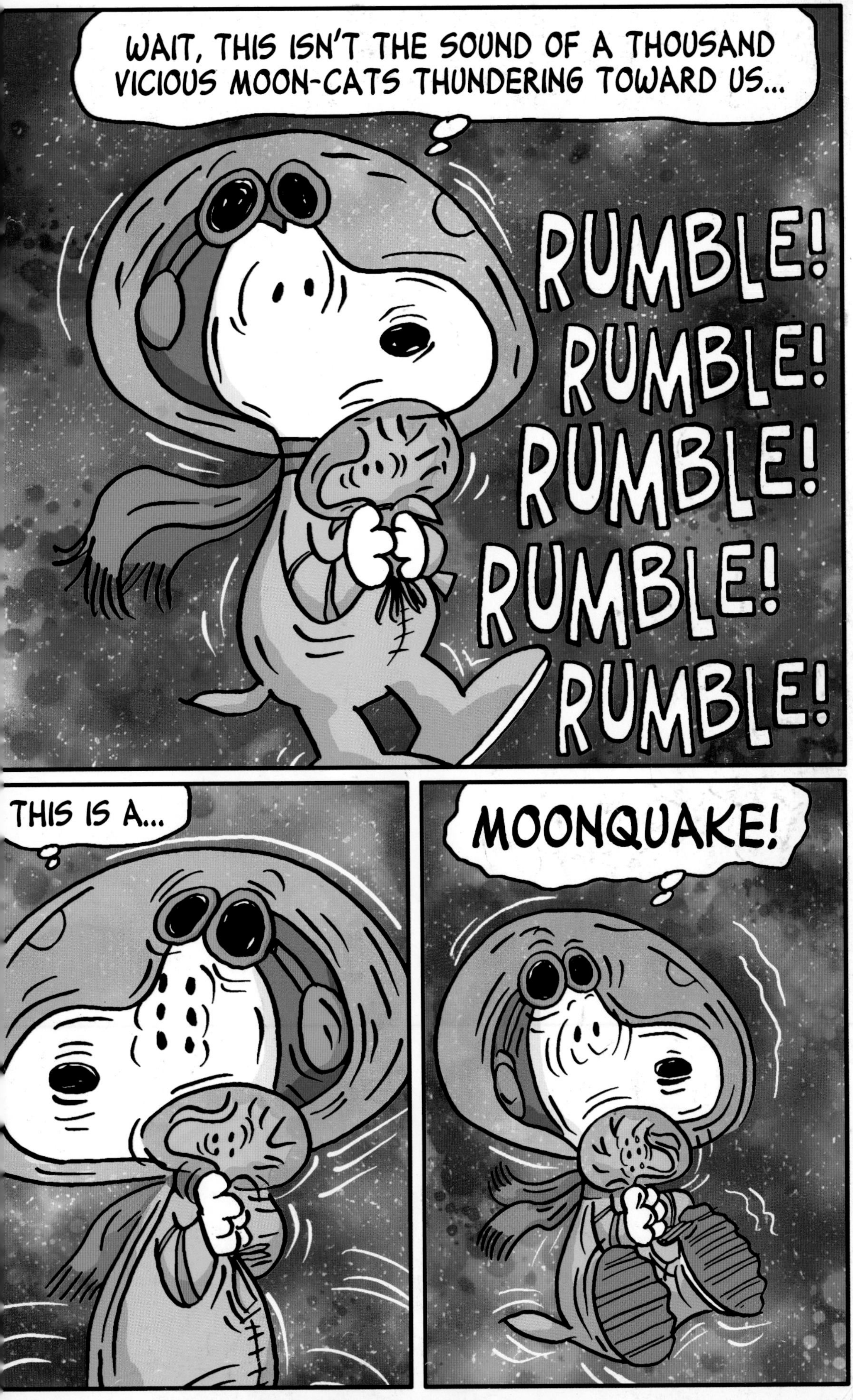
WAIT, THIS ISN'T THE SOUND OF A THOUSAND VICIOUS MOON-CATS THUNDERING TOWARD US...
RUMBLE! RUMBLE! RUMBLE! RUMBLE! RUMBLE!
THIS IS A...
MOONQUAKE!

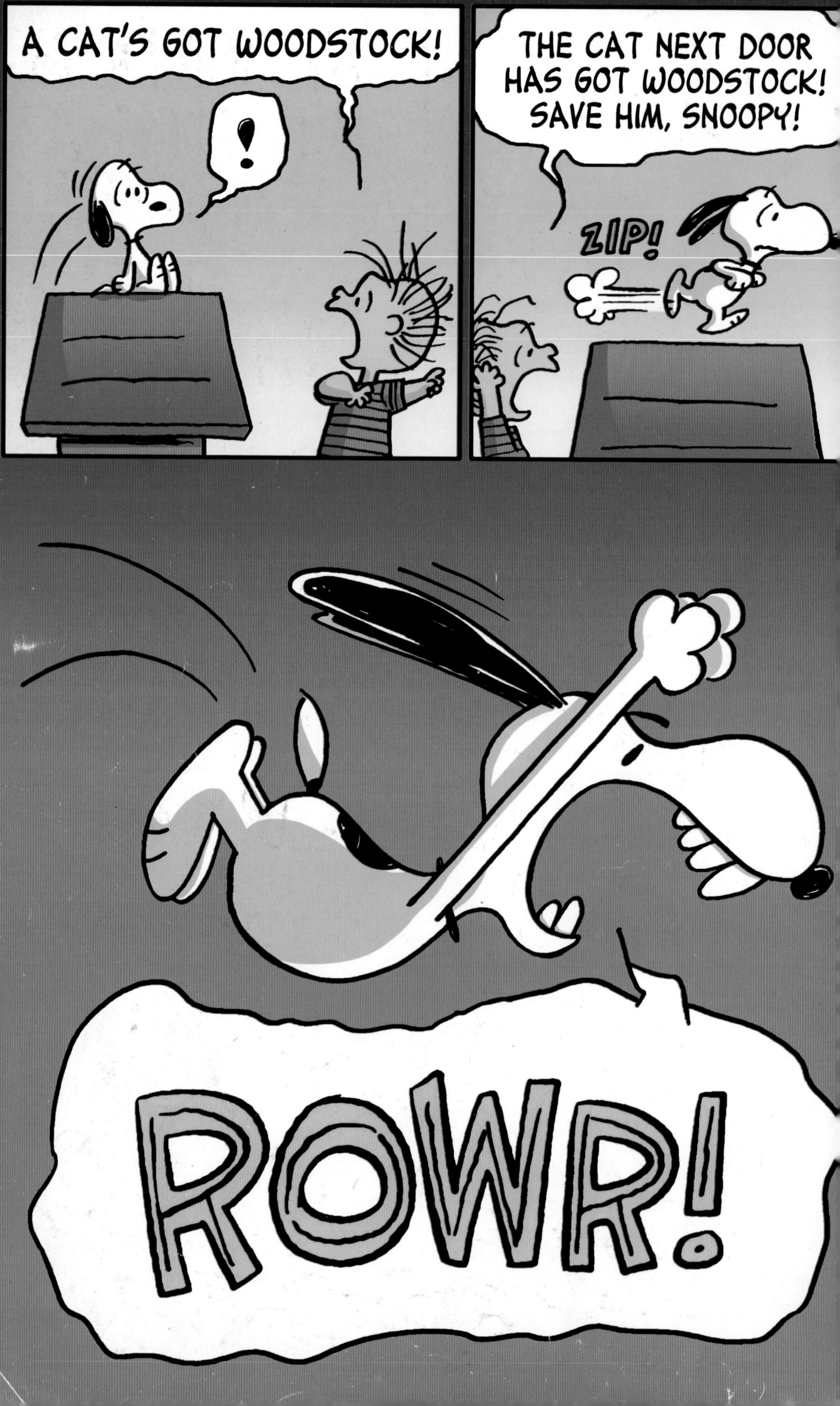
A CAT'S GOT WOODSTOCK!
!
THE CAT NEXT DOOR HAS GOT WOODSTOCK! SAVE HIM, SNOOPY!
ZIP!
ROWR!

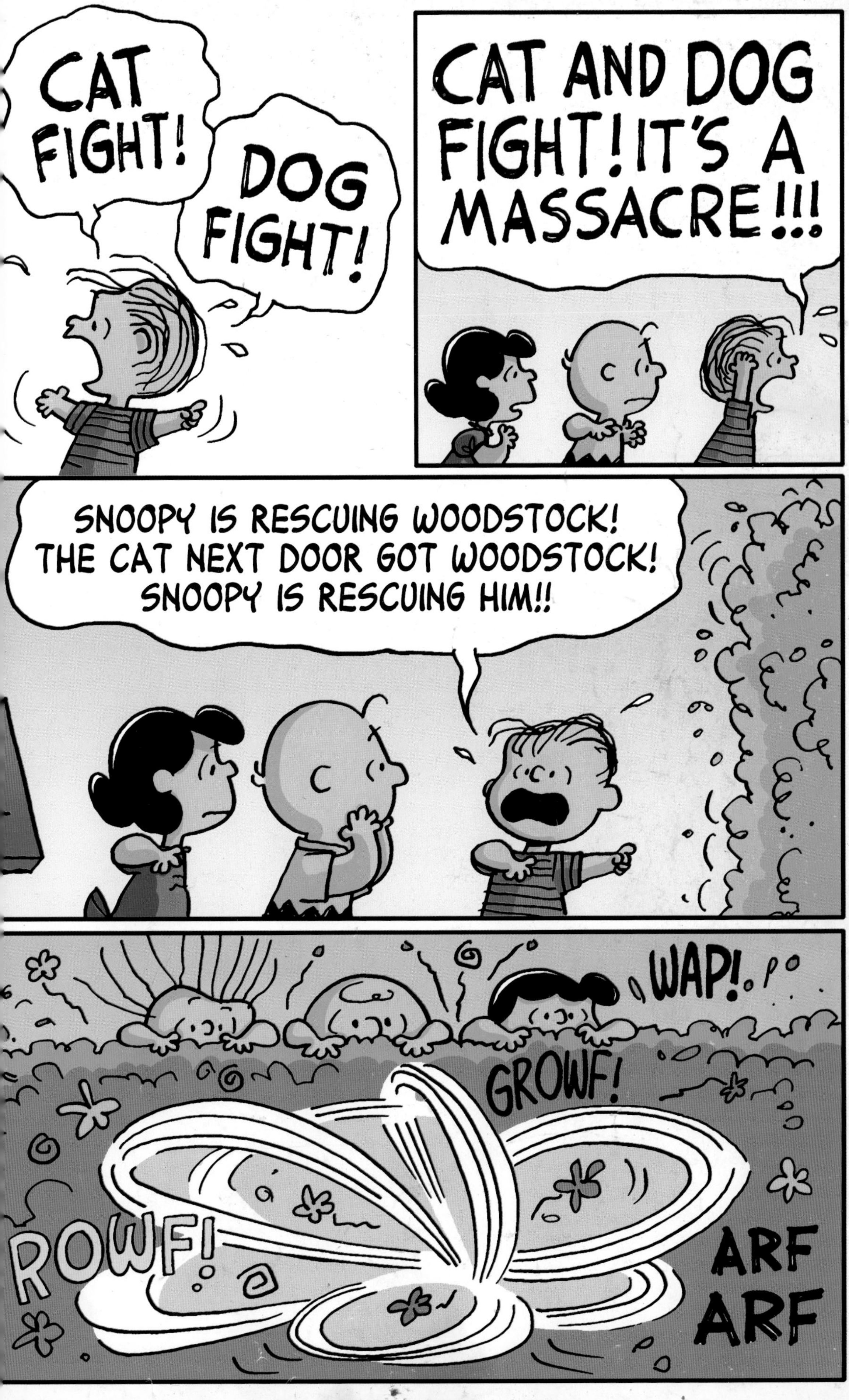
CAT FIGHT!
DOG FIGHT!
CAT AND DOG FIGHT! IT'S A MASSACRE!!!
SNOOPY IS RESCUING WOODSTOCK! THE CAT NEXT DOOR GOT WOODSTOCK! SNOOPY IS RESCUING HIM!!
WAP!
GROWF!
ROWF!
ARF ARF

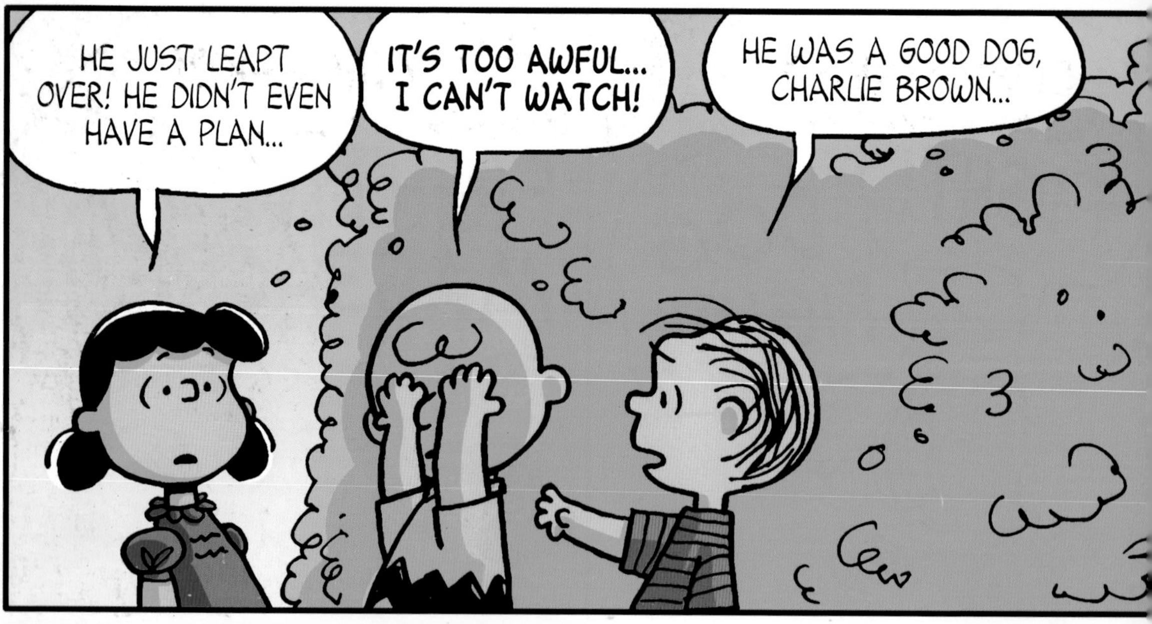
HE JUST LEAPT OVER! HE DIDN'T EVEN HAVE A PLAN...
IT'S TOO AWFUL... I CAN'T WATCH!
HE WAS A GOOD DOG, CHARLIE BROWN...

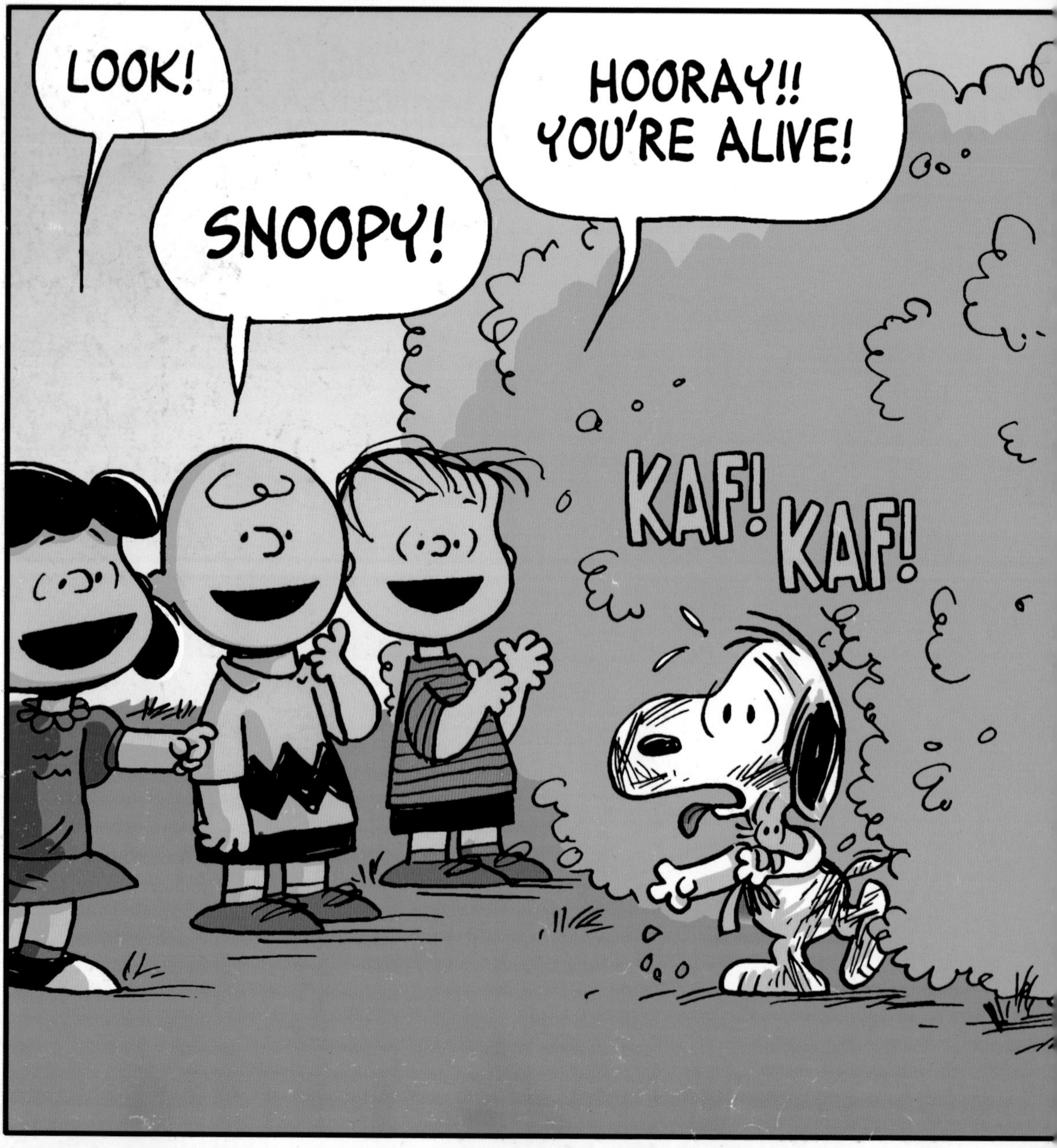
LOOK!
SNOOPY!
HOORAY!! YOU'RE ALIVE!
KAF! KAF!

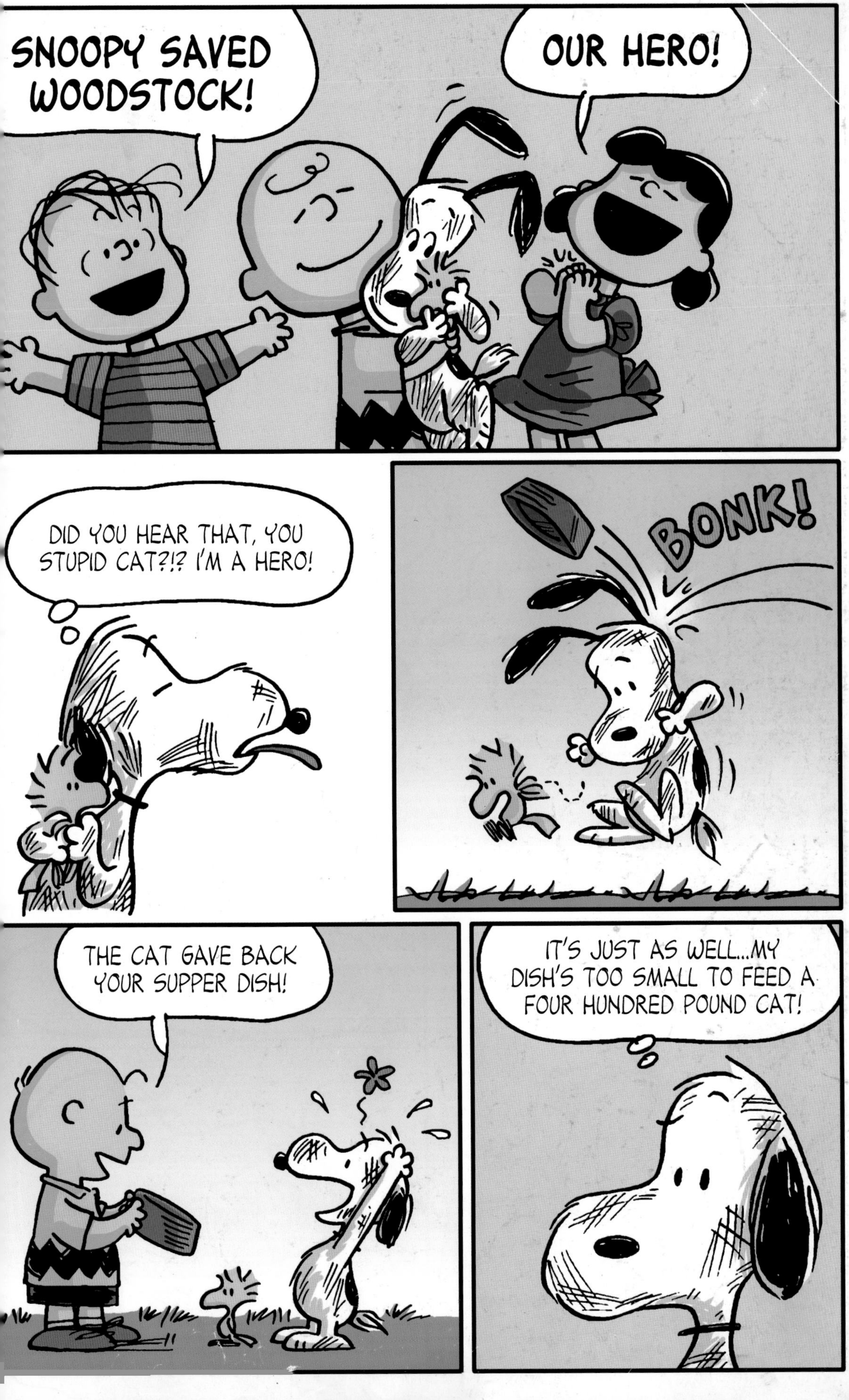
SNOOPY SAVED WOODSTOCK!
OUR HERO!
DID YOU HEAR THAT, YOU STUPID CAT?!? I'M A HERO!
BONK!
THE CAT GAVE BACK YOUR SUPPER DISH!
IT'S JUST AS WELL...MY DISH'S TOO SMALL TO FEED A FOUR HUNDRED POUND CAT!

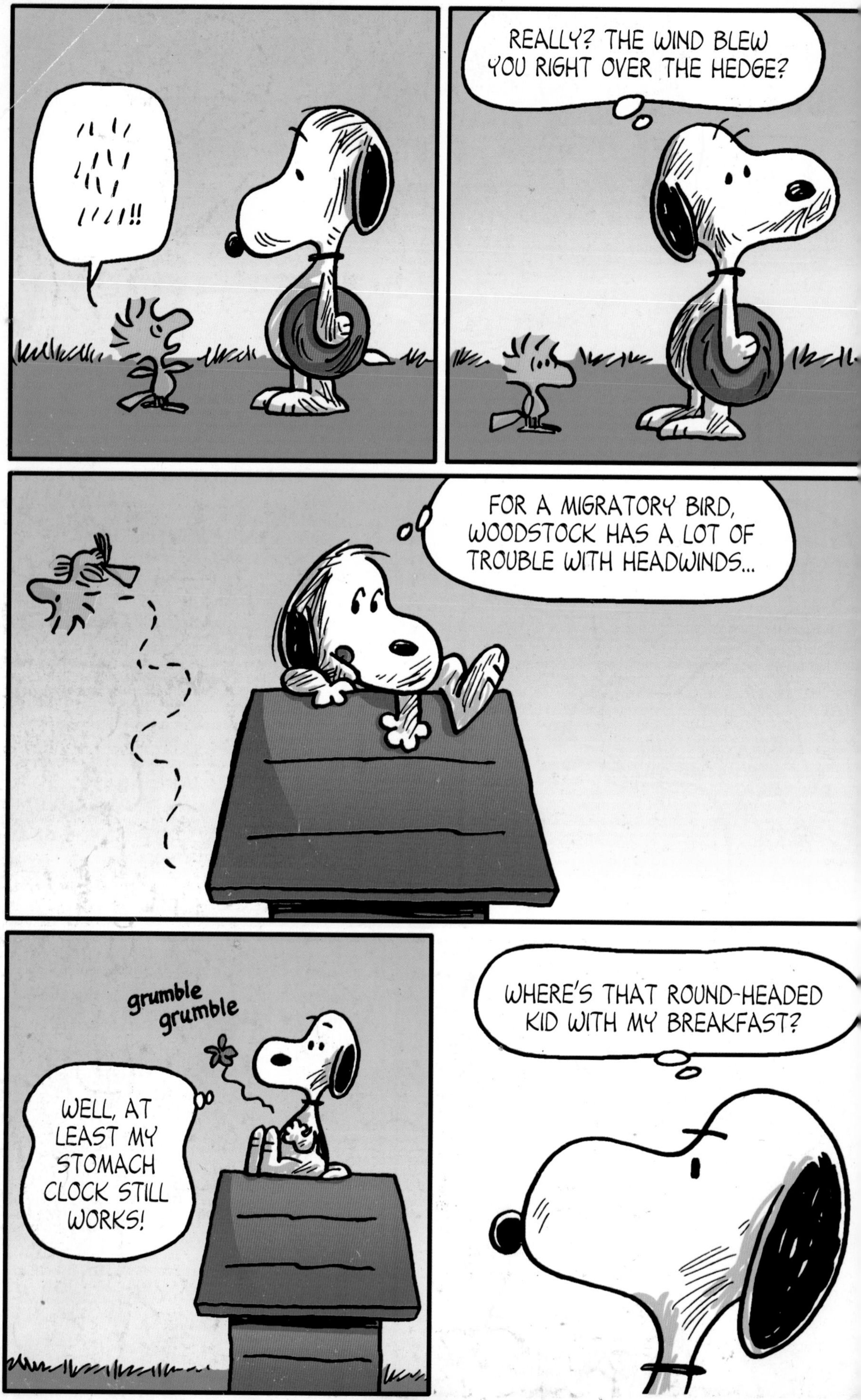
REALLY? THE WIND BLEW YOU RIGHT OVER THE HEDGE?
FOR A MIGRATORY BIRD, WOODSTOCK HAS A LOT OF TROUBLE WITH HEADWINDS...
grumble grumble
WELL, AT LEAST MY STOMACH CLOCK STILL WORKS!
WHERE'S THAT ROUND-HEADED KID WITH MY BREAKFAST?

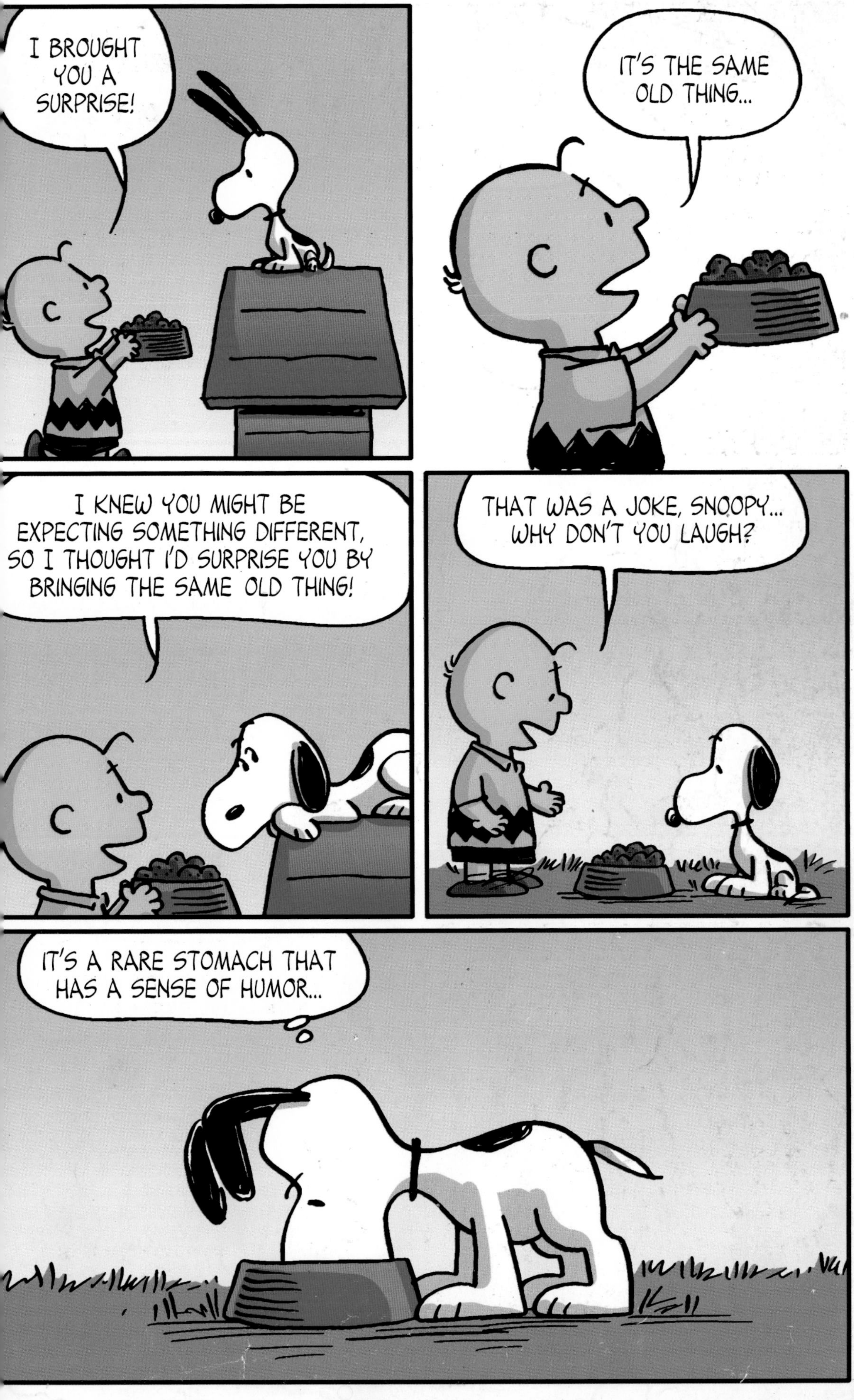
I BROUGHT YOU A SURPRISE!
IT'S THE SAME OLD THING...
I KNEW YOU MIGHT BE EXPECTING SOMETHING DIFFERENT, SO I THOUGHT I'D SURPRISE YOU BY BRINGING THE SAME OLD THING!
THAT WAS A JOKE, SNOOPY... WHY DON'T YOU LAUGH?
IT'S A RARE STOMACH THAT HAS A SENSE OF HUMOR...

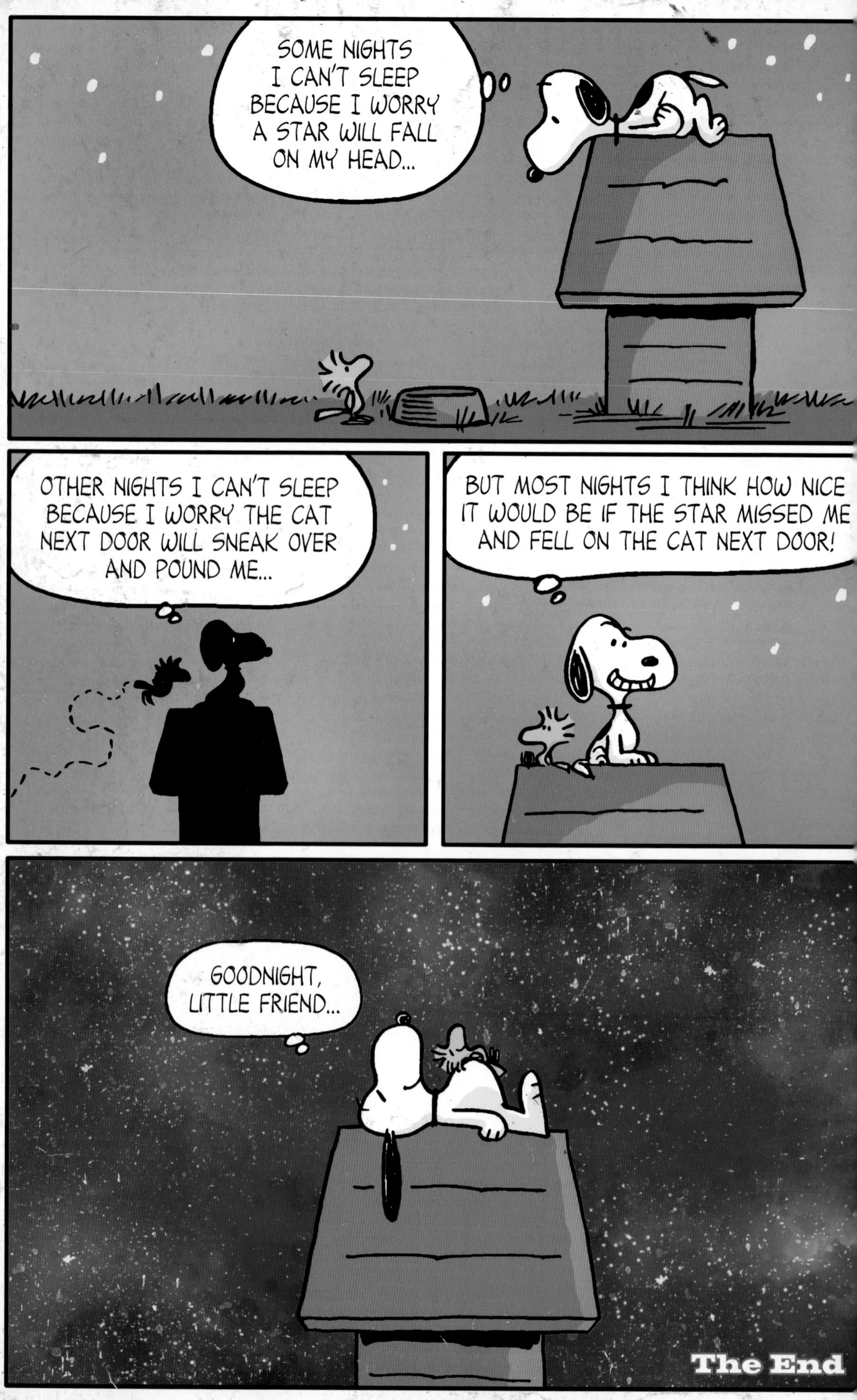
SOME NIGHTS I CAN'T SLEEP BECAUSE I WORRY A STAR WILL FALL ON MY HEAD...
OTHER NIGHTS I CAN'T SLEEP BECAUSE I WORRY THE CAT NEXT DOOR WILL SNEAK OVER AND POUND ME...
BUT MOST NIGHTS I THINK HOW NICE IT WOULD BE IF THE STAR MISSED ME AND FELL ON THE CAT NEXT DOOR!
GOODNIGHT, LITTLE FRIEND...
The End

Behind-the-Scenes

The Beagle Has Landed, Charlie Brown!

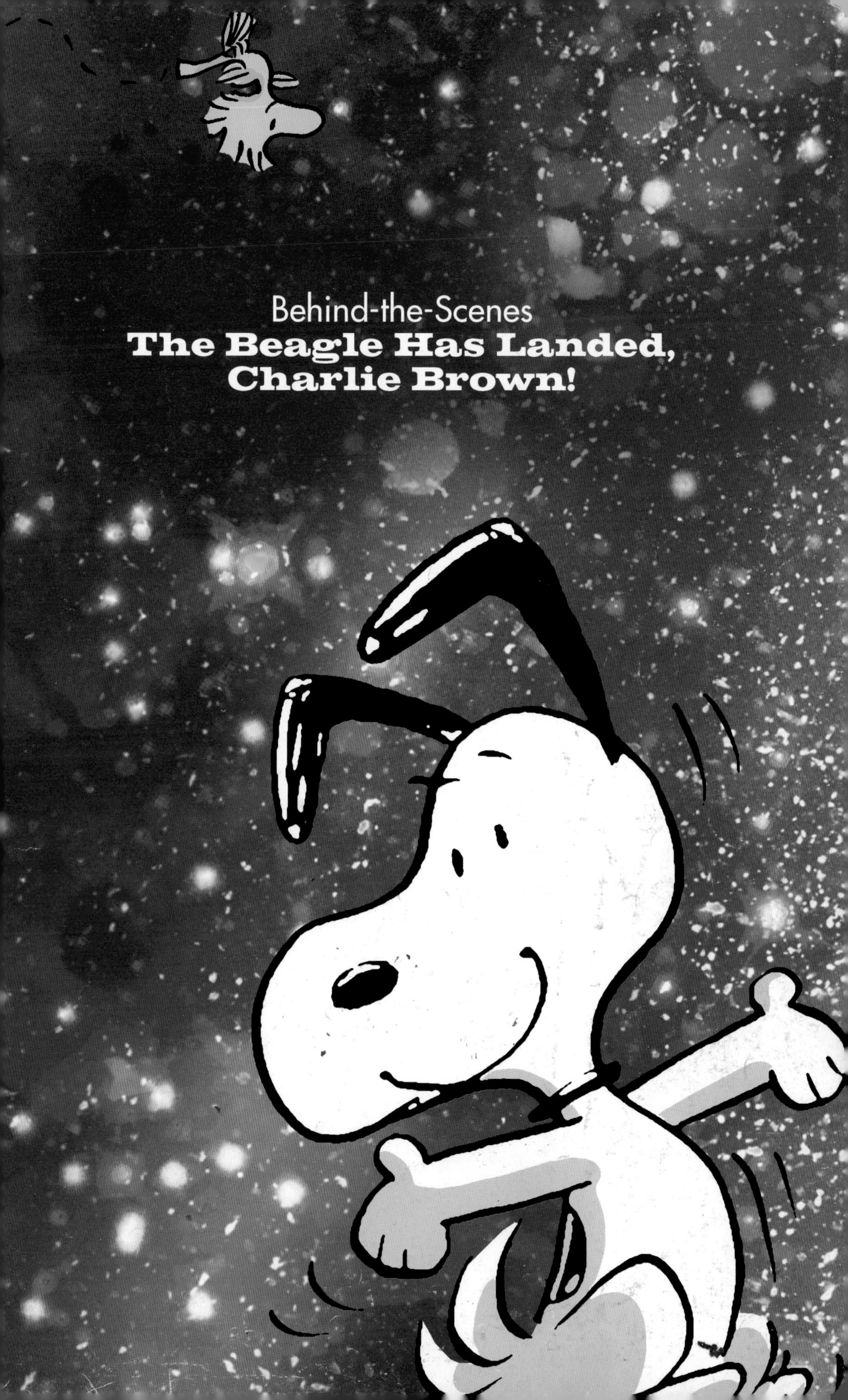

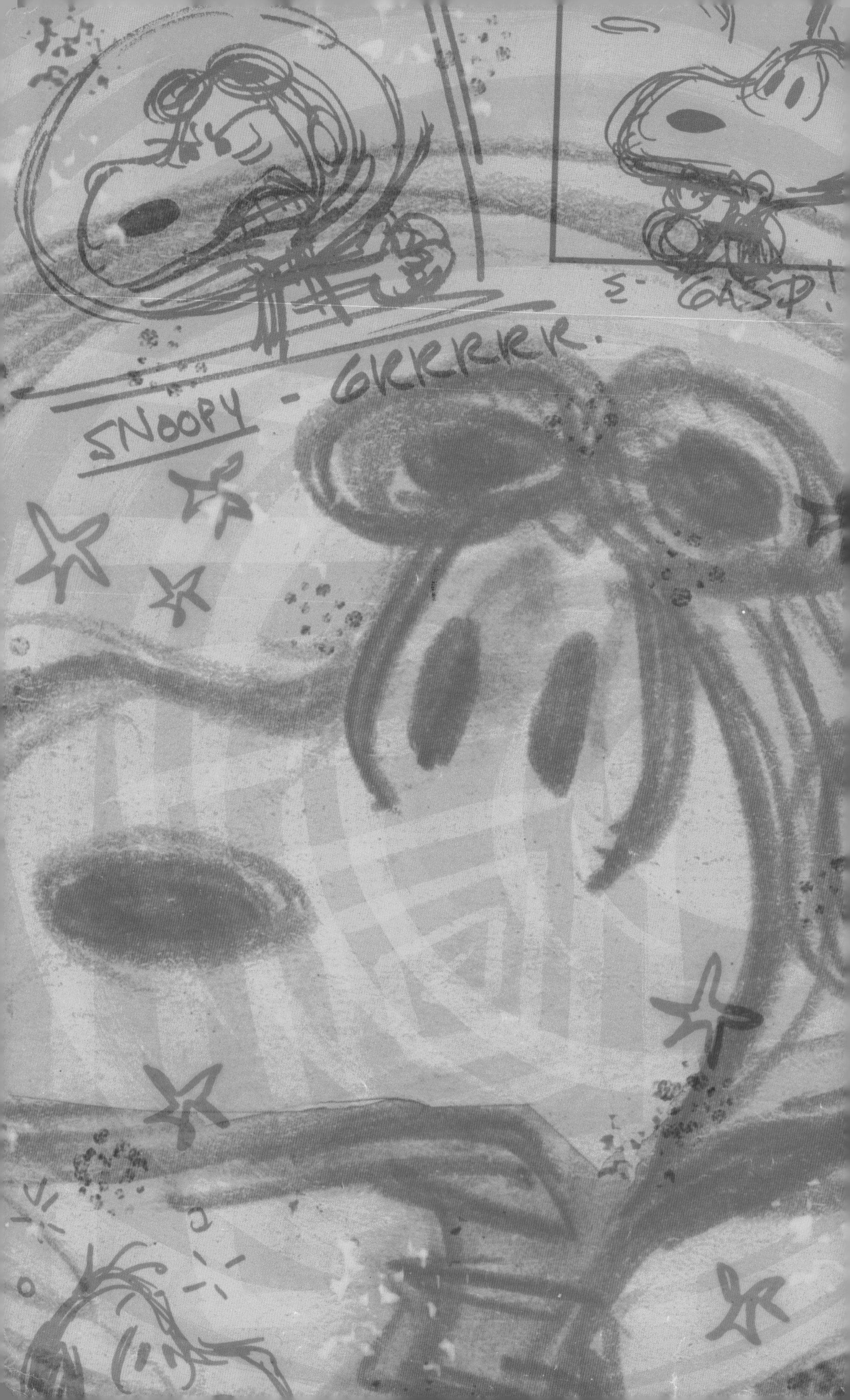
SNOOPY - GRRRRR.
GASP!

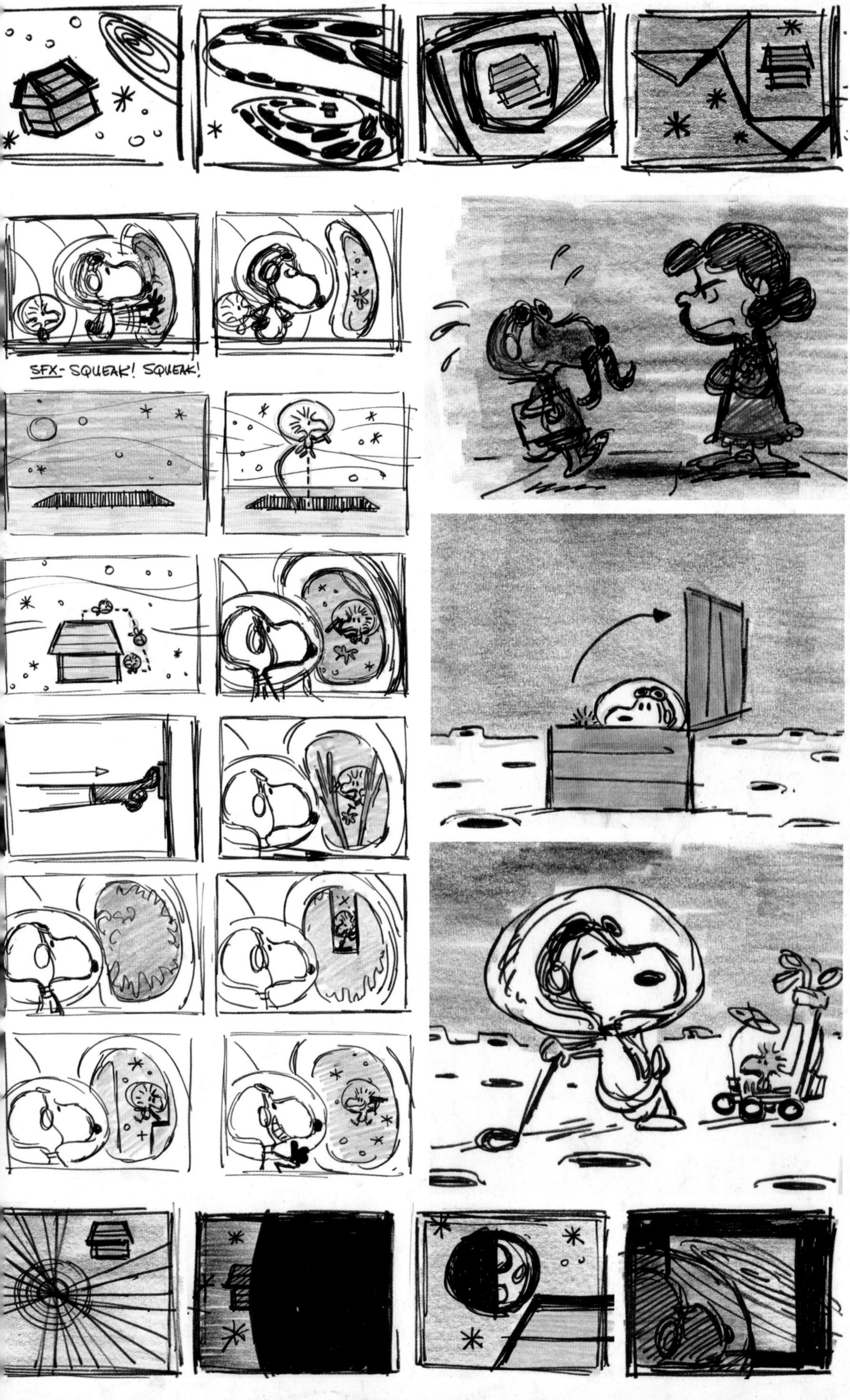
SFX- SQUEAK! SQUEAK!

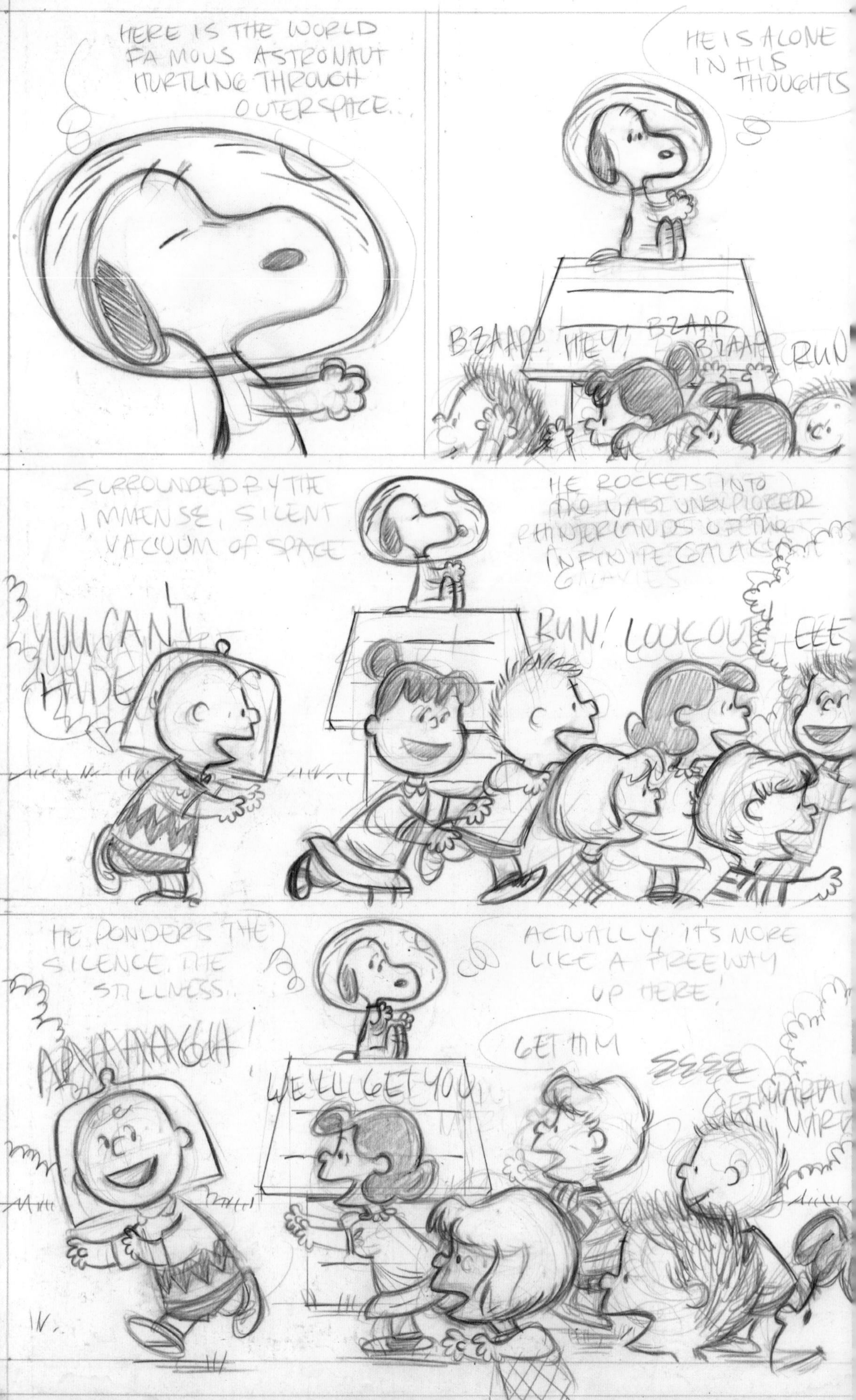
HERE IS THE WORLD FAMOUS ASTRONAUT HURTLING THROUGH OUTER SPACE...
HE IS ALONE IN HIS THOUGHTS
BZAAP! HEY! BZAAP BZAAP
RUN
SURROUNDED BY THE IMMENSE, SILENT VACUUM OF SPACE
HE ROCKETS INTO THE VAST UNEXPLORED HINTERLANDS OF THE INFINITE GALAXY
YOU CAN'T HIDE
RUN! LOOK OUT! EEE
HE PONDERS THE SILENCE, THE STILLNESS...
ACTUALLY IT'S MORE LIKE A FREEWAY UP HERE!
AAAAAAGH!
WE'LL GET YOU
GET HIM
EEEE

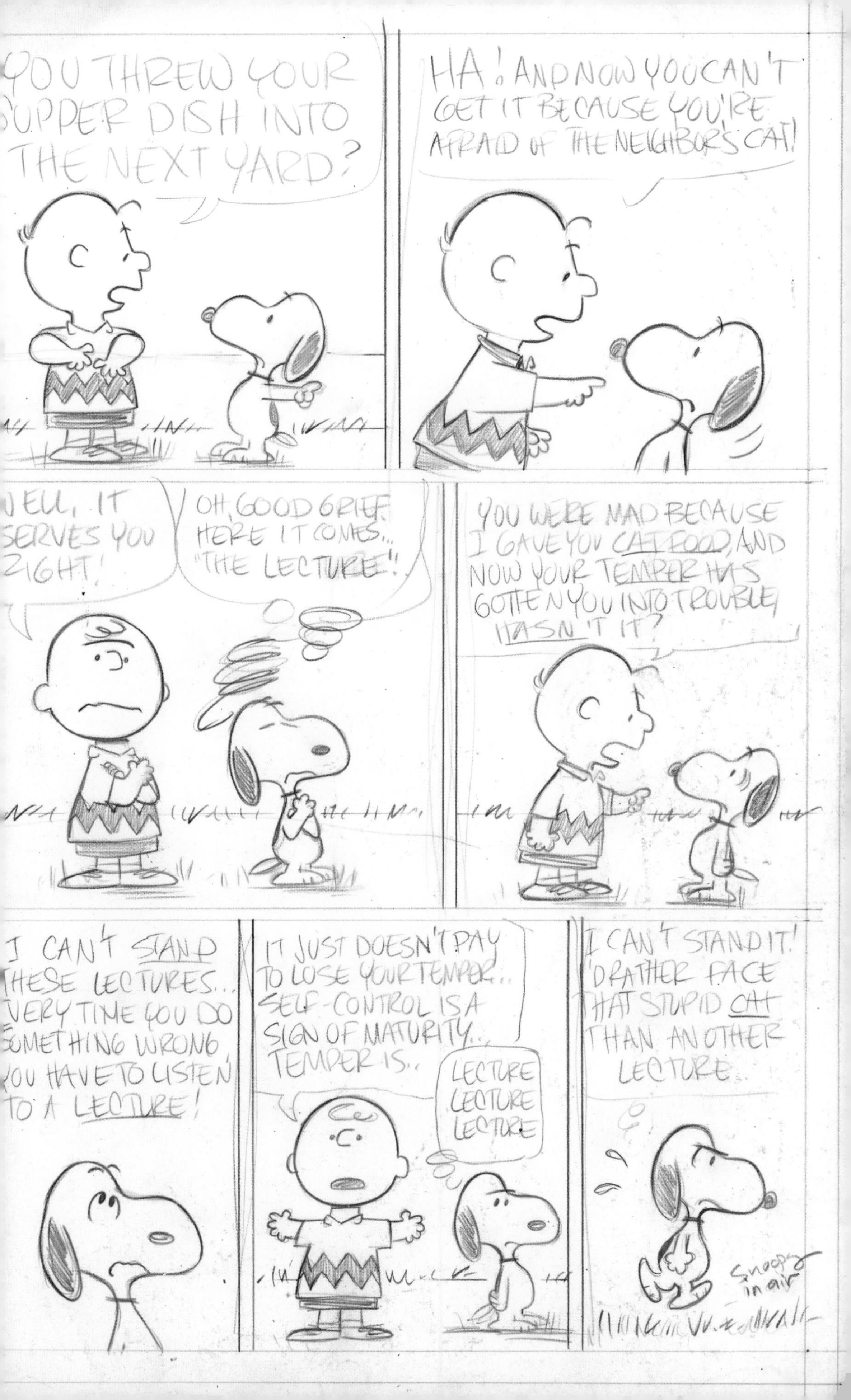

YOU THREW YOUR SUPPER DISH INTO THE NEXT YARD?
HA! AND NOW YOU CAN'T GET IT BECAUSE YOU'RE AFRAID OF THE NEIGHBOR'S CAT!
WELL, IT SERVES YOU RIGHT!
OH, GOOD GRIEF. HERE IT COMES... "THE LECTURE"!
YOU WERE MAD BECAUSE I GAVE YOU CAT FOOD, AND NOW YOUR TEMPER HAS GOTTEN YOU INTO TROUBLE, HASN'T IT?
I CAN'T STAND THESE LECTURES... EVERY TIME YOU DO SOMETHING WRONG YOU HAVE TO LISTEN TO A LECTURE!
IT JUST DOESN'T PAY TO LOSE YOUR TEMPER... SELF-CONTROL IS A SIGN OF MATURITY... TEMPER IS...
LECTURE LECTURE LECTURE
I CAN'T STAND IT! I'D RATHER FACE THAT STUPID CAT THAN ANOTHER LECTURE.
Snoopy in air

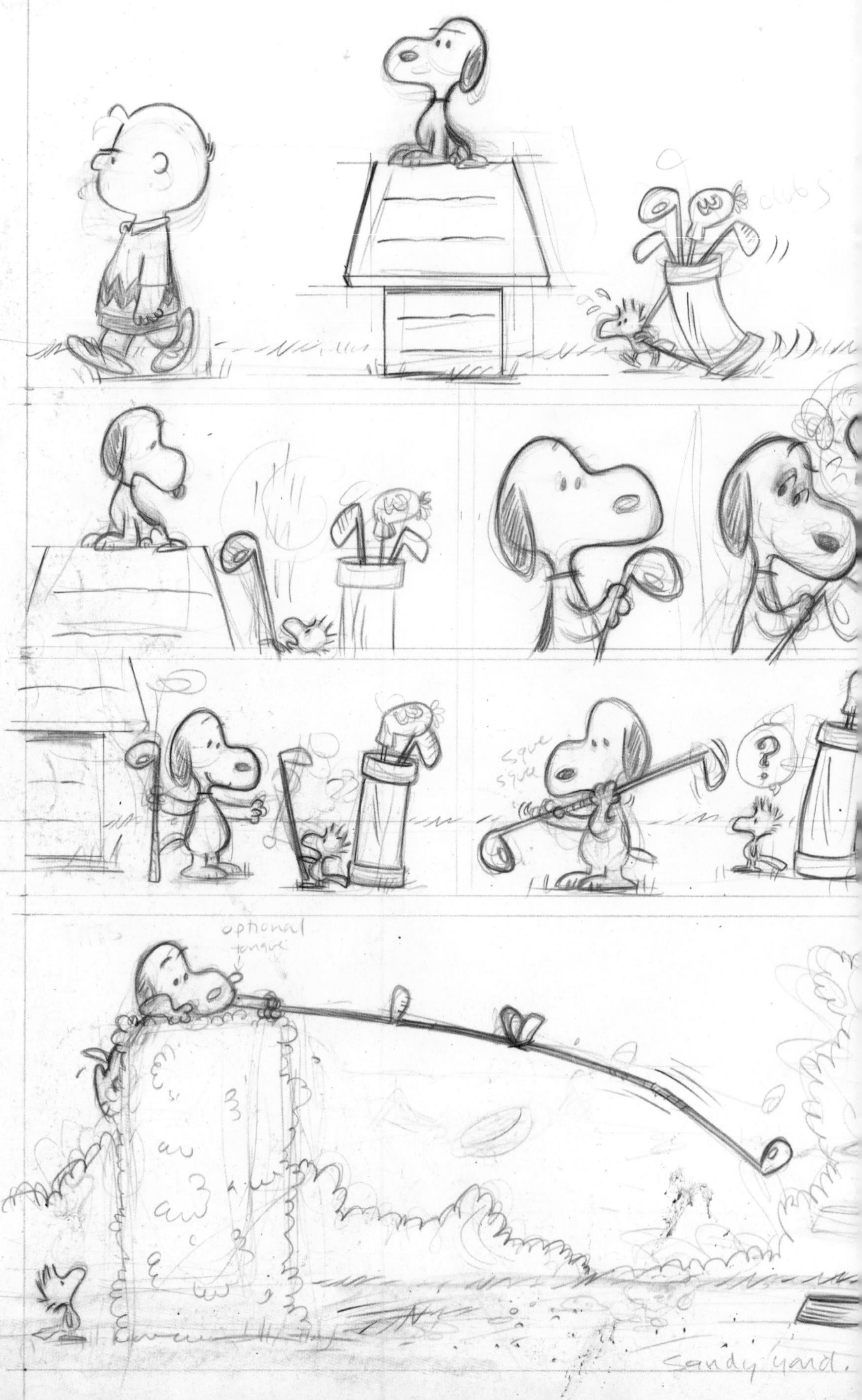
clubs
sque
sque
?
optional
tongue
sandy yard.

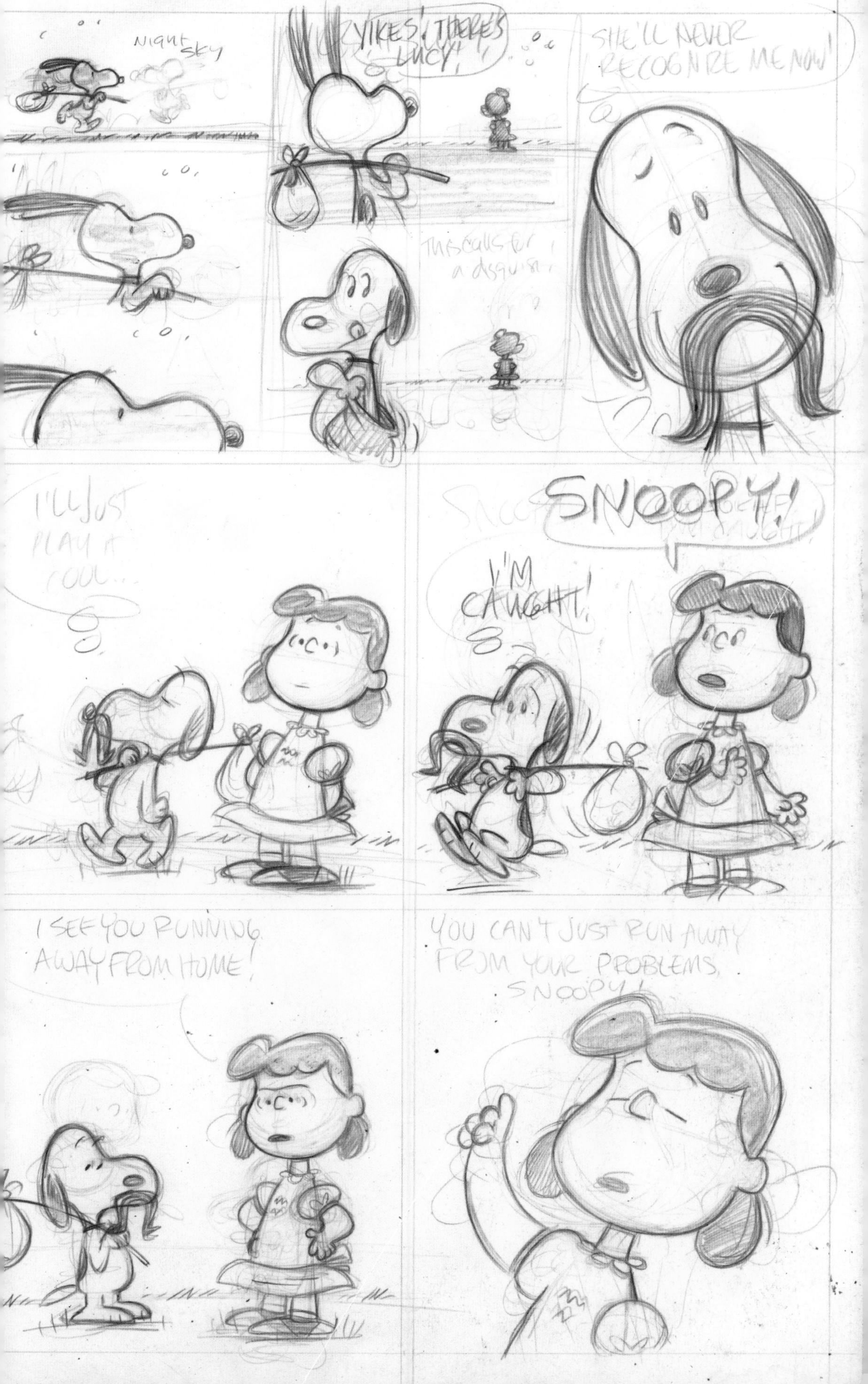

NIGHT SKY
YIKES! THERE'S LUCY!
SHE'LL NEVER RECOGNIZE ME NOW!
This calls for a disguise!
I'LL JUST PLAY IT COOL...
SNOOPY!
I'M CAUGHT!
I SEE YOU RUNNING AWAY FROM HOME!
YOU CAN'T JUST RUN AWAY FROM YOUR PROBLEMS, SNOOPY!

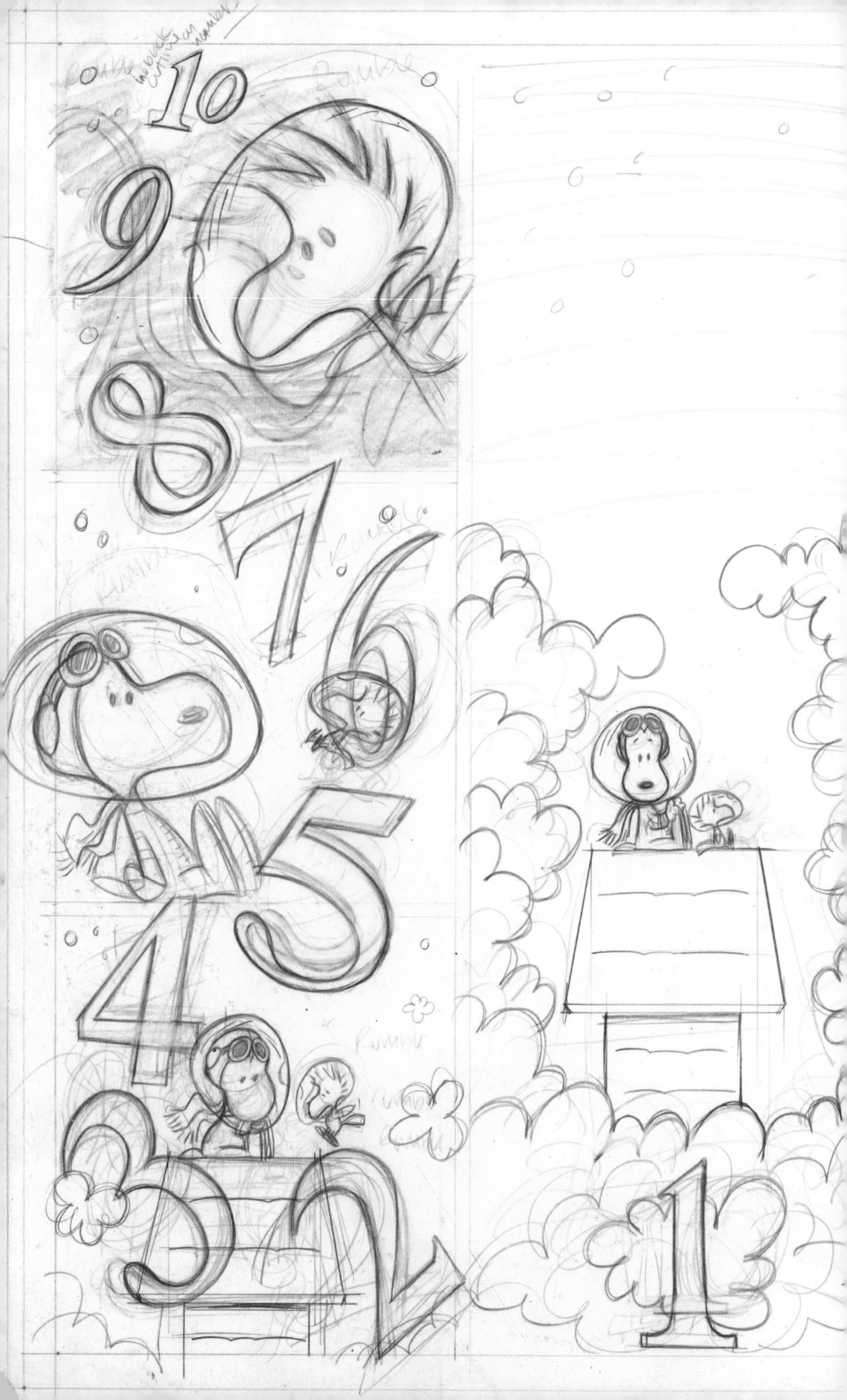
10
9
8
7
6
5
4
3
2
1

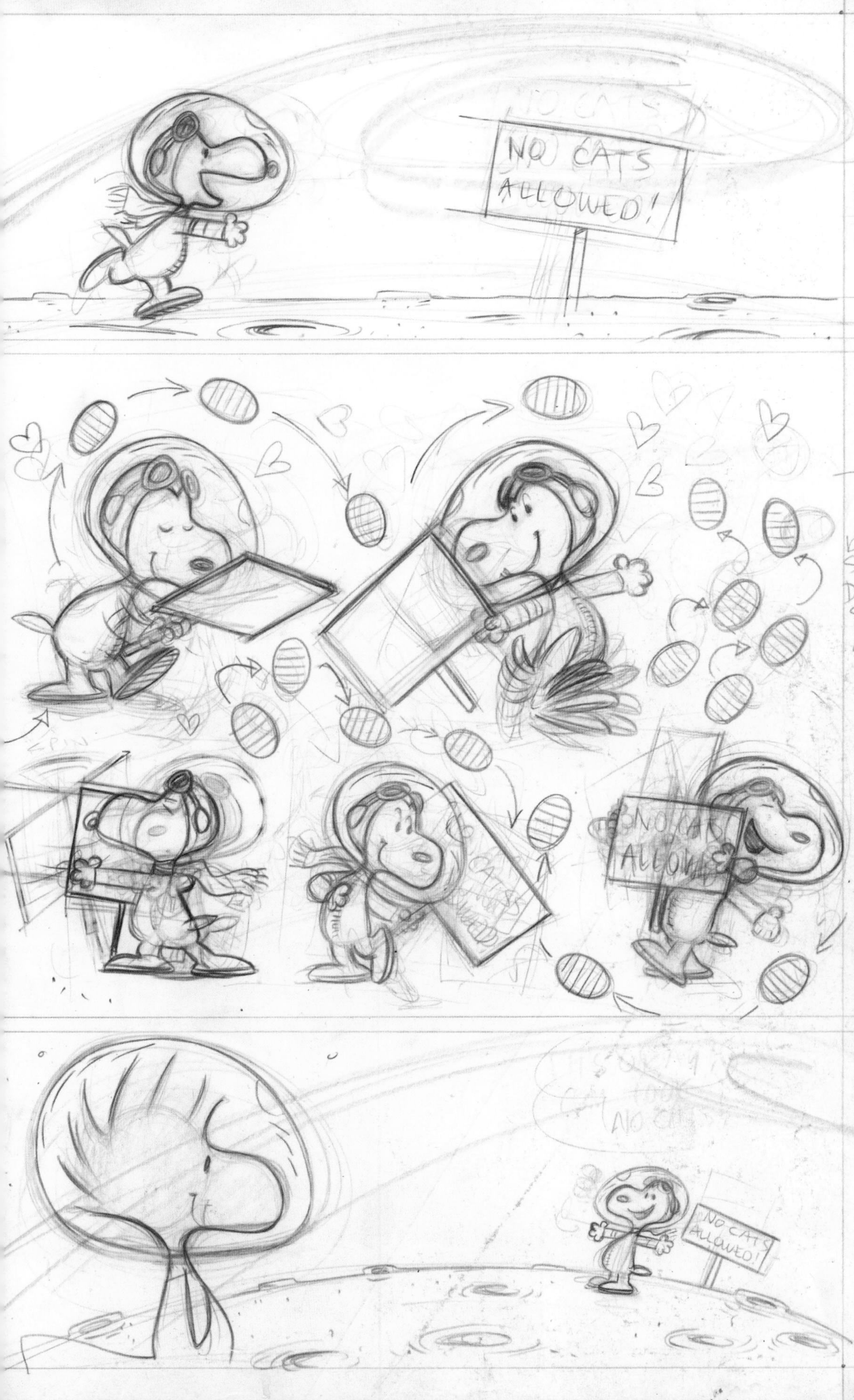
NO CATS ALLOWED!
NO CATS ALLOWED!

Charles M. Schulz once described himself as "born to draw comic strips." Born in Minneapolis, at just two days old, an uncle nicknamed him "Sparky" after the horse Spark Plug from the Barney Google comic strip, and throughout his youth, he and his father shared a Sunday morning ritual reading the funnies. After serving in the Army during World War II, Schulz's first big break came in 1947 when he sold a cartoon feature called "Li'l Folks" to the *St. Paul Pioneer Press*. In 1950, Schulz met with United Feature Syndicate, and on October 2 of that year, PEANUTS, named by the syndicate, debuted in seven newspapers. Charles Schulz died in Santa Rosa, California, in February 2000—just hours before his last original strip was to appear in Sunday papers.

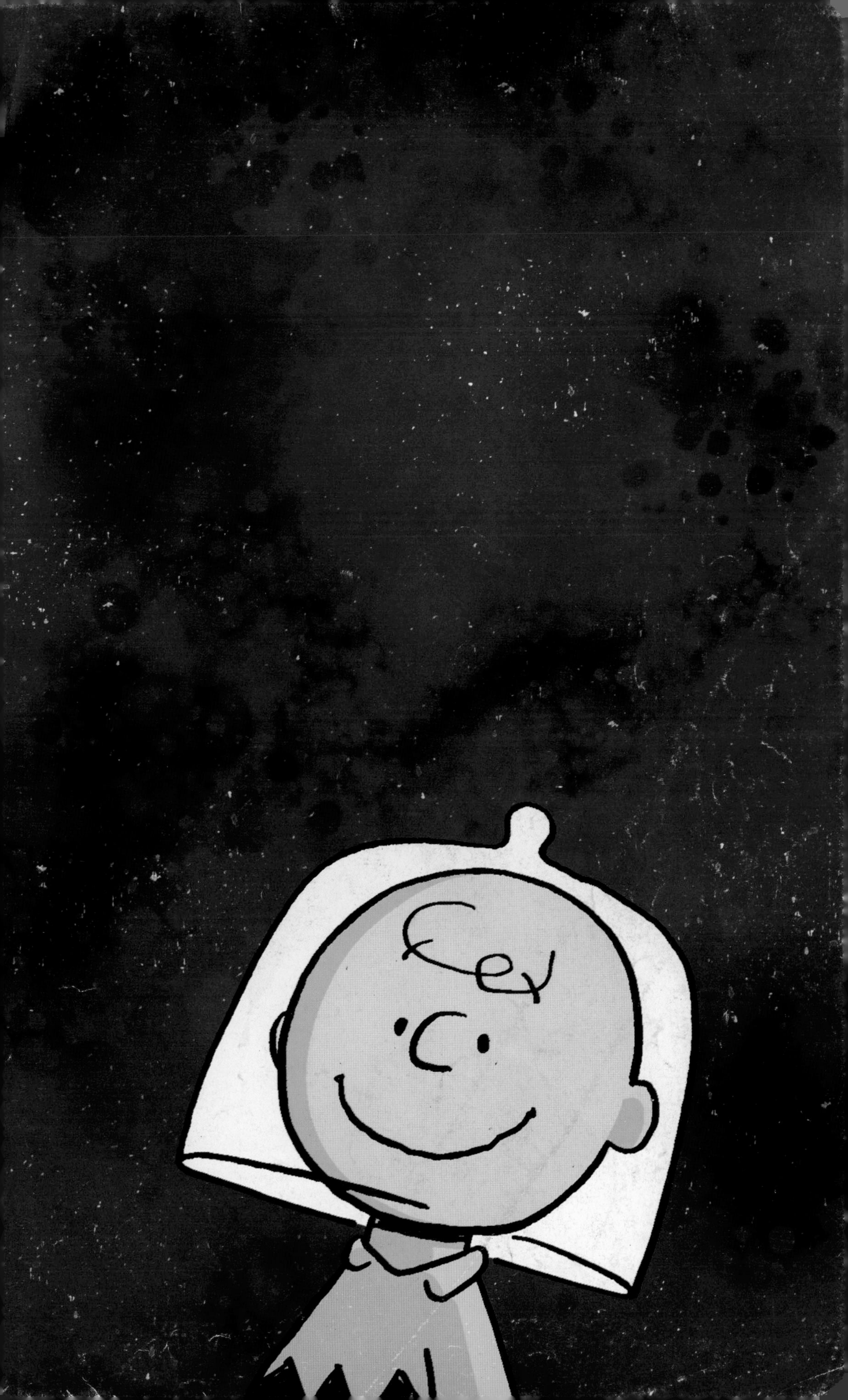

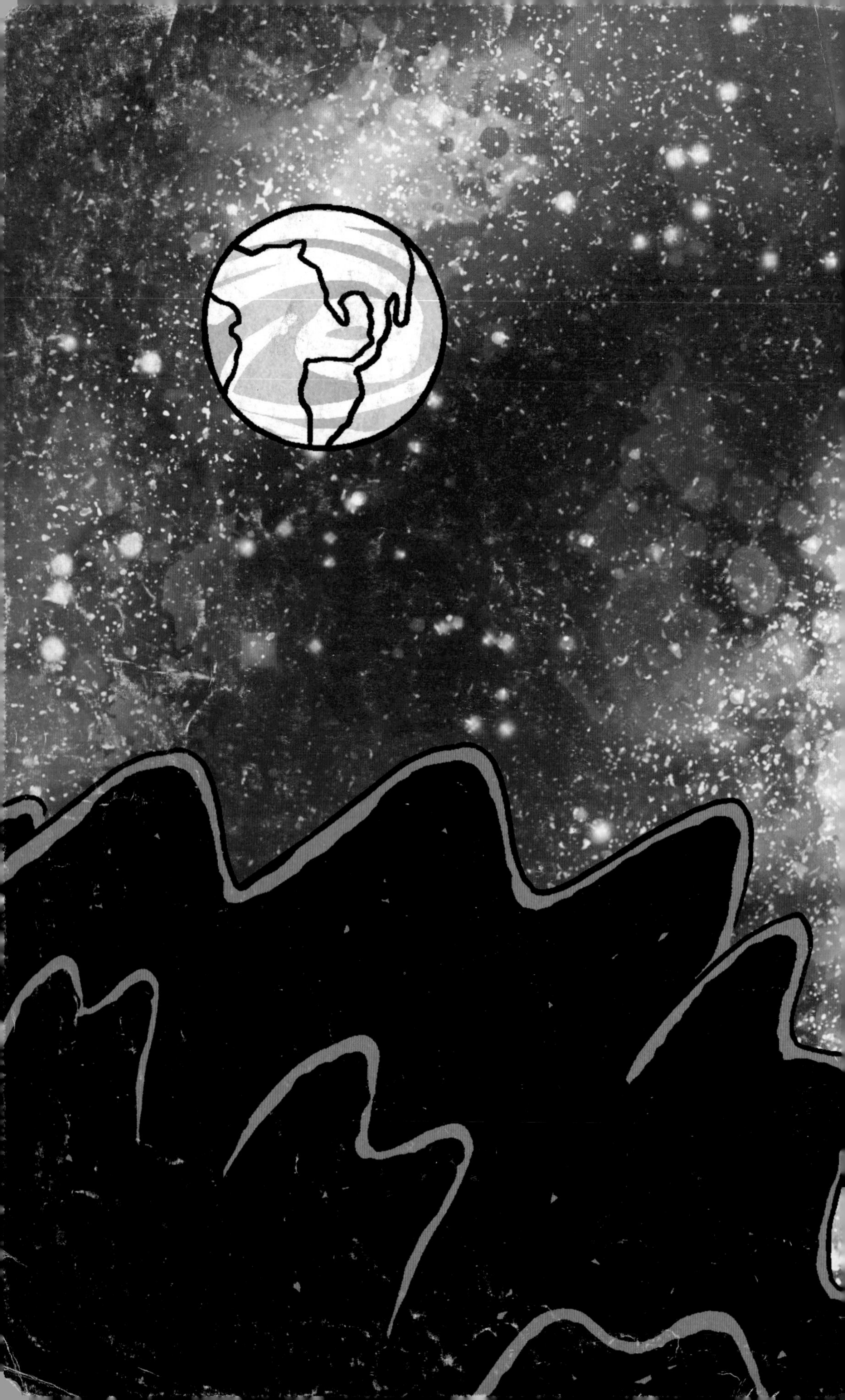